Take the Long Way Home

Take the Long Way Home

A Lineage Series Novel

Michael Paul Hurd

lineage Independent Publishing
Marriottsville, MD

ISBN (paperback): 9781958418406

Publisher: Lineage Independent Publishing, Marriottsville, MD, USA

To my family and especially our grandchildren,

William, Nolan, and Madelyn

Charles II

King of Scotland (1649-1685)

Charles II, by the Grace of God,

King of Great Britain, France, and Ireland,

Defender of the Faith (1660-1685)

Contents

1: Near Wroxeter, Shropshire, UK
September, 2011

My name is Aaron Shepherd. I am the current leader of the archaeological dig at Wroxeter, United Kingdom, the site of a Roman settlement in what was known to the Romans as Brittania. The latest digs at Wroxeter had been going on for over a decade and its leadership passed to post-doctoral researchers on fully funded fellowships from Cambridge University.

As a post-doctoral researcher in archaeology, I moved frequently from one dig to another. The mobility had made me an opportunist in all things romantic, and I had never married. It just didn't seem to be in the cards for me and I was not one to go down the same paths as some of my academic colleagues, leaving a trail of discarded wives and alimony checks in my wake. I was more of a "love the one you're with" kind of guy and made sure the objects of my temporary affection understood that from the start.

I hailed from Michigan Technical University and was a tenured professor of archaeology there. I won the Cambridge fellowship with a proposal to bring modern technology, namely ground penetrating radar, or GPR, to bear on the

Wroxeter excavation. Armed with GPR technology, it was my intent to "work smarter, not harder" and focus our efforts where the GPR showed a higher likelihood of retrieving large (and intact) artifacts.

I have always been interested in history and archaeology as I am descended from one of the first groups of English emigrants to the New World, arriving on board the *Hector* in the 1630s. My father, too, was an archaeologist – so it seemed as if I were in the family business, so to speak.

My predecessors at the digs had successfully mapped the remnants of the Roman city known as *Viroconium Cornoviorum*, adjacent to the modern English village of Wroxeter. In its heyday, *Viroconium* was believed to have had a population of over 15,000 citizens – making it the fourth-largest Roman settlement in Britain.

I had been in charge for a little over six months when our GPR technician, James Hudson, discovered an unusual metallic object roughly six feet below the surface. Circular in shape, we deduced that it could be a *parma* (round shield) from the Third Century. The only way to be sure, as the GPR was only capable of presenting a two-dimensional image relative to the surface of the ground, was to extricate the object from its earthly confines. A careful dig would be necessary.

I would personally supervise the tedious dig, which was in a previously undisturbed area of the Roman settlement outside the known wall boundaries. It was to be my first dig of a Roman site, and I had been studying the Roman occupation of Britain for several months. I was now intimately familiar with Hadrian's Wall, the garrison at *Eboracum* (known in modern times as York), and had studied the theories surrounding the disappearance of the mysterious Ninth Legion.

For safety reasons and to completely document the site, the size of the hole to be dug would be approximately twice the size of the buried object, or six feet by six feet square; the suspected *parma* was roughly three feet in diameter. A total of 8 cubic yards of earth and buried detritus would have to be loosened, sifted for other smaller artifacts, catalogued and moved.

If this were a simple "dig a hole" operation, it would take approximately eight man-days to dig. Archaeology, however, requires significant attention to detail and a whole lot of paperwork. That generally multiplies the time and effort required by a factor of three. In other words, it could take about 24 man-days to reach the buried artifact, English weather permitting, of course.

To prepare for the dig, I convened a meeting of my technicians, fellow archaeologists, students, and laborers at 4 p.m. on the afternoon the artifact was discovered.

"Mr. Hudson, I want a daily GPR scan of the excavation at noon. Can you do that?" I asked.

"Of course, sir. I will make sure to be here at noon every day until we reach the artifact," Hudson replied.

"What a sanctimonious ass," I thought to myself.

Michelle Whitcomb, a PhD candidate at Western Michigan University, was my second-in-charge and leading field archaeologist. I turned to her and gave more instructions.

"Miss Whitcomb, *you* are in charge whenever I am not at the dig." Please set up a rotational schedule for the others to ensure that no one is digging for more than two hours at a time. I've found that two hours is about the maximum attention span before errors in judgment start to affect how the person works, especially in the close confines of a dig." My tone made it clear that there would be no usurpation of her authority, especially not by James Hudson.

"Yes, Aaron. That's an easy assignment. At the moment, we have plenty of staff on hand," Whitcomb replied.

My mind wandered more than a little bit as I took in her voice and smile – and a teasing wink that gave me a moment's pause and a brief detour into the realm of possibilities with the comely Michelle Whitcomb.

"Tonight, we can relax and let our hair down a little bit," I said with a smile, "but tomorrow morning, it will be noses to the grindstone until we unearth whatever it is that Hudson found with his GPR."

"What do you propose for the evening, Aaron?" Michelle Whitcomb asked with another almost seductive wink.

"I think a few pints at the pub are in order. The first round's on me," I replied, knowing that a round of drinks would go a long way to cementing working relationships for the next few days. I called ahead to the pub to be sure that the snug would be available for our use; its intimate privacy would provide an environment for more relaxed and candid conversations.

As the group drank, speculation on what we were going to find ran rampant. Was it a full-size *parma* as I suggested, or was it something else even more valuable? We had no way of knowing until it was unearthed. It could just as easily be a piece of junk.

"I think it is just a large serving platter, the kind they would use for a whole suckling pig," one laborer suggested, trying to make it sound like such discoveries were everyday things. The food provided by our canteen was acceptable, but not remarkable, and the vision of a roast suckling pig had everyone salivating.

Other team members' speculations ranged from my own assessment to more sinister or ribald suggestions. One person suggested it was for transporting human or animal sacrifices. Another mumbled that it had to have some sort of erotic connection. We wouldn't know until the item was retrieved from its resting place.

When the proprietor called for last orders, the entire team was well on its way to inebriation, me included. There was no way we were going to begin work at the crack of dawn. It would be copious amounts of hot coffee and at least an attempt at eating breakfast before any work would get done.

We returned... staggered is probably more accurate... back to our quarters adjacent to the site. Michelle Whitcomb's accommodation was directly across the hall from my own and I escorted her there. I don't remember much about the hallway encounter other than that she slapped me quite firmly, bid me a gruff "Good night, Doctor Shepherd!" and slammed the door in my face. My face was still stinging from that slap as I fumbled to open my own door.

By noon the following day, my hungover team had assembled at the dig site. Despite the hangovers, the excitement in the air was palpable as it had been a very long time since an artifact of this size had been retrieved from its subterranean repose at a dig anywhere in the known Roman Empire. Most of what we had discovered in recent months was shards of broken pottery or metal fragments so disfigured by oxidation that they were unrecognizable as to their form or function.

The dig to uncover the suspected *parma* was painstakingly slow. There were times that I could not hide my own impatience. I lashed out at Michelle Whitcomb in particular.

"Miss Whitcomb, can't we move this along any faster?" I pushed. The irritation in my voice was obvious. Perhaps it was my own pounding hangover talking.

"*Doctor* Shepherd," she began in a contemptuous tone, "you yourself laid down the guidelines we have been following for site documentation. I shall not... I will not... deviate from those guidelines and compromise the integrity of our work under any circumstances." Her continued frosty tone stopped me cold, and the memory of last night's slap suddenly reared its head. *"What had I done?"* I wondered almost aloud. My memory of the previous evening stopped when we left the pub.

"Of course, Michelle... Miss Whitcomb... you are absolutely correct. I am sorry for letting my own impatience get the best of me," I said apologetically, almost meekly. She remained in high dudgeon for the rest of that day, never offering an explanation for her foul mood.

The dig continued for approximately twelve hours every day. Each discovered artifact from the layers above the object was sketched and photographed *in situ* and its precise position according to GPS was catalogued before it was moved. Only then was it carefully and reverently extracted from the surrounding soil.

Surprisingly, the excavation was two or three days ahead of expectations at the end of the first week. Michelle Whitcomb, who was now back to her normal self, assured me that no corners were being cut and that my own rigorous standards for documentation were being followed. I don't know if my constant fidgeting was a subconscious response to the tedium or in anticipation of making a significant discovery when we got down to the final layer above the suspected *parma*.

It was noon on Day 14 of the dig and Hudson was making yet another of his daily GPR scans.

"Aaron, I think you are about a foot above the artifact, and I recommend that the diggers be even more careful than they already have been. Remember, we still haven't confirmed what the buried object is – but my scans have remained consistent for its size and position," Hudson explained. I nodded my acknowledgement and approval.

Within minutes after Hudson stepped away from the hole, the digging technician summoned me to the rim.

Pointing to a partially uncovered fragment, he explained, "Dr. Shepherd, I think what we have here is a human bone fragment."

Carefully, I climbed down into the hole with my bristle brush and magnifying glass to examine what the technician was talking about. It took only a matter of seconds for me to confirm that it was indeed a human bone fragment, likely the lower portion of a femur.

The dig was now being slowed by the discovery of human remains. Though the bone was at least 1700 years old, we still had a standing policy of treating all human remains with reverence until we determined without a doubt that it was not an intentional burial site. This apparent femur was no different.

Taking over from the technician, I carefully eased the dirt away from the bone. About three inches below the surface, I breathed a sigh of relief: I could clearly see that the partial femur was the result of an intentional amputation. The end of the bone was more or less clean cut; it was likely that its owner had been seriously injured in some way. I did wonder, though, what had become of the rest of the leg and perhaps the person attached to it.

Cataloguing and photographing was completed, and I removed myself from the hole, allowing Michelle and the on-duty team to resume their digging. I knew from Hudson's earlier GPR scan that we were less than a day away from revealing the buried whatever-it-was.

Once again, I faced another sleepless night of anticipation. Never in my time as an archaeologist had I been given the opportunity to recover a full artifact. Sure, I had unearthed more than my share of broken pottery, disintegrating weapons, partial skeletons, and even preserved clothing – but nothing of the magnitude of the disc that Hudson said lay buried beneath our feet. Cambridge was certainly getting their money's worth from me!

Returning to my quarters and logging the events of the day into my electronic journal, I began to feel the exhaustion of field work. I knew that after a hot shower, I would be ready for bed. Sleep, I assured myself, would come easily.

*   *   *   *   *

Around 2 a.m., I awoke with a start. It must have been a nightmare – something that happened to me when I was on active digs, albeit infrequently. The nightmares usually took over when we were close to making a significant recovery. As I lay in my bunk staring at the ceiling, I tried to reconstruct the nightmare.

The frantic screams of the wounded man pierced the afternoon calm as I watched the physician do his work. From my bird's eye perspective, I realized that I was not an active participant in the operation; rather, I was an invisible observer sympathetic to the poor man's plight.

Through the primal screams, I heard the physician explain to his assistant that the poor man's leg had been crushed under an ox cart and that the only way to save his life was… abscindere… cut it off. The assistant blanched at the suggestion and did his best to control the urge to vomit.

The man's wife was more stoic than the assistant as she offered her husband to drink freely from a goatskin of wine. In due time, he would become inebriated and pass out, even with the pain he was experiencing. It was then – and only then – that the physician would begin the amputation.

I noticed that the techniques for amputation had not changed significantly in centuries, perhaps even millennia. Overall, it was a quick procedure: cut the skin, cut the muscle, saw the bone, tie off the bleeders, and suture the flap to close the stump. A skilled surgeon could complete the procedure in just a few minutes and it was no different in Roman times.

With the nightmare deconstructed in my subconscious, it didn't take me too long to fall back asleep. My slumber from that point forward was deep and uninterrupted. It wasn't until approximately 6:30 a.m. when Michelle Whitcomb knocked on my door that I awoke.

"Aaron, it's time to get up. You need to eat before we start work today. Once we get close to the object, you will forget to eat. I know you too well," she said playfully.

When I opened the door to confirm that I was indeed upright, I was greeted with an electric, captivating smile.

"Thank you, Michelle, for your concern. I shall be along shortly." I was now beginning to wonder if she was interested in more than just a platonic work relationship. She was definitely mothering me more than she ever did the rest of our team and whatever had happened after the night at the pub seemed to have been forgotten.

"After that the battell was so absolutely lost as to be beyond hope of recovery, I began to think of the best way of saveing myself: and the first thought that came into my head was that (if I could possibly) I would get to London, as soone (if not sooner) than the newes of our defeate could gett there; and it being neere dark, I talked with some (espetially with my Lord Rochester, who was then Willmott) about their opinions which might be the best way for me to escape..."

As told to Samuel Pepys by Charles II, October 1680, twenty-nine years after the battle of Worcester. From the Trent University Library collection.

2: Out the Back Door

September 3, 1651

"Your Majesty," Colonel Charles Giffard whispered, "we need to depart *now*. Cromwell's Roundheads are almost at the front door."

"Charles is dead! Charles is dead!" the mob of battle-weary and very thirsty soldiers outside were shouting. The unison chant was getting louder and louder and Charles wisely chose not to make as hasty an exit as Giffard was stridently insisting upon.

"To depart in fearful haste and clamor," Charles admonished, "would draw undue attention to ourselves and our plight."

"What do you suggest, Your Majesty?" Giffard asked, his voice barely above a whisper.

"Discretion. I will depart first for the necessary and meet you in the woods immediately adjacent, where the rest of our men are in hiding," Charles instructed, "and it is time to stop calling me 'Your Majesty'. I am certain that the Parliamentarians would like to separate us from our heads, just to claim the £1000 reward. I think it best if everyone would just call me either 'sir' or 'Charles'."

Slowly and singly, the royal entourage slipped out the back door, meeting the rest of their meager band in the woods as Charles had instructed. None of the arriving Parliamentarians suspected anything; they were preoccupied with the freely-flowing ale and the complement of wenches coming quickly to their sides, insistent on offering pleasures of the flesh – for a reasonable fee, of course.

Before the Battle of Worcester and their defeat, the band of more than sixty mounted Royalist soldiers would have made a lot of noise as they moved. The metal of their weapons and armor would have clanked and clanged annoyingly – giving away their position. Colonel Giffard recognized this and insisted that all armor be removed and weapons concealed as much as possible.

Now able to move more stealthily, but still not in silence, the Royalists headed north for White Ladies Priory. It was a dangerous 50-mile trek that would take the entourage through territories controlled by Cromwell's New Model Army and its agile cavalry. Any misstep by one individual could compromise the entire group.

Charles and his attendants arrived at White Ladies in the early morning hours of September 4. There, Charles had to stifle a chuckle when one of the unusually tall 'female' servants dropped 'her' frock and removed 'her' wig to reveal the cassock and tonsure of an outlawed Catholic priest. Despite the comedy of the situation, Charles, now disguised as a common woodsman himself, knelt with his men in reverence as the priest began a recitation of the Mass and celebration of the royal party's safe arrival.

"In nomine Patris, et Filii, et Spiritus Sancti, Amen," the priest intoned, making the sign of the Cross over his clandestine royal congregation. Because the Catholic liturgy had been outlawed since the reign of Elizabeth I, only the spoken *missa privata*, or Low Mass, was said, in a further effort to conceal the practice of their Catholic faith.

Within a couple hours of daybreak and just after the final *"Deo gratias"* was said by the congregants, the estate's watchmen observed a small red banner being waved from the top of a pollarded oak tree at the entrance to the estate. The red banner, unseen by those passing below the tree, meant that a force of Roundheads was approaching.

"Sir, we haven't a moment to waste," said Richard Penderel, a tenant farmer loyal to the Giffard family.

"Then we shall be on our way," Charles II replied, in a manner that did not show his internal panic.

Within minutes, the entire entourage had spirited itself out through the kitchen garden and into the dense woodland adjacent to the priory. They were undetected by the small Roundhead force and turned southeast towards the Severn River, where a crossing had been arranged at Madeley.

Penderel's knowledge of the area made him a logical choice to put in the vanguard position well ahead of the main party. He reached Madeley first and determined that the town was no longer safe; in fact, the river crossing was controlled by a detachment of heavily armed Roundheads.

Before he could be noticed by the Roundhead sentries, Penderel turned back to the main group, where he made his breathless report, "Colonel Giffard, we must return to Boscobel at once. The Roundheads have ransacked Madeley, and likenesses of His Majesty are posted all over the town – along with the offer of a reward of £1000, dead or alive."

Turning to Charles II, Giffard said, "Sir, my man Penderel would not give bad advice. I recommend that we proceed with great haste back to the relative safety of my estate."

Charles II thought for a moment, then nodded as he spoke, "Agreed. Let us be on our way!"

Penderel was now exhausted and could no longer lead the group. It thus fell to Colonel Giffard. Initially, the king insisted on riding next to Giffard, but was quickly relegated to the more defensible main body of the entourage out of concern for his safety.

Charles II was a difficult man to disguise. He was over six feet tall and had very distinctive facial features, especially his larger-than-life nose. It was a face that, once seen, was never forgotten. Their best hope was to continue the ruse of Charles as a woodsman or gamekeeper, complete with the associated odors of his profession.

The king's entourage reached Boscobel on the morning of September 6 without incident. Regardless, Colonel Giffard remained vigilant for another Roundhead visit to his estate, once again posting sentries in the row of pollarded oak trees on either side of the lane leading to the manor house.

Posting the sentries was as serendipitous as it was wise. Within hours of the return to Boscobel House, a sentry signaled that a Roundhead unit was approaching. Giffard dispatched his man, Penderel, to escort Charles II to a suitable hiding place.

Richard Penderel knew just the place. It had been his idea to place the signal sentries in the tops of the pollarded oak trees. Their placement had successfully warned the royal party of approaching Roundheads on two occasions. Perhaps he could use that success to hide the fugitive king.

"Sir, would you please follow me quickly?" Penderel said to Charles II, handing him a green cape to use as camouflage.

At the edge of Boscobel Wood was a separate large pollarded oak tree probably more than a century old. With only minutes to spare, Penderel helped Charles II and another accomplice, William Careless, up into the tree and into hiding among the dense foliage and thick branches. It was a good thing that Charles was in excellent physical condition as the quick climb required both strength and agility.

Charles and Careless remained silent and undetected as Roundhead soldiers passed beneath them. The pair would remain in the tree for the next several hours as the Roundheads diligently searched Boscobel House and the surrounding grounds. Inside, the search was so thorough that one of the two priest's holes was discovered, leading to a lengthy but unsuccessful interrogation of the senior servants. By nightfall, with no evidence of Charles's presence, the Roundheads abandoned their futile search.

Though the Roundheads had departed the Boscobel estate, both Giffard and Penderel felt it best for the fugitive king to stay hidden overnight. At first, they considered sleeping rough in the woodlands.

"That will never do," Giffard said succinctly and deferentially as his glance caught Charles's eye, "the king deserves to be sheltered indoors for the night."

"The only place that is safe is the second priest's hole," Penderel offered, "but I doubt the king's size would make for a very restful experience."

"Your Maj… Sir…" Giffard started his explanation to the rapidly tiring king, "we shall hide you away in the undiscovered priest's holes here in Boscobel House. It won't be the most accommodating of spaces, but you will at least be indoors."

"Whatever you suggest, Colonel Giffard," the king replied.

Giffard continued with his security plan, "First, sir, we need to work out a system of communication. One of the three of us – myself, Penderel, or Careless – will be armed and outside your hiding place at all times."

"Will I be forced to use a chamber pot, or will I be given the opportunity to visit the necessary overnight?" the king asked.

"A Roundhead patrol could return at any moment throughout the night, so it will be at our discretion," Penderel said, jumping in on the conversation. Giffard, his superior, frowned at the unintentional affront to the established protocols of position.

"Of course," the king agreed, with a twinkle in his eye, "but I would prefer not to use the pot in the hole. By morning, it will certainly be quite ripe and ready for emptying."

3: What the Hell is That?

Wroxeter Digs, September 2011

As we anticipated yesterday, we were within inches of the artifact when James Hudson did his GPR scan at noon. It was at this point I took over complete control of the dig, relegating Michelle to sketch artist and photographer. She was none too pleased that she had been removed from the active part of the dig, even though I was her superior and responsible for any results we produced. Archaeology is a competitive field and any archaeologist worth his salt was always clamoring to be first at something other than relegation to obscurity. We all felt tensions rising as our implied success approached.

We had already assumed the object was metallic and probably magnetic. If that was indeed the case, it should also conduct electricity. To confirm that assumption, I used a microbore, similar to a gardener's plugging tool, to create two holes approximately two feet apart but well within the projected circumference of the buried object. Into those holes, I inserted conductivity probes and made sure I heard a muffled clank of metal against metal at the bottom of each hole. Once the probes were in place, I connected them to the voltmeter.

Turning the device to its lowest voltage, the meter registered almost immediately: our artifact was indeed metallic and conductive. The reading also suggested that the material was not badly corroded and oxidized.

I looked up at Michelle and smiled. She was beaming. All we had to do now was to carefully uncover the artifact and remove it from its resting place.

Working outwards from the center of the hole, I slowly and carefully uncovered the artifact. At first, it did look like it might be a full *parma*, preserved since Roman times. It had all the right characteristics, at least on the surface. It was the right diameter, somewhat convex, and embossed with some sort of emblem – as any soldier's shield from that period would have been. It likely pre-dated the Roman Empire's full acceptance of Christianity in AD 380 as there was no cross embossed on its surface.

I carefully brushed away the dirt and expanded the exposure of the item. As the day presented with a nearly cloudless sky, I asked that a shade tarp be erected over the hole to protect the item from direct sunlight.

Under the protection of the tarp, I worked slowly and deliberately, using my brush and can of compressed air to enlarge the exposed surface even more, stopping at fifteen-minute intervals to allow sketching and photography.

As more and more of the artifact was uncovered, I sensed something vaguely familiar about the emblem. I just couldn't put my finger on it. I had seen it before, but where?

By dinner time, I had uncovered the entire surface of the object. Because the convex shape of the object was causing some adhesion to the compacted dirt beneath it, I decided that it would be best to leave the final extraction until the next morning. Michelle wholeheartedly agreed with my recommendation.

"Michelle, do you have any idea what the symbol is on the object?" I asked.

"Like you, I've seen it before," she replied, "and like you, I don't think it has any military significance. Outwardly, it does look like a shield, but we won't be certain of that until we see the underside. There should be places – or even straps – for a soldier to grab… otherwise, what good would it be?"

"After dinner, maybe we should do some research against the photographs and sketches to see if we can come up with a theory," I suggested.

Normally a consummate professional, Michelle blushed at the suggestion of us spending time alone doing research. It would be the first time since our arrival at the site that we had been without the watchful eyes of the rest of our crew. Her blush finally confirmed that she had more than a professional interest in me.

"What the hell is this thing?" I asked after a couple hours of searching through Michigan Tech's archaeological databases. From there, we moved on to Michelle's undergraduate school, William and Mary, whose database was more extensive. As an alumna, she retained access. It was there that we found what we were looking for.

It turned out that the symbol on the object had mystical and religious significance. It was a symbol known to the Romans and Greeks alike as "Hecate's Wheel." In ancient Greek deism, Hecate was the goddess of magic and witchcraft and the guardian of crossroads and entryways. In Roman times, she was known as Trivia and associated with Diana, among other Roman deities.

Michelle and I spent the next several hours reading everything we could find about Hecate/Trivia. The more we read, the more confused her legends became. It seemed that her followers were just as confused as we were. What was consistent throughout our research was the symbol itself. In fact, Hecate's Wheel had connections to neopaganism and Wiccan rituals in modern times.

One of the interesting tidbits we uncovered was that a representation of Hecate's Wheel was often hung on the exterior wall of a Roman fortification near an entrance, usually to mark the location of a concealed postern gate. We wondered if the one we had discovered buried several feet down had at one time been affixed to the wall encircling the settlement.

We became so engrossed in our research that we lost track of time, even neglecting to look at the tiny digital clock in the corner of the computer screen.

I looked at Michelle and asked, "Do you realize it is after 2 a.m.?"

"Oh, my God… I didn't. We need our rest. Tomorrow is going to be busy once we remove the object from the pit," she replied. "I think I will turn in." I was disappointed when she nonchalantly got up and left for her own room without so much as saying "good night."

Now alone, I tried to decipher as many of the myths associated with Hecate/Trivia as I could. Before long, I felt myself being drawn back to the pit for a closer examination of the object. We normally enforced a strict buddy system when working on a dig site; normally, I would have been accompanied by either Michelle Whitcomb or James Hudson – but I was the man in charge and could do as I pleased.

Taking a flashlight fitted with a red lens to preserve my night vision, I walked towards the dig. About halfway there, I sensed a force of some kind propelling me onward and closer to the artifact. As I walked zombie-like through the Roman ruins towards the pit, I no longer had control of my own movements. *"What is happening?"* I thought to myself, *"I've read about mystical phenomena at dig sites, but in all my years have never experienced anything like this."*

Reaching the edge of the pit, I could see the object literally glowing in the light of the nearly full Harvest Moon. An irresistible and unseen force was compelling me to climb down into the pit. My heart raced.

Down the ladder I went, being careful not to disturb anything as I descended. As part of our dig, we made sure there was a working rim of about two feet all the way around the object; it was on that rim that I knelt, facing Polaris, the North Star.

I reached out to touch the object and as I did, I was aware of a deep hum surrounding me. Touching the object at the northern opening to the interior labyrinth, my fingertip seemed to be stuck to it with cyanoacrylate but at the same time still mobile around the circumference. I tried to pull my hand away – but couldn't.

My hand was forced in a counterclockwise direction around the perimeter. I had no control over my hand as it moved around the circle. With each ninety degrees of arc, the volume and intensity of the humming increased.

I began to panic as my hand passed through the compass points of west, then south, then east – when the humming became almost too painful to endure.

My finger touched top dead center, the point of origin, once again. There was a loud crack, a blinding flash of blue light, and I was plunged into the darkness of unconsciousness.

*   *   *   *   *

Back in the sleeping quarters, Michelle Whitcomb was jostled awake by the blue flash and loud crack. She assumed that it was a passing thunderstorm like the ones she remembered from her childhood in Michigan. Not hearing the sounds of high winds or the freight train roar of a possible tornado, she promptly turned over and returned to her fitful slumber.

Little did Michelle know at the time that no one else quartered at the dig site had heard or felt the disturbance. She was the only one, but would not find out about that until the next morning.

4: Strange Things In Boscobel Wood
September 4-5, 1651

The light of the nearly full Harvest Moon illuminated Boscobel Wood to a twilight-like brightness. Sentries loyal to the Giffard family and King Charles II had been stationed throughout the forest with orders to sound an alarm if anyone without the password tried to approach.

Despite their best efforts to the contrary, the four sentries eventually fell asleep at their posts. Around 3 a.m., they were awakened by a low rumbling followed by an intense blue flash and what would have been termed a sonic boom in later centuries. Stunned, the four men thought the end of the world was near and trembled in panic, crossing themselves in prayer. One of them involuntarily voided his bladder.

"William, are you okay?" Philip Thatcher whispered *sotto voce* to the sentry approximately 50 yards to his right.

"Yes, Philip. I am not harmed," William Throckmorton replied.

The other two sentries, James MacBride and Seumas Fraser, both Catholic Scots loyal to the king, engaged in the same confirmation of their condition.

Thatcher, the sentry in charge, gathered the men together to determine what they had just experienced. There was stifled laughter as they all realized Fraser had wet himself.

"Did you see the blue flash?" Thatcher asked; the other men all nodded their heads.

"What about the rumbling under our feet?" Again, the men agreed.

It was at that point the quartet heard a noise in front of them in the underbrush. It sounded like a large animal, but wolves and bears had not been seen in England for many, many years. Maybe it was a badger?

After slowly drawing his sword, Thatcher decided to call out. "You there, in the woods, show yourself with your hands above your head and you will not be harmed."

*   *   *   *   *

I don't know how long I had been unconscious. As my disorientation faded, the last thing I could recall was a blinding blue flash and a ground tremor like a low-intensity earthquake. My red-lensed flashlight was nowhere to be seen and… wait a minute… I was completely naked. Had I fallen asleep in the pit and was this a dream?

The night air was cool and damp around me. I began to shiver – which confirmed I was awake and not dreaming. I also desperately needed to relieve myself. A few yards away, I heard male voices with distinct British accents – not the educated accents to which I had become accustomed during my time as an academic, but more rural and clipped. Finally, I was able to understand that one of the men was calling me to remove myself from the underbrush. I decided it would be best to comply – after voiding my bladder, of course.

"Bloody 'ell, mate, it sounds like 'e's takin' a piss!" Thatcher said to no one in particular.

Raising my hands above my head, modesty be damned, I slowly stepped out into a clearing illuminated by the moonlight. I was puzzled by what I could see in the moonlight. The men before me were dressed in battle garb of the mid-17th Century. They were armed with swords and daggers and only one carried a pistol; I assumed he was the man in charge.

Seeing my nakedness and obvious lack of weapons, the four sentries lowered their swords, stifling laughter.

"Are you alone, sir?" Thatcher asked.

"Yes," I responded.

Looking around one last time in anticipation of a Roundhead ambush, Thatcher sheathed his sword; the other three men followed suit. Then it dawned on me: Hecate was the guardian of gateways and crossroads. The labyrinthine symbol on the artifact must have been a gateway... a portal across time.

Checking my potential captors again, I estimated from their dress and weaponry that I was probably in the 17th Century.

"Where do you hail from, sir?" Thatcher asked.

"I am from... uhh... Cambridgeshire," I answered. It was the best I could do under the duress of the moment.

"You don't sound like anyone from Cambridge that I know," Thatcher said. Even in the dim moonlight, I could see his quizzical expression.

I had to think fast. My 21st Century American accent was about to get me into trouble. Perhaps he would believe that I had learned English on the continent. My mind raced to find a suitable linguistic origin.

Though I was an archaeologist by profession, I was also a Civil Affairs Officer in the United States Army National Guard. I had been mobilized and deployed several times after the United States invaded Iraq late in 2001 to protect and recover any antiquities discovered by Coalition forces on the ground. We were taught in pre-deployment training that, if captured, an easy-to-remember story would be much more believable and defensible than an elaborate ruse. It was time to put my training into practice.

"I was not born there. I was born in… in… I think you call it Jutland, in Denmark"

It was the best I could think of at the time. I hoped that I would remember it as my cover story if I was subjected to any interrogation – or even torture to the point of death, as was often the case with interlopers accused of being spies. I knew from my own historical research that experienced torturers of the period could exact a confession from anyone about any accusation – and I certainly did not want to be their next poster child.

"What brings you here, good sir?" Thatcher asked, "and why are you naked as the day you were born?"

"I became lost in the darkness and was set upon by thieves who knocked me senseless," I explained, "and left me for dead. They stole everything I had. My clothes. My sword. My horse…" I stopped right there, as most common men did not own horses. Thinking fast, I added, "She was an old nag retired from pulling a plow and not much good for anything other than plodding along at a walk." I hoped they believed it.

Thatcher turned to one of the other men and gave some instructions. "Throckmorton, give the man your blanket roll so he can cover himself. We can't take him back to Colonel Giffard stark naked."

I wrapped the itchy wool blanket around me like a toga and was more or less frog-marched down the lane towards the manor house where I assumed Colonel Giffard was waiting. I was rudely pushed through the doorway into the servants' area, "downstairs" as it was euphemistically known. It was there that I waited for the Colonel.

Though I was in the servants' part of the home, I could clearly hear Giffard bellowing his displeasure at being awakened in the middle of the night.

"Thatcher, I thought I told you not to wake me unless it was the Roundheads coming up the lane," Giffard huffed.

"Sir, the man we captured appeared out of nowhere and dressed in nothing at all. He was starkers when 'e came out of the woods towards us... and... I think 'e might be a Jew besides," Thatcher said with a perceptible downward nod.

I decided not to engage on the allegation about my ethnic heritage. It would do no good and would likely inflame my captors to the point that I would be summarily executed. Instead, I chose to allow my ignorance of time and place guide my next words.

"Gentlemen, if I may," I began in as conciliatory a tone as I could muster, "I seemed to have taken a bump on the head and cannot remember what year this is. Could you please tell me?"

Giffard spoke over the guffaws of his men, "Good sir, it is the Year of Our Lord One Thousand Six Hundred and Fifty-one."

"*Oh, my God,*" I thought to myself, "*that's 360 years in the past. How the hell did I get here?*"

Just then, a trap door opened in the floor and the aroma of an unwashed body and human waste assaulted my nostrils.

"Colonel Giffard, what is the meaning of this?" a voice of authority bellowed. "Why was I awakened at this ungodly hour?"

Giffard began to respond, "Your Maj… Sir… my men captured this man in the wood adjacent to this house and brought him in for questioning. They suspect he might be a Jewish spy for the Roundheads."

The form arising from the trapdoor turned to face me. I was dumbstruck as I realized I was in the presence of none other than Charles II. I had seen his unmistakable likeness on many paintings from the period. No wonder Colonel Giffard started off with the honorific that he immediately shortened to "sir." Giffard did not wish to confirm for a potential spy that the wanted monarch was indeed present.

At that point, Charles spoke directly to me. "Good sir, on the threat of pain of death, do you swear that you are not a spy for the Parliamentarians?"

I decided that I would finish what Giffard had started with the honorific form of address, "Your Majesty, indeed I am not a spy for Mister Cromwell nor his forces. As I told Colonel Giffard's men, I was set upon by highwaymen who took all my possessions, my horse, and even my clothing. I mean no ill will nor am I a spy for the Roundheads. I simply wish to be clothed and sent on my way."

Charles tented his fingers under his chin as he thought of a possible solution. After what seemed like an eternity, he pursed his lips and nodded – as if he was agreeing with his own thoughts.

"What do they call you, sir?" Charles asked.

"My name is Shepherd… Aaron Shepherd," I answered.

"And from where do you hail, Aaron Shepherd?" Charles queried. "Your manner of speaking tells me you are not of English origin."

"Your Majesty, I told your sentries that I was from Cambridgeshire, but I really come from Jutland, in Denmark. I studied at the University of Copenhagen," I answered.

Colonel Giffard interrupted, without permission from Charles, "How and why would a learned man such as yourself be in England during time of war? It seems an odd story to me." The king raised a single eyebrow inquisitively, waiting for my reply.

I had violated one of the basic precepts of my military training: keep the story as simple as possible. Now here I was fabricating an elaborate story to which there was no logical or plausible exit. How would I, how could I explain my presence on British soil? Any delay on my part would be interpreted as uncertainty.

"Your Majesty, I hope you will understand that a woman's reputation is at stake. She is the daughter of one of my professors and took refuge in a convent to await her days of… ahem… confinement."

"So, the woman of which you speak was with child, Mister Shepherd?"

"Indeed, she was, Your Majesty, but I was not the father," I asserted.

"The woman was carrying another man's bastard child and yet you chose to follow her to the ends of the earth. How strange," said Charles, the tone of his voice suggesting he wanted more salacious details than I was willing or able to provide. "Was she betrothed to the other man?" Charles asked.

"Your Majesty, there was no betrothal. She explained to me that it was a moment of passion, not love, that resulted in their tryst," I explained.

Colonel Giffard interrupted the conversation. "Sir, I have an idea. Mister Shepherd has just given us a believable story for you to be spirited away to France… a lady's honor."

"Do tell, Giffard," Charles replied.

"Sir, my niece is with child and her husband was taken by sickness before our last battle. Her belly is showing her condition," said Giffard.

"I still do not understand your suggestion, Colonel," Charles said tentatively.

"You will assume the role of her guardian, charged with delivering her to a convent in Normandy, where she can await her confinement," Giffard explained.

"A splendid idea, Colonel Giffard," Charles replied. "Find this young lady at once and bring her to me."

5: Missing

Michelle Whitcomb awoke on the morning of September 5 feeling as if she had not slept at all the night before. First, there was her late-night with Aaron Shepherd… *"What was that, really?"* she asked herself. Then there was the lightning flash and thunder that roused her briefly about an hour before dawn.

After her morning ablutions, Michelle dressed slowly and methodically and prepared to walk across the compound for coffee and a continental breakfast. Should she knock on Doctor Shepherd's… Aaron's… door and invite him to join her? A very inappropriate fleeting thought of dalliance passed from her mind as quickly as it entered, and she decided against making the invitation – for now.

Reaching the outer door of the dormitory, she stepped outside. Strangely, the ground was bone-dry; there was no way it could have rained overnight. Michelle now wondered if what she had heard and seen was actually thunder and lightning after all.

It was a cool, crisp morning and hardly a cloud in the sky, unseasonably cool even for England. As the shock of the morning chill hit her, Michelle self-consciously crossed her arms in front of her chest and wished she had not left her lightweight jacket back in her quarters. She was obviously the first one up and about besides the kitchen crew and the compound, thankfully, was eerily silent.

At the refreshment tent, she filled her insulated leakproof mug with hot, black coffee. No milk or sugar for her today. She needed the bitterness and the undiluted caffeine after being up well past her normal bedtime. She also grabbed a green Granny Smith apple and a single serving packet of peanut butter – something that the Americans on the dig demanded – from the snack table. It was the only thing she could think about eating without being nauseated; even the wonderful bakery-fresh pastries turned her stomach.

It was a quick walk to the active dig, where the team hoped to loosen and retrieve the round artifact perhaps before lunch. Somewhat absentmindedly, she peered over the edge of the hole, now several feet deep, and froze. In the bottom of the hole was a pile of clothing that looked an awful lot like what Aaron Shepherd had been wearing when she last saw him around 2 a.m.

She looked around hoping to find Aaron somewhere else nearby, perhaps coming out of the men's toilet in clean clothes. After a few minutes, no one had emerged from the men's loo (as the Brits called it). Maybe he was still in his quarters…

Michelle strode quickly back to the dormitory and walked down the hall to Aaron Shepherd's combined office and sleeping area. After knocking loudly on the door, she stopped, hoping to hear Aaron rousing from a deep sleep. After all, they had been up most of the night and she knew he was one of those men who could sleep anywhere, anytime, and fully disregard his surroundings.

After a second round of knocking, Michelle tried the doorknob and was surprised to find it unlocked.

"Doctor Shepherd? Aaron? Are you here?" she said *sotto voce.*

Michelle Whitcomb carefully entered the room, making sure not to touch anything other than the doorknob she had already touched. As she looked around Shepherd's quarters, they looked the same as they did when she had left just a few short hours ago. The only difference was that a screen saver was active on the large format computer monitor on the desk.

Nervously, she moved through the office and into the sleeping area. The bed did not appear to have been slept in.

Nearing panic, she went to the other end of the dormitory building and began knocking on James Hudson's door. He seemed to be the closest to Aaron of anyone on the team; Aaron often confided in James – sometimes to Michelle's chagrin.

"James? Are you there?" she said as she knocked. The tension in her voice was obvious.

"What's the matter, Michelle?" she heard a sleepy voice answer – followed by a playful female giggle. James obviously had entertained overnight company.

"I think Aaron... Doctor Shepherd... is missing," Michelle replied. "Have you seen him in the past couple of hours?"

"Just a moment... I'll be right out," he said.

The dormitory was a repurposed and reconditioned World War II barracks building that had been moved from a nearby base made redundant in a recent round of budget cuts. Its walls were anything but soundproof. Michelle could hear everything that was going on in Hudson's room.

"Babe, please don't go!" a female British voice whined.

"I have to. Doctor Shepherd is my boss," James answered.

Michelle stifled a laugh as she recognized the female voice. It was one of the barmaids from the local pub, one who was known for her frequent libidinous escapades. "*After all, he's single and entitled to a little companionship now and again,*" she thought to herself.

James Hudson opened the door and stepped into the hallway, using his body to block the view into the room. "Why do you say he is missing?" he asked.

"We were up late, working through the William and Mary archaeological database and I left his *office* a little after 2 a.m.," she explained, putting extra emphasis on the word 'office'. She was sure that some members of the crew had suspected, if not openly gossiped about, a romantic relationship between her and Aaron Shepherd. "That was the last time I saw him."

Hudson didn't believe her for a moment but played along with her. "Tell me more, Miss Whitcomb."

She spent the next several minutes recounting her morning, even confiding that she had entered Shepherd's room to find him "… and then I found his clothes in a rumpled pile at the bottom of our active dig."

Hudson was now thinking that Whitcomb was acting like a jilted lover and perhaps had done something to fake Shepherd's disappearance. True, it was all circumstantial, but why would someone remember all the details of what a work colleague had been wearing the day before?

"I am thinking we should call the local police," Hudson suggested. "We may be able to follow historical clues, but they have the knowledge, skills, and technology to investigate whether foul play was indeed involved."

Michelle readily agreed with him, but also was afraid that she would become a suspect and be taken to the precinct for questioning. Though British law generally ascribed to the premise of "innocent until proven guilty" and had a concept similar to Miranda rights in the United States, local constabularies often handled things as they saw fit. As an unmarried American woman, she was concerned how she would be treated.

Knowing that an archaeological dig on the verge of discovery was generally akin to a crime scene anyway, Michelle Whitcomb and James Hudson agreed that they should cordon off the area to await the police arrival. This way, the scene would remain undisturbed and the evidence, what little there appeared to be, remained intact.

Hudson dialed the national emergency number, "999," and handed the mobile phone to Michelle. The polite and thorough dispatcher took down the details, starting with the name of the missing person. The dispatcher repeated each question twice to be certain that there was no discrepancy in Michelle's answers.

"Alright, Miss… Thank you very much. Constables are on their way," said the dispatcher, "they should be there presently. Please do not allow anyone to go near the site of the suspected foul play."

Despite knowing that no one would enter the dig without her permission, Michelle helped James set up exclusion ropes around the hole. They both wanted to be sure they had adhered to the dispatcher's instructions to the letter. As they were both Americans, the West Mercia Police were likely to take a dim view of any deviation from their expectations.

An hour after Hudson's 999 call, two detectives and a crime scene expert arrived from the West Mercia Police offices in nearby Shrewsbury. Their demeanor as they alighted from their vehicles was all business. A smartly dressed woman in her early thirties approached Michelle Whitcomb and James Hudson, extending her hand.

"I am Detective Sergeant Royce-Smallworth, from the West Mercia Police. Who rang with the report of a missing person?" she asked.

Michelle extended her own hand in greeting. "Michelle Whitcomb, Supervising Archaeologist. I made the call."

James followed suit. "James Hudson, Ground Penetrating Radar technician."

Detective Sergeant Royce-Smallworth took out her notebook and began taking details, starting with their names.

"I can tell you are Americans. Where are you from, Miss Whitcomb?" Royce-Smallworth asked.

"I am a doctoral candidate at Western Michigan University in Kalamazoo, Michigan. That's my registered home as well," Whitcomb replied.

"And you, Mister Hudson?"

"I am originally from New Hampshire," Hudson began, "and was trained by the military to use ground penetrating radar to locate potential burial sites in Southeast Asia after the Vietnam War. Since then, I've used my skills at archaeological digs around the world."

Turning back to Michelle, Royce-Smallworth asked another question, barely above a whisper as she spoke, "Miss

Whitcomb, what was your relationship with the missing man, a Professor Aaron Shepherd, was it?" The Detective Sergeant was probing for subtle hints that might help her investigation.

Michelle Whitcomb blushed deeply in response to the question. "*Doctor* Aaron Shepherd," she said indignantly.

Detective Sergeant Royce-Smallworth had received extensive training in reading subliminal cues like the ones Michelle Whitcomb had just given her. The combination of the deep blush and quick correction on Shepherd's title told her all that she needed to know: Michelle Whitcomb was – or maybe wanted to be – more than just an assistant to Doctor Aaron Shepherd.

"Miss Whitcomb, do you have access to Doctor Shepherd's living quarters?" Royce-Smallworth asked.

"Normally, I would use my passkey. This morning, though, his door was unlocked," Michelle answered.

"Why do you have a passkey?" the Detective Sergeant asked.

"As Doctor Shepherd's assistant, I often have to return to his quarters – which double as his office – to retrieve research materials and supplies."

Royce-Smallworth nodded. It was an acceptable and believable answer, but something still wasn't quite right.

"I'll need to take a thorough look around his quarters, if you don't mind," she told Michelle.

"Of course," Michelle answered with no emotion in her voice whatsoever.

"Miss Whitcomb, do you know where Doctor Shepherd keeps his identification, credit cards, and perhaps his passport?"

"They should be in a waterproof zip bag in the center desk drawer," said Michelle.

"Would you please wait outside, Miss Whitcomb? Doctor Shepherd's quarters could be a crime scene and we do not want it to be contaminated any more than it already has been."

After donning latex exam gloves, Royce-Smallworth opened the desk drawer and found Shepherd's documents right where Whitcomb said they would be. That ruled out a voluntary disappearance. Anyone planning on a departure, even within the United Kingdom, would have at least taken their credit cards and identification with them. Someone planning on leaving the country would have taken their passport as well.

The outer office area was devoid of anything untoward or suspicious. It was a typical academic's office: somewhat disorganized to the outsider but organized enough that its occupant would know exactly where to find just about anything. Royce-Smallworth had seen similar offices during her time studying Criminology and Law Enforcement at the University of Leeds.

Moving on to the sleeping quarters, Royce-Smallworth carefully opened each of the two wardrobes and bureaus. There she found Aaron Shepherd's clothing, toiletries, and an assortment of "top shelf" gentleman's magazines that he had apparently been collecting while in countries where such publications were legal.

"Why does he need these when he can get that and more on the internet?" she rhetorically asked her assistant.

Nearly an hour and a half later, Detective Sergeant Gemma Royce-Smallworth had completed her search of Doctor Aaron Shepherd's office and living area. Michelle Whitcomb was now a suspect as Royce-Smallworth was convinced that Shepherd's disappearance was the result of foul play or misadventure. She would have to wait until her superiors had reviewed her findings and recommended a course of action before tipping her hand.

Once back out in the hallway, Royce-Smallworth gave instructions to Michelle Whitcomb.

"Miss Whitcomb, if you have any plans to leave the area in the next three days, I suggest that you cancel them. We need you to remain available as we continue our investigation."

6: In Disguise and On the Move

September 6-8, 1651

Charles II was not a small man. He stood over six feet tall, generally a head taller than the average man of the day. His nose, more of a proboscis, really, was one that people rarely forgot. In my time, he probably would have had a rhinoplasty to reduce its prominence and a septoplasty to clear his nasal passages.

Charles's regal bearing was another "tell" that would give him away to his Parliamentary adversaries, so he needed a disguise; simply dressing him as a common farm laborer wasn't enough. Charles needed to walk the walk and talk the talk. The fugitive king also had very large feet – another trait that would be recognizable to potential captors. If I didn't already know the outcome of his wanderings, I would not have given him any chance at all of completely escaping recognition. My cogitations were interrupted by Colonel Giffard, who seemed to have been reading my mind.

"Mister Shepherd, you are an educated man and seem to be familiar with different dialects. Do you think you could teach His Majesty how to speak like a common man?" Giffard asked.

I was dumbfounded. It was only yesterday that I had literally appeared out of thin air and here I was, being asked to assist with Charles II's escape from England.

There was a pensive silence as I pondered my answer. "Yes, Colonel, I believe I can. Charles... His Majesty... is himself highly educated and should be a quick study," I replied. "However, to make this happen, I will need unfettered access to the king at all times."

"Of course," Giffard confirmed.

"Colonel, I do have to ask: why are you trusting me with the king's training? If I were armed, I could do grave damage to his person," I said in a very somber tone.

"We do not have a choice but to trust you, Mister Shepherd," said Giffard, "and unless you have purloined a weapon since your naked arrival, I know that you are unarmed."

Interrupting our discussion, a breathless sentry came running into Boscobel House, reporting that the Parliamentarians were searching house-to-house in hopes of finding the wanted fugitive king. It looked like we would be leaving early the next morning after deciding our next destination would be Moseley Hall, a little more than ten miles away. Like Boscobel, Moseley was owned and occupied by another Catholic family. I was also told the family kept a priest in residence, himself disguised as a farm hand.

"Mister Penderel," Giffard barked, "please go fetch my niece and head for Moseley Hall forthwith."

"Aye, sir," Penderel acknowledged.

Because of this new development, the time I would have to teach Charles how to look and sound like a farm laborer would be short. Fortunately, he was indeed a quick study and by the time we reached Moseley Hall, he sounded like a native of the Midlands and walked with the stooped shoulders of an overworked field hand. I would later find out that his gait had also been affected by shoes that were way too small for his feet, causing no small amount of discomfort with every step. Now I understood where his pained grimace originated. Regardless, it was appropriate for a common laborer or farm hand to have ill-fitting shoes.

We reached Moseley Hall around midday and our hosts, the devoutly Catholic Whitgreave family, were most hospitable. Thankfully, lunch was still available. There was a large cauldron of soup on the boil and a selection of cured or dried meats for us to choose from. There was also ample bread and plenty of very potent farm-brewed ale. After we had all eaten and drank our fill, Charles invited the priest to say Mass.

In my youth, I attended an all-male Catholic school where Mass was a part of nearly every school day. I knew that in 1651, it likely would be in Latin – a subject I grudgingly studied under Sister Mary Bernadette, or "Sister Mary Burn-a-dick" when she was not within earshot. Rumors ran rampant through our school – and others – that she became a nun after a dalliance that left her with a case of the clap. I was one of the few students who did not believe the rumor, but went along with the moniker just to fit in.

Why were these old and sometimes painful memories flooding back to me now? My time in Catholic High School was not pleasant and I was mercilessly bullied for being a "quota kid," one that the archdiocese allowed to attend on a full scholarship as a result of financial need. My family, thanks to a couple of factory closures, almost lost our house and Catholic school was an extravagance they could ill afford.

The priest took his place at the head of the assembly, raised his right hand in the gesture of St. Peter, and recited the opening invocation, making the sign of the cross in unison with the small congregation:

"In nomine Patris, et Filii, et Spiritus Sancti, Amen"

I noticed that the rituals of the Mass were not significantly different than what I had experienced in high school – except that again there was no singing. To me, without music, Mass seemed lifeless and formulaic and I wondered if the traditional expression of a priest "saying Mass" had its origins in post-Reformation England.

When the priest began the Mass, I did notice that Charles only halfheartedly participated and merely went through the motions. I would later learn that he was not yet a professed Catholic; rather, that he was simply tolerant of other religions that were outside the scope of the official Church of England, of which he was the titular head. In his mind, it would have been impolite to not at least make some effort at participation.

At the end of the Mass, the priest intoned in Latin, "*Benedícat vos omnípotens Deus, Pater, et Fílius, et Spíritus Sanctus.*" May Almighty God bless you: the Father, the Son, and the Holy Ghost.

The group responded with a soft "*Amen.*"

The Mass now over, our group dispersed into the workings of the farm – except for the sentries. As they were at Boscobel, the sentries were responsible for alerting

Colonel Giffard to approaching Roundheads. They seemed to have a knack for materializing out of thin air when we least expected it.

On the morning of September 8, Charles awoke from his slumber in good spirits. Before retiring the night before, he had allowed the priest, Father Huddleston, to clean and bandage his badly blistered feet. It was also the first time since the Battle of Worcester that he had been able to sleep for more than a couple of hours at a time.

With the additional manpower from our entourage, the farm hummed with activity. Cows were milked, stalls mucked out, eggs gathered, and a dozen non-laying hens slaughtered for the mid-day meal. Charles, too, assisted wherever he could, but shied away from the mucking and slaughtering; he had very sensitive gag reflex and retched almost immediately when the chickens' entrails were drawn. *"What a wimp,"* I thought to myself, shaking my head in disbelief.

We made it through breakfast and the midday meal without incident. Lady Whitgreave herself supervised every aspect of feeding the royal entourage as she did not want to be embarrassed by a servant's missteps. Under her capable hand, the household ran like clockwork. What I found even more amazing was that Lady Whitgreave, because of a debilitating medical condition, depended on a crutch to move around Moseley – and was not afraid to use the crutch as a "motivating tool" when the need arose.

Not long after the midday meal, we heard the boys at the upstairs window shouting repeatedly, "The Roundheads are coming!" With our narrow escape from Boscobel still fresh on everyone's mind, I knew the boys were not raising a false alarm.

Once again, Charles found himself heading down into a priest's hole. Fortunately, it was early enough in the afternoon that the encounter with the Parliamentarian patrol would be brief, and Charles would not have to remain there overnight as he had at Boscobel House. Thomas Whitgreave's ability to convince the Roundhead soldiers that Charles was not on the grounds was a masterpiece; had he been an attorney in the 21st Century, he could have convinced any jury of a defendant's innocence, even with insurmountable evidence.

We left Charles in the priest's hole for another hour after the patrol left just to be certain there was not a larger force nearby. Before nightfall, Whitgreave himself rode the boundary of his estate and returned to report that he had seen no evidence that other Roundheads were anywhere nearby.

Returning with Whitgreave was Penderel, who accompanied Colonel Giffard's niece. They had unexpectedly joined up with each other while Whitgreave was making his evening rounds. Giffard had been correct that her "delicate condition" could no longer be concealed; I guessed she was in her third trimester. Still, she was a strikingly beautiful woman and reminded me of my comely assistant, Michelle Whitcomb, back in the 21st Century. *"That was a reminder I certainly didn't need right now,"* I thought to myself.

After introductions, when I would learn Giffard's niece was named Mary, the household assembled for the evening meal. Once everyone was seated, Charles rose to speak.

"Tomorrow, we must begin our next chapter and move once more. The Roundheads are too close for comfort and I do not wish for my head to be soon separated from my body." The assembly groaned loudly at the suggestion before Charles continued, "Colonel Giffard, whose niece is now part of our band, will ensure that everything is ready immediately following the morning meal."

Had it been up to me, we would have been on our way before dawn and not dependent on Charles's rigid meal schedule. His concept of the "morning meal" was radically different from the working men on the farm, who ate their meager rations long before heading to their work across the estate. In the winter, this was usually before sunrise. Charles, on the other hand, considered it an inconvenience if he was awakened before 9 a.m. We would have to work on that...

His speech concluded, Charles sat back down, and the room buzzed with muted conversations. From my place in the center of the banquet room, I sensed that not everyone was happy with the constant moving and uncertainty of Charles's flight. I hoped that he would be able to keep the group loyal and not have to worry about a traitor in our midst turning him over to the Parliamentarians for the reward.

Roughly an hour into the banquet, Colonel Giffard motioned for me to join him. It appeared that he wanted to speak with me about our preparations for the next morning, as we had not really spoken since I had been tasked with teaching the king how to act and sound like a common man from the local area.

"Mister Shepherd," Giffard said, "when we depart in the morning, you will be the one responsible for my niece and the story that you are taking her to a convent in France. The king will be your servant and bodyguard."

I gave him a quizzical look before replying, "the original story was for the king to be her escort. What has changed?"

"If His Majesty fills the role of bodyguard, it is less likely that he will have to talk. Though you've done an admirable job teaching him to speak like a commoner, I am not yet convinced that he will be able to continue the ruse under pressure," Giffard explained.

"I understand now," I acknowledged.

"What is more important is that Charles is capable with a sword and dagger. He proved that on the battlefield," Giffard said, beaming from ear to ear, "and it is more appropriate if he assume the role of defender and protector."

"You are quite correct, Colonel. I would probably cut off my own... well..." glancing down to my private parts, "you get the idea."

Giffard roared with laughter at the ribald suggestion and returned to his place at the king's table.

7: Persons of Interest

Wroxeter, September 8, 2011

Michelle Whitcomb had been detained at the Shrewsbury police station since the morning of September 7, roughly 48 hours after she reported Doctor Aaron Shepherd's disappearance. Her basic nutrition and hygiene needs had been met, but it seemed as if the detectives, and especially Detective Sergeant Royce-Smallworth, were simply trying to wear her down and extract a confession.

"*Illegitami non carborundum*," Michelle repeatedly said to herself. Don't let the bastards grind you down. Even in isolation, her grit and determination were undaunted.

Sitting in the interrogation room opposite Detective Sergeant Royce-Smallworth once more, Michelle finally began demanding that she be visited by a representative from the American Embassy in London and that she be provided with a solicitor immediately.

"We have just a few more questions for you, Miss Whitcomb," Royce-Smallworth said yet again. It was the same opening line that had been used in each interrogation session. Michelle knew instinctively that the Detective Sergeant was trying to find chinks in the story of Aaron's disappearance and that Royce-Smallworth was hell-bent on closing the case with an American suspect in custody.

"I'll ask you one more time, Miss Whitcomb: were you romantically involved with Doctor Aaron Shepherd?"

Michelle still blushed crimson whenever this question was posed to her. It was the same physical cue that Royce-Smallworth had assessed was the linkage between Michelle and Shepherd's disappearance.

However, Michelle knew that uncontrollable blushing had betrayed her feelings ever since her first serious crush on the high school football team's quarterback nearly two decades earlier. No matter how hard she had tried, she could not control her physical response, which she knew even had a medical name, erubescence. She was going to have to admit that yes, she was indeed romantically interested in Doctor Aaron Shepherd – but that the interest did not appear to be reciprocal.

Michelle tried to stall answering the question. "Could I have a drink of water, please?" she asked Royce-Smallworth.

"PC Lambert, would you please fetch Miss Whitcomb a bottle of water?"

66

In the next interrogation room, a male detective named Rowan was questioning James Hudson. His alibi was that he had spent the night with the barmaid from the pub, something they constabulary would have to corroborate before letting him go.

"Mister Hudson," Rowan began, "what was the name of the barmaid you took back to your quarters at the Wroxeter archaeological site?"

"Her name was… is… Lucy," Hudson replied.

"No surname?" Rowan asked.

"We didn't get that far into our discussions," Hudson answered with a sly grin and a wink, "if you know what I mean."

"Still, we will have to interview her as well, to corroborate your story and remove you from suspicion," Rowan explained. "Is this woman the only 'Lucy' that works at the local?"

"As far as I know, that is correct," Hudson answered.

"Please stay here for just a while longer," Detective Rowan instructed as he stepped out into the hall and closed the door.

As he walked out of the interrogation room, Detective Rowan nearly collided with PC Lambert.

"Mind how you go, PC Lambert!" Rowan chided. "The last thing we need is to fill out an accident report in the middle of a murder investigation."

"Yes, Detective," Lambert responded.

"Where are you off to in such a hurry?" Rowan asked.

"DS Royce-Smallworth sent me to get a bottle of water for our suspect," said Lambert.

"When you go back to the interrogation room, could you give DS Royce-Smallworth this note?" Rowan took out a pen and wrote on the last sheet of his notepad, "Male suspect has alibi. Slept with barmaid Lucy from The Gladiator. Need to prove alibi."

"Yes, Detective," Lambert confirmed before heading to the refrigerator for the requested bottle of water. A few moments later, he handed the note to Detective Sergeant Royce-Smallworth, who read it with a single raised eyebrow.

"PC Lambert, will you remain here with Miss Whitcomb while I step outside for a moment?" DS Royce-Smallworth asked. Lambert nodded in assent as Royce-Smallworth stood to leave the room.

Out in the narrow corridor, Detective Rowan was waiting for his superior. Speaking in hushed tones, they decided that bringing Lucy in for questioning would be appropriate. In her more than a decade of police work, Royce-Smallworth had encountered numerous situations where a male suspect had invented a story of dalliance to use as an alibi. She hoped that this would not be the case with James Hudson.

"Rowan, please send a female constable to The Gladiator and have Lucy whatever-her-name-is brought in for questioning."

"Yes, Detective Sergeant," he acknowledged.

The female constable, Eliza Robertshaw, returned less than an hour later with Lucy Penderel, barmaid at The Gladiator, and asked her to corroborate James Hudson's alibi. PC Robertshaw had completed an A Level in British History and recognized the Penderel name for its connection to the old families of the area.

"Miss Penderel," Robertshaw began, "did you spend the night of September 5 with an American, Mister James

Hudson, at his quarters adjacent to the Wroxeter Roman digs?"

"Indeed, I did, PC Robertshaw, and please call me Lucy. 'Miss Penderel' sounds more like me spinster auntie."

"So… you were in his quarters all night and did not have the opportunity to see anything untoward taking place either in the dormitory or the dig site?" Robertshaw asked.

"I didn't leave his room all night, not even to go to the loo. The only thing I remember other than the hows-your-father, if you know what I mean, was a blue flash and a rumble like thunder about an hour or so before sunrise. Jimmy wasn't *that* good, I tell ya'," Lucy explained.

"Approximately what time did you leave Mister Hudson's room?" Robertshaw asked.

"It was just after Miss Whitcomb came by the room all in bits…" Lucy answered. "I was still starkers… Jimmy got up, put on his underpants, and went to the door."

DS Royce-Smallworth had been observing through the two-way mirror in the anteroom that separated two adjacent interrogation rooms. She had no reason to disbelieve Lucy's story as the barmaid's reputation of being "a bit of a tart" was well-known throughout the jurisdiction. In fact,

Lucy Penderel had been detained on more than one occasion for public disorderly conduct after licensing hours. Those charges generally involved "lewd and lascivious behaviour," according to the police reports.

Royce-Smallworth walked around to the door of the interrogation room and knocked once, followed by two more quick knocks, the prearranged signal for PC Robertshaw to step outside.

"Robertshaw, I need you to go back in there and ask her if she ever saw Doctor Shepherd and Miss Whitcomb alone in the pub, perhaps in a seemingly romantic situation. She may be able to rule out the possibility of Miss Whitcomb being a jilted paramour," Royce-Smallworth said.

"Yes, Detective Sergeant," Robertshaw acknowledged.

Back in the interrogation room, PC Eliza Robertshaw posed that very question. The response was about as evasive as it could be.

"I'm tellin' ya'… those two always seemed a bit dodgy to me," Lucy Penderel said with conviction, "and it was obvious they fancied each other."

"Go on," Robertshaw urged.

"Even with everyone else about, Michelle... Miss Whitcomb always seemed to be on the pull. I know a randy bird when I see one," Lucy explained.

"What about Doctor Shepherd?" Robertshaw probed.

"The bloke seemed to be a posh fuddy-duddy. I'm tellin' ya', he wasn't the type to be snogging in the snug!" Lucy said, stifling a giggle.

Once again, there was a coded knock on the door. PC Robertshaw stepped outside and closed the door.

"PC Robertshaw, I think we can release both Mister Hudson and Miss Penderel. Their stories seem to check out," Royce-Smallworth instructed in hushed tones.

Back in Michelle's interrogation room, Detective Sergeant Royce-Smallworth sat down and busily scribbled on her notepad before speaking once more to Michelle Whitcomb.

"I am asking you again, Miss Whitcomb, if you were romantically involved with Doctor Aaron Shepherd."

During Royce-Smallworth's absence, Michelle had constructed an explanation of her romantic intentions for Aaron Shepherd. What was not certain was how the Detective Sergeant would respond to Michelle's explicit and descriptive explanation of her lust and feelings, perhaps interpreting the situation as that of a jilted lover looking for revenge.

"Detective Sergeant Royce-Smallworth, I would be lying to you if I said I was not interested in Doctor Shepherd. He was... is... a good-looking man and a catch for any woman. There were times when I wanted to take him to my room and... well... you get the idea. Those thoughts kept me awake many nights."

"Was Doctor Shepherd aware of your interest?" Royce-Smallworth asked.

"I believe he was aware, but he always came across as disinterested in anything long-term," Michelle answered.

"Did that make you angry, Miss Whitcomb?" the Detective Sergeant asked.

"At first, yes, but after a while, I understood that the interest was not mutual and my feelings for Doctor Shepherd would never be reciprocated," Michelle replied.

"Miss Whitcomb, I will ask you one more time: did you have anything to do with Doctor Shepherd's disappearance? You had motive... You had opportunity...

and you certainly had the means," Royce-Smallworth insinuated.

"Look, Detective Sergeant, the last thing I wanted was for any harm to come to Aaron... Doctor Shepherd. All I wanted was for him to notice me, beyond our professional relationship."

9: An (Un)Likely Story

September 9-11, 1651

After leaving Moseley Hall, Charles's entourage was joined by another friend, Lord Wilmot. I was now concerned that his band of merry men was becoming too large and likely to draw attention from locals sympathetic to Cromwell and the Parliamentarians. I remained confident, though, that my efforts to make Charles seem like a common laborer had been successful and that he would not be outed by the next Roundhead patrol.

Reaching Bentley Hall near Walsall, we were accommodated by a Colonel Lane and joined by his unmarried sister, Jane, who had a travel permit to visit a pregnant friend in Abbots Leigh. Lane suggested we have Charles and me disguise ourselves as Jane's servants and accompany her on the journey. There, we would surreptitiously try to find a vessel, any vessel, headed for France. With this new ruse, we no longer needed Colonel Giffard's gravid niece, so she was sent home with her uncle. Interestingly, a man named Lascelles was part of the Lane party; I recognized the name from numerous documentaries I had seen about Elizabeth II in my own time.

After a restful evening without disturbance from Parliamentarian patrols, we departed on the morning of September 10. Besides Charles and me, the party consisted of Jane Lane, Lord Wilmot, his second daughter and her husband.

Bristol lay almost 100 miles south of Walsall. On horseback, it would take about three days to cover the distance – less if we could acquire a change of horses from a willing stable. Along the way, we would pass through Worcester, the site of Charles's defeat not quite a week earlier, and other burgeoning towns to the east of the River Severn.

I knew from my studies in the 21st Century that Worcester was particularly bloody, with approximately 3,000 of Charles's army killed in battle. Another 10,000 were taken prisoner, several thousand of whom were sent to the New World to work as indentured laborers. Another group of approximately 1,200 Scottish fighters were force-marched to London, where many died of disease and starvation in makeshift prison camps.

As we approached Worcester, a breeze was blowing from the southwest over the field of battle. The stench of decomposing human bodies and equine carcasses was almost unbearable despite a huge quantity of quicklime having been scattered over much of the carnage. Charles was so affected by the smell that he had to excuse himself to vomit in the bushes adjacent to the roadway.

The two ladies, safe in their carriage, simply doused their linen handkerchiefs with heavily scented French lavender *parfum* and held them over their noses to mask the sickening smell, far worse than any I had encountered during my archaeological digs and opening centuries-old graves.

The *parfum* handkerchiefs worked for only a short period before the ladies, too, were in the bushes losing the contents of their stomachs. It was everything I could do to suppress my own urge to join them; the sound of so many people retching and vomiting all at once made it extremely difficult.

South of Worcester, we came to a burned-out livery stable where we could have exchanged our horses for fresh steeds. Ideally, we should have fresh horses every 40 or 50 miles to maintain anything faster than a leisurely pace.

However, the stable was empty and silent except for the flies buzzing around the composting detritus of equine habitation. The aroma of manure was more tolerable than that of the decomposing human flesh remaining unburied on the battlefield.

On the largest exterior wall of the stable, which miraculously had remained intact following the conflagration, was a Parliamentary Proclamation. It was dated two days previously, meaning that a Roundhead patrol had just recently passed through the area.

Charles was still a wanted man. The proclamation read, in part:

"Whereas CHARLS STUART Son to the late Tyrant, with divers of the English and Scotish Nation, have lately in a Trayterous and Hostile maner with an Army invaded this Nation, which by the Blessing of God upon the Forces of this Commonwealth have been defeated, and many of the chief Actors therein slain and taken prisoners; but the said Charls Stuart is escaped: For the speedy Apprehending of such a Malicious and Dangerous Traytor to the Peace of this Commonwealth, The Parliament doth straightly Charge and Command all Officers, as well Civil as Military, and all other the good People of this Nation, That they make diligent

Search and Enquiry for the said Charls Stuart, and his Abettors and Adherents in this Invasion…

The proclamation continued:

And if any person shall knowingly Conceal the said Charls Stuart, or any his Abettors or Adherents, or shall not Reveal the Places of their Abode or Being, if it be in their power so to do, The Parliament doth Declare, That they will hold them as partakers and Abettors of their Trayterous and Wicked Practices and Designs: And the Parliament doth further Publish and Declare, That whosoever shall apprehend the person of the said Charls Stuart, and shall bring or cause him to be brought to the Parliament or Councel of State shall have given and bestowed on him or them as a Reward for such Service, the sum of One thousand pounds…

It took me a few moments to understand the importance of what I had just read. Parliament had declared a nationwide manhunt for Charles and his accomplices, promising a reward of £1000 – roughly equivalent to £200,000 in 2021. Whoever turned Charles over to the authorities would immediately be a wealthy person. That amount of money would keep an extended family fed and sheltered for a long time.

We would all be in deep trouble if the identity of my fellow masquerading servant were to be revealed. I pointed the broadsheet out to Charles as we passed. He stopped briefly to read it and laughed out loud before turning to me once more:

"Mister Shepherd, you have no obligation to continue, knowing the peril in which you put yourself. You could just as easily turn me over to the next Roundhead patrol and collect the reward on my head," said Charles, pausing for effect, "and I do appreciate your loyalty."

I thought to myself, *"Turning you over to the Roundheads would change the course of history... I'm not prepared to do that and I certainly don't want to see the consequences of my actions three centuries into the future."*

Though his vocabulary was that of an educated man, Charles's accent and diction were now more like that of a local farmer or tradesman. I finally was convinced that I had done my job and that we should be able to maintain the ruse as we journeyed south.

Our masquerade was put to the test sooner than I had expected. Passing over a particularly rough stretch of roadway, which was more like a rutted path than a road, one of the horses threw a shoe. *Somebody* would have to take the horse into the next village and avail themselves of the services of the village smithy.

Charles willingly volunteered for the errand. "I need to know if I can dupe the average fellow," he said quite convincingly.

At the blacksmith's, Charles engaged in conversation with the blacksmith and his apprentice, all joking about how many Scots had died at Worcester. As the conversation continued, Charles actually asked if there had been any news of the "rogue prince" since the battle. When the blacksmith replied that there had been no news, Charles later recalled that he laughed and suggested the fugitive prince should hang like a dog. The blacksmith and his apprentice both readily agreed.

In the next village, we had to convincingly pass through an entire regiment of Roundheads who were drinking outside the town tavern. Deciding not to press our luck after successfully navigating through the regiment, we elected to remain overnight at a relation of Jane Lane's in hopes that the Roundheads would depart at first light the next morning.

At our overnight accommodation, Charles and I were billeted as if we were common servants. In fact, because we had no household standing, we were relegated to the kitchen and scullery and assigned straw mats under the back stairs. Charles was given the menial task of turning a side of mutton on a spit and I was literally up to my ears in dirty dishes and crockery. We had to earn our keep, after all.

Charles proved to be inept at spit-turning, so much so that a jocular teen boy provided some training.

"You've never turned a spit before, 'ave you?" the boy asked. "One turn, you go too slow and the next, too fast."

"We are poor folk and never get a side of meat such as this," Charles answered in an impeccable regional accent. I had taught him well.

"If you keep doing it that way, the mutton won't be cooked through for a fortnight!" the boy chided. "'ere, turn it like this…" Within minutes of the demonstration, Charles was turning the spit like an expert and smiling from ear to ear at his accomplishment.

As night fell, the cooking fires in the Roundhead camp flickered and sputtered from the wet wood they were burning. If we assumed that each of the twenty visible cooking fires would be shared by as many as six men, we estimated that there were approximately 120 men plus their officers in the encampment. We were the safest staying where we were, even if it was in the least desirable of the servants' quarters – with nothing more than the straw mat and a threadbare blanket for comfort.

As if on cue, the sounds of so many men breaking camp reverberated through the village just after sunrise. If they were as well-trained and as disciplined as Cromwell wanted them to be, they would be on their way within a couple of hours.

Getting that many men fed in the morning was a a logistical nightmare. First, the officers were rationed the best of the food on offer, then the sergeants, then the foot soldiers. The officers were served by their orderlies and the sergeants by the camp-following women. The lowly foot soldiers fended for themselves, often suspending a cut of meat from a pike propped over a fire.

I wondered what sort of meat they ate. My guess was that it was some sort of cured meat, like ham or bacon, which had a longer use window. Oh, how refrigeration would have benefitted military men of the day!.

When the village clock struck 8 a.m., a cacophony assaulted our ears. That many men, their support equipment, and officers on horseback are anything but quiet. Sergeants barked orders, equipment clanked against equipment, and before we knew it, the regiment was passing out of sight, heading southeast towards London. We were safe… for the moment.

10: Michelle's Plight
Through September 11, 2011

Michelle Whitcomb remained in the custody of the West Mercia Police. Because she could not produce a believable alibi, nor could she control her deep crimson blushing at the mere mention of Aaron Shepherd's name, Detective-Sergeant Royce-Smallworth remained firm against releasing Whitcomb. In fact, Royce-Smallworth had successfully petitioned the local magistrate for authorization to hold Michelle as a murder suspect for the full 96 hours authorized by law. That 96-hour window was quickly coming to a close.

Because of her gender and the scrutiny that would be given to any perceived misstep on her part, Royce-Smallworth followed protocols to the letter, providing Michelle's information to the United States Embassy in London. Within six hours of that notification reaching the Embassy, a representative arrived at the Shrewsbury constabulary demanding to see Michelle Whitcomb.

Upon the arrival of the Embassy official, Michelle was immediately taken from her cell and guided to a separate room where she could speak with the Embassy representative in private; these rooms were generally reserved for attorney-client discussions, not equipped with two-way mirrors, nor fitted with audiovisual recording equipment. The only condition on the use of the room was that the Embassy representative go through an extensive screening for metallic objects or recording devices and an invasive pat-down.

In their first session, on September 9, Michelle explained to the Embassy representative, G. Hamilton Lee, the circumstances of her detention. She went through the entire litany of her whereabouts and actions before Aaron Shepherd's disappearance – and admitted that she had an unrequited romantic interest in Shepherd. Michelle blushed deeply at this revelation and explained to Mister Lee that her involuntary erubescence was one of the reasons she was being held.

"Why, in God's name, would I want to do harm to someone I wanted more than a friendship with?" Michelle exclaimed in frustration. She was on the verge of tears.

Lee's smirk told Michelle everything that she needed to know: he, too, thought she had taken revenge on Dr. Aaron

Shepherd for neither acknowledging nor returning her romantic intentions.

At the end of the meeting, Lee provided Michelle with a list of solicitors who had worked on legal matters for the Embassy in the past, one of which was right in Shrewsbury. Michelle agreed to the suggestion but asked that Lee make the initial contact and share with the solicitor the particulars of the case. G. Hamilton Lee agreed that he would. She hoped that he would suspend judgment and provide the Shrewsbury solicitor with an objective portrayal of her circumstances.

By dinnertime on September 9, the solicitor arrived. Miss Victoria Sulgrave, the British equivalent of a public defender, at first seemed disinterested in the case and was focused solely on procedural issues like how much longer the West Mercia police could hold Michelle without charges being officially filed. After listening to Michelle's story, Sulgrave's interest and demeanor changed dramatically.

"Miss Whitcomb," Sulgrave began, "are you absolutely certain of your actions and whereabouts on the night that Doctor Shepherd disappeared?"

Michelle's reply conveyed a sense of defeat. "I have nothing more to tell you than I have already told Detective Sergeant Royce-Smallworth. I was with Doctor Shepherd doing research in his office until just after 2 a.m. before retiring to my own quarters. When I arose not much more than four hours later and went to Doctor Shepherd's quarters to awaken him, he was nowhere to be found."

"And when you went to the dig site, Doctor Shepherd's clothing was at the bottom of the active dig?" Sulgrave asked.

"I already told the police the same thing," Michelle answered. "It was after I went to James Hudson's room to ask for his help in finding Doctor Shepherd."

"Is there anything you are not telling me about your relationship with Doctor Shepherd? Just like in the United States, we have attorney-client privilege and anything you share with me cannot be brought up in court," Sulgrave explained.

Michelle was once again near tears when she answered. "I flirted with Aaron... Doctor Shepherd... in hopes of sparking some sort of romantic relationship. I was always politely rebuffed." Michelle paused for a moment to collect her thoughts before continuing, "But there was one time we were coming back from the pub and had had a little too much to drink. Aaron... Doctor Shepherd... pulled me close and rudely squeezed my *derriere* – at which point I slapped him pretty hard. Before that, I was beginning to wonder if he was already married and remaining faithful – or that maybe he might not like women at all..."

"Miss Whitcomb, were you aware that Doctor Shepherd listed you as his emergency contact in his grant paperwork at Oxford?" Sulgrave asked. "It is logically possible that you, in the absence of close family members, could also have been named beneficiary on his life insurance policy. In other words, you would have something to gain both professionally *and* financially by his demise. Such a relationship will come up in pre-trial discovery – assuming, of course, that your case does make it onto the court's docket."

Now in high dudgeon, Michelle's reply was less than cordial. "Doctor Shepherd's personal affairs are no concern of mine. He never intimated the details of his emergency contacts nor his life insurance beneficiary to me at any time."

Sulgrave scribbled furiously on her legal pad, speaking as she wrote, "Miss Whitcomb, the police cannot hold you more than 96 hours without charging you, except in cases involving acts of terrorism. We have a simple missing person, not a terrorist act. Our laws on your detention fall under the Habeas Corpus Act of 1679... yes, that's 1679... and its basis goes back to the Magna Carta. I will petition the magistrate for a release order forthwith. I suggest, though, that you offer to voluntarily surrender your passport to the United States Embassy in London for 'safekeeping' until your case is resolved. Without a passport in hand, you will not be able to leave the United Kingdom. I am also going to promise that you will not discuss the particulars of the case – or your detention – with anyone other than me or the police."

"I'll do whatever it takes to be out of this place and return to work. We were on the brink of a breakthrough discovery the day before Doctor Shepherd disappeared. The dig site was made a crime scene when I was arrested," Michelle replied. "With my release and the time that has transpired since Doctor Shepherd's disappearance, I hope the police will allow our work to resume at the dig site."

Within a couple of hours, Victoria Sulgrave had secured Michelle Whitcomb's release; she was driven by PC Robertshaw back to the Wroxeter site. The patrol car had not even come to a full stop before James Hudson came running to the carpark, ecstatic that Michelle was coming back to work. He would tell her in their initial discussion that morale at the site had reached a new low following Aaron Shepherd's disappearance and her subsequent detention.

"Let's get back to work first thing in the morning," Michelle said with a smile. "We will take a moment to acknowledge Aaron's disappearance and then pick up where we left off, extracting that thing, whatever it is, from the dig."

"Tell me about what happened when you were in custody," Hudson prodded.

"James, as a condition of my release, I am not allowed to discuss the particulars of the case nor anything to do with my detention," she answered.

James acknowledged with a nod and a crooked wry smile, acknowledging that Michelle Whitcomb was probably one of the most ethical people he had ever encountered.

"I hope there's still food in the commissary tent," Michelle said, "I'm famished. I've had enough of jail food. That much I *can* tell you!"

The serving line for hot food had closed down for the day; they only served breakfast and lunch, leaving the archaeologists and the laborers to fend for themselves for their evening meal. However, the caterer had agreed when they signed the initial contract that properly chilled food and hot drinks would be available until at least 6 p.m. every day. It is from this cold assortment that Michelle chose the watercress and cucumber finger sandwiches, plus smoked salmon and dill on cream crackers. The afternoon fare was never intended to replace a full meal; rather, to tide a worker over until they could get someplace to eat a proper meal.

Michelle consumed her food in silence, contemplating her situation. Aaron was gone. She was now in charge. James Hudson seemed genuinely glad to see her and was a little more exuberant than she was comfortable with; she had, after all, caught him *in flagrante delicto* on the morning of her detention.

Her hunger now partially satisfied, Michelle suggested to James Hudson that she wanted some solitude. The past few days had been overwhelming and she needed to be alone with her thoughts. Michelle's tone and demeanor told Hudson she was on the verge of a meltdown at his expense, so he excused himself and headed off-site for the local pub.

Michelle Whitcomb was now alone in the commissary building. She finished her tepid coffee and stood up, ready to leave. As she began to walk, she felt a low rumbling under her feet and a sensation that she was being pulled to the active dig – and the metallic disk at the bottom where she found Aaron Shepherd's clothes several days earlier.

11: And Then There Were None
Mid-September

2011

Following Aaron Shepherd's disappearance and during Michelle Whitcomb's detention, no further progress had been made on recovering the metallic disk from the bottom of the dig. In fact, the technicians, including James Hudson, and the local laborers had spent the entire time idle except for the seemingly never-ending impromptu soccer games and heated discussions on British vs. American politics. Tempers frequently flared, and cooler heads stepped between the belligerents to prevent physical violence. The verbal altercations were the worst when alcohol was involved.

The low rumbling under Michelle's feet continued, urging her towards the active dig where the compulsion to touch the disk was overwhelming. Almost catatonic, she climbed down into the hole for the first time since Aaron's disappearance and stared unblinkingly at the ornate emblem embossed onto the disk's surface. From her last night working with Aaron and slaving over a computer, she already knew it was a representation of Hecate's Wheel;

she just didn't know what it meant in this particular instance.

The intensity of the low rumbling steadily increased as an unseen force took control of Michelle's right hand, molding it into a pointing gesture with her index finger extended. Try as she might, she could not resist the force. Her hand was drawn closer and closer to the north side of the design. Like a magnet, her index finger was fixed to the perimeter of the emblem and then drawn around the emblem in a counterclockwise direction.

With each 90 degrees of arc, Michelle felt herself becoming more and more detached from the reality she knew as 2011. As her hand passed through the south point, or 180 degrees of arc, a lavender aura surrounded her. She looked at her left hand and saw it pixelating between the lavender and a sparkling gold; she immediately thought of Tinkerbell's "pixie dust" and smiled. For some strange reason, she was happier than she had been since childhood and her first visit to Walt Disney World in Florida.

Her finger came full circle and once again reached the north point of the emblem. With a blinding blue flash, she lost consciousness.

Across the compound, James Hudson was in his room with Lucy Penderel, the promiscuous barmaid from The Gladiator. He had just consummated their tryst when he felt a seismic shudder and loud bang, as if a thunderclap and earthquake had happened simultaneously. He laughed out loud and muttered something about the earth truly moving when he was alone with Lucy.

Lucy, too, felt the shudder and heard the bang but did not make the same erotic connection that James Hudson had. She thought that something was truly amiss and pushed him off her naked, prostrate form.

"What the bloody 'ell was that?" Lucy asked.

"I have no idea," James replied.

"Wait a minute, will ya'? I remember the same thing 'appning when Doc Shepherd disappeared!" Lucy exclaimed. "Ya' don't spose someone else is gone, now, too, do ya'?"

"I don't know what you are talking about, Lucy," Hudson said. He was not lying: the last time, when Aaron Shepherd disappeared, he was at the point of no return and not entirely aware of his surroundings. The memory made him smile – only briefly.

"James Hudson, wipe that smirk off your face, will ya'? You ain't God's gift to women in the sack. That's how I know about the blue flash. I couldn't wait for you to be finished, that's for sure."

Lucy's sudden change in attitude was puzzling for Hudson. Up to that moment, he thought their physical relationship was satisfying for them both. He obviously had made the wrong assumption. She was the first woman to ever have criticized his bedroom performance to his face.

"Get out, you little whore!" he bellowed. "Never come back here again. I will tell our security guards that you are no longer welcome."

The barmaid headed for the door and, reaching it, turned back to James to give him the two-fingered '*up yours!*' salute. She got her comeuppance when she quickly turned around and planted her left cheek firmly against the door frame with enough force that was sure to cause a black eye.

Lucy recognized the mishap as an opportunity. Knowing that the West Mercia Police had an active interest in the goings-on at the Wroxeter dig, she rang the local precinct. Once she was connected to Detective Sergeant Royce-Smallworth, Lucy filed a report of being assaulted by James

Hudson. Royce-Smallworth only half believed Lucy's assault allegations, knowing first-hand of her promiscuity.

*   *   *   *   *

1651

Michelle Whitcomb slowly regained consciousness and realized she was lying naked on a small sandy beach adjacent to a waterfall. The surroundings were not familiar to her, and she couldn't remember how she got there. She even wondered if she was still in England. Panic was quickly setting in.

Michelle quickly snapped back to reality hearing the giggles of what sounded like a group of schoolgirls. To preserve her dignity and modesty, she quickly eased herself into the water, which was quite a bit warmer than the air. The temperature difference was almost comforting.

When Michelle first saw the sources of the giggles, she realized they were four adult women. However, their attire was quite puzzling. It was not like anything she had ever seen before, and Michelle wondered if perhaps the women were involved in some sort of sorority initiation.

Hiding behind a screen of bullrushes and still undetected, Michelle strained to hear what the women were talking about, but their conversation was almost drowned out by the sounds of the waterfall. Watching as the women undressed and prepared to enter the water, Michelle noticed that not a single one of them wore a bra, despite being amply endowed, and their underwear looked more like pantaloons than panties. "*Strange…*" she thought to herself.

Once naked and fully into the water, the women began what seemed like a bathing routine. Finally, Michelle was able to hear and understand their conversation. She immediately realized that the women had British accents. Whatever subjects they were talking about elicited louder and louder giggles. "*This is no sorority initiation. They're having too much fun!*" she thought.

Michelle sensed that a sneeze was imminent. It came on so suddenly that she could do nothing to stop it.

"Ahhh-choo!"

"*Oh, shit…*" Michelle thought to herself.

"Who's there?" one of the women asked.

"Ahhh-choo!" Michelle sneezed a second time, more forcefully than the first.

"Have you been there this whole time watching and listening to us?" a second woman asked.

Though she was an archaeologist by both vocation and profession, Michelle had also dabbled in musical theater during her undergraduate years, performing once as Mary Poppins. It was during this performance that Michelle learned to passably mimic a posh British accent.

"Yes, love. I haven't a choice right now. I came by here to wash myself and while I was in the water, some boys came by and stole my clothes. I have been in the water perhaps for more than an hour since," Michelle explained.

"What is your name?" the first young woman asked.

"I am Michelle." Given the circumstances of this meeting, surnames were not really important.

The oldest of the women introduced herself and her companions.

"I am Elizabeth, and these are my friends, Mary, Alice, and Katherine," pointing to each one in turn.

"I am pleased to make your acquaintances, ladies," Michelle answered, "and I would appreciate it if you would help me find suitable attire so I can remove myself from the water. Are there no men with you? I would be embarrassed if they were to see me in a state of dishabille."

"My home is nearby," Katherine responded, "and we can go there once our ablutions are finished."

"Thank you so much," Michelle replied.

"Mary, Alice, would one of you please offer your shift to Michelle so she can enjoy some modesty on our way to Katherine's home?" Elizabeth asked.

*   *   *   *   *

2011

"James Hudson, I am arresting you for the murders of Aaron Shepherd and Michelle Whitcomb," Detective Sergeant Royce-Smallworth said in a tone that was all business. "Anything you say from now on will be written down and could be presented in a court of law. Do you understand?"

Hudson was in shock that he had been taken into custody. The reality of it was slowly sinking in and caused him to be quite circumspect about providing any answers to Royce-Smallworth. For several minutes, he stared blankly at nothing in particular.

"I do understand my rights as you have explained them to me and I would like to speak with an attorney, Detective Sergeant Royce-Smallworth," James finally said. "I know I have that right – even here in England – before answering any of your questions."

Had Hudson been placed under arrest in the United States on similar charges, he would have been immediately handcuffed by the Detective Sergeant's assistant. The UK, on the other hand, considered routine handcuffing of non-resistant suspects an unreasonable use of force. Instead, the assistant took firm control of Hudson's arm to emphasize that he was being detained.

"Come along now," the constable urged.

As they walked towards the waiting patrol car, Royce-Smallworth gave James Hudson information on acquiring the services of an attorney.

"Unless you have a particular attorney in mind, we will provide one for you. In fact, Miss Whitcomb herself worked with Miss Victoria Sulgrave, the equivalent of what you Americans call a 'public defender.' I'm sure Miss Sulgrave will be more than capable of handling your situation." Royce-Smallworth's contempt for Americans and the American legal system was obvious from her condescending tone.

James's thoughts were running wild. He knew he was being accused of murder, yet he had no recollection of any violent encounters with either Aaron Shepherd or Michelle Whitcomb. He also recognized that he had been drinking more than usual lately and wondered if he had begun suffering blackouts. James discounted that thought almost immediately as there were no blocks of time that he could not remember. Some, like his recent spat with Lucy Penderel, he would just as soon forget.

12: Now What Do I Do?

September, 1651

As Michelle Whitcomb walked away from the river with the four women, she was trying to figure out exactly where and when she was. Their clothing told her that she wasn't in 2011 anymore and her undergraduate minors in cultural anthropology and English history provided her with more insight.

She had noticed when the other four women disrobed for their bath that they all had an unusual amount of body hair. Their legs, their armpits, and other areas were more hirsute than any woman she had seen in 2011, even in field conditions. Puzzled, Michelle wondered if the young ladies found her own lack of body hair odd. She would soon find out.

Back at Katherine's home – which Michelle noticed was devoid of any male clothing or other accoutrements – the five women sat in front of a warming fire over which was suspended a cauldron of soup. The aroma wafting from the stockpot was heavenly and Michelle suddenly realized she was very hungry.

Katherine went to the kitchen and gathered five carved wooden bowls, five hammered pewter spoons, and a loaf of crusty bread; Michelle guessed it was probably a day old. Inviting each woman to the cauldron in turn, Katherine ladled a generous portion of the soup into each bowl before filling her own. The crusty loaf of bread was then passed from woman to woman, each tearing off a sizeable portion.

"My Sisters in Christ, shall we pray?" Elizabeth asked; it was more of a command than a request.

The women, Michelle included, bowed their heads as they made the sign of the cross.

Elizabeth intoned, "May this meal nourish our bodies, as Your Word nourishes our souls. We thank You for the hands that prepared this food and for the fellowship we share at this table. Let our hearts be filled with gratitude, and our conversations be seasoned with grace. Guide us in Your ways, and help us to remember those who are less fortunate. In Jesus' name, we pray. Amen." The remaining four repeated the "Amen" after Elizabeth.

The women began eating in silence; Michelle assessed that meals were a time of quiet reflection, not conversation. She stifled a giggle as slurping sounds filled the small eating area near the fire. She also noticed that there were shreds of an unidentifiable meat in the soup; she decided not to ask what type of meat it was. Her best guess, from its texture, was that it was mutton.

Elizabeth broke the silence and started an inquisitive conversation. "Lady Michelle, and I assume you are a lady from how your body is groomed, where do you come from?"

Michelle was somewhat prepared for this question and knew she had to give a believable response. She quickly took another spoonful of soup to delay responding, then pretended to have burned her mouth on the piping hot broth.

"Katherine, this soup is delicious!" Michelle exclaimed through her gasps, "I have never tasted anything so good."

"Surely you cannot be serious," Katherine replied, "it's no different than any other soup in any other hut in any other village, and I am sure, as a Lady, you are accustomed to fancier fare."

"I am not a Lady, as you suggest. I was born in France, schooled in England, and was sent back to France to enter a convent," Michelle said as convincingly as she could before adding a little more embellishment. "When I found out that my father had died of his war wounds and my mother dead of a fever, I had no choice but to return home and delay taking my vows." Michelle also had fluency in French, so if they challenged her on that point, she was ready.

The four women looked at each other knowingly. They knew "taking vows" should mean that their new acquaintance was probably Catholic and practicing Roman Catholicism in England was illegal. One of them had to ask the question.

"Lady Michelle," Alice began, "you said you were about to take your vows. May I ask why you were being sent to a convent?"

"Alice, please call me 'Michelle' as I have neither land nor title," Michelle replied, pausing for a moment before continuing her story. "My parents learned that I had fallen in love with a Protestant and had… umm… given him my body before we were wed." She hoped that this fabrication would stop further questions.

Michelle's story elicited stifled giggles from the other four women; they knew exactly what she was talking about.

Elizabeth replied, "Michelle, it will please you to know that you are among friends here. We are Catholics ourselves and practice our faith in secret. And… you should know that we were all well aware of the pleasures of the flesh before we took our own vows of chastity and poverty."

The other three women whispered to each other, with Katherine speaking up. "Elizabeth, we have consulted each other and agree that you should tell Michelle the truth."

Elizabeth glared at the other three. Her anger was obvious.

"Michelle, if you must know, we are all Sisters in the Augustinian order. Our order has existed in secret for over 100 years, since the time of King Henry VIII," Elizabeth explained. "When we had an abbey of our own, our sisters were known as White Ladies – and our former priory is on lands now owned by the Giffard family. The Giffards are secretly Catholic as well."

Michelle now had a better approximation where she was on the timeline of history. Her mind raced through a timeline that resided in her memory: Henry VIII broke with Rome in 1534 after Pope Clement VII refused Henry's request to divorce his first wife, Katherine of Aragon. Michelle also knew that Henry died in 1547. With those dates, Michelle calculated that she was now sometime during the mid-17th Century. She also now understood why there were no men living in the cottage: the four women were, as they would say in the 21st Century, "Brides of Christ."

Thanks to her secondary minor in English History, Michelle was familiar with some of the terms used by Elizabeth in her explanation. What Michelle lacked was context and how Henry VIII's break with the Roman Catholic Church over a century earlier was still affecting English religious life. She got that context almost immediately.

Elizabeth continued, "When Henry VIII dissolved the monasteries and abbeys, our order forfeited its lands, and they were deeded under Royal Warrants to friends of the King. That is how the Whorwood and Giffard families took ownership of our lands there. The two families have a large following and placed the rest of our minor holdings into the protective care of fellow Catholics. We are free to visit those holdings any time and use them for our own purposes whenever it is necessary."

"How has your order existed for so long without being discovered?" Michelle asked. She was also curious about the contradiction of the Giffards receiving land under a grant from the Crown despite their secret practice of

Catholicism. That question might have to wait for another day, she thought.

"We are very careful who we associate with," Elizabeth explained, "and I was amazed that my Sisters wanted to take you into our confidence without being more acquainted with your background or your beliefs."

Michelle nodded in understanding of what she was being told. She was raised in a devout Catholic home, attended Mass regularly, was educated in Catholic schools, and had been forced to learn Latin as part of that Catholic education. If these so-called "White Ladies" were ever visited by a priest for Mass, Michelle knew she would be prepared. She would not have to wait that long until her knowledge of the Latin liturgy was put to the test.

As twilight fell, several candles were lit around the cottage, Katherine lifted a floorboard and brought an ornate crucifix out of hiding, placing it on the table. All five of the Sisters knelt and genuflected once the crucifix was in its place of honor; after a brief hesitation, Michelle followed their actions.

Elizabeth explained that it was now time for Vespers and invited Michelle to join them.

As the elder Sister, it fell to Elizabeth to lead the liturgy. Chanting and singing were discouraged, so the Rite of Vespers was spoken in voices barely above whispers:

"Deus, in adiutorium meum intende. Domine, ad adiuvandum me festina. Gloria Patri, et Filio, et Spiritui Sancto. Sicut erat in principio, et nunc et semper, et in saecula saeculorum. Amen. Alleluia."

"O God, come to my assistance. O Lord, make haste to help me. Glory to the Father, and to the Son, and to the Holy Spirit. As it was in the beginning, is now, and will be forever. Amen. Alleluia."

Michelle instinctively joined the Latin recitation, completing it from memory and making the Sign of the Cross at the appropriate places. When the White Ladies began the recitation of the Magnificat, again Michelle was convincingly engaged. She did feel somewhat odd speaking rather than singing the Rite of Vespers as she had only ever participated in its musical form.

With Vespers complete, the ladies were free to relax and prepare for sleep. As Michelle was a guest, she was afforded the best accommodations in the small cottage and would not be sharing her bed with any of the other women, who would be doubling up in the remaining beds.

As the women returned from the privy and prepared to retire for the evening, Elizabeth knelt, made the Sign of the Cross, and offered one final prayer in English:

"In your mercy, Lord, dispel the darkness of this night. Let this household sleep in peace and awaken with joy at the dawn of a new day in Your name, through Jesus Christ our Lord, who taught us to pray…"

The other four women joined Elizabeth in the recitation of the Lord's Prayer. In keeping with the Catholic tradition of the time, it ended with the final petition, "… but deliver us from evil. Amen."

Evening prayers complete, it was Alice's job to bank the fire for the night. This simple task ensured that there would be sufficient embers in the morning to restart a blaze for cooking and to warm the room from the chill of the night.

Alice first found the glowing embers of the last piece of firewood from the day. She then covered the embers with warm ashes, finally placing two logs atop the ashes. That final important step provided the embers with enough oxygen to keep smoldering through the night so that fresh kindling and more logs would quickly catch fire in the morning simply from stirring the glowing embers.

Except for Michelle, the women fell asleep quickly. It wasn't long before snoring resonations filled the cottage. Michelle was able to pinpoint the source to Elizabeth and Katherine, the older of the four Sisters. Alice and Mary seemed to be asleep as well, but they were restless, tossing and turning for several minutes. It appeared almost as if their bodies moved as one under the blankets. Michelle stifled a laugh at the absurdity of their movements, reminiscent of some of her own encounters during her dormitory life as an undergraduate.

Michelle's mind raced as she stared at the ceiling. She wondered how she got here, why she was here, and what was going to happen to her if her story did not hold up to further scrutiny. Though none of the Sisters made an issue of it, Michelle was traveling alone, something that a woman just would not do in the 17th Century – unless she was running from something. Her story, unconvincing as it was, provided a societally correct explanation for her plight.

13: More Deception and Subterfuge

September, 1651

I was beginning to resent the way Charles was treating me like his personal valet and servant. My responsibilities of teaching him to speak in the local dialect and to walk like a common farm hand had morphed into something else entirely. I was also concerned that the elaborate ruses we were constructing to hide his identity were so complex that some of the foot soldiers like MacBride and Fraser would unintentionally reveal the true identify of the man we were now calling "William Jackson."

Once again, we were on the move to evade Roundhead patrols – and our entourage had become so large that it was hard to move unnoticed. Charles knew this, too, and suggested to Colonel Wyndham that a vanguard of at least two lightly armed men be sent ahead on foot anytime we approached a village. That duty up to this point had fallen on MacBride and Fraser, but their Scottish brogues were likely to draw suspicion if they were to engage in conversation with anyone outside of our group; Scots were generally assumed to be loyal to the Crown, not the Parliamentarian cause.

As we approached Halesowen, Colonel Wyndham checked the village with his spyglass. Through it, he could see that a unit of Roundhead cavalry was outside the village inn. Convinced that a common man and his wife would not get much attention, Wyndham sent the Petres ahead to observe the cavalry and to find a route through the village. If John Petre believed that safe passage was possible, his wife was to drop her red headscarf as a signal.

Less than a mile away, in a copse of evergreens, the remainder of our group waited impatiently for the red headscarf to fall. Colonel Wyndham, too, trembled with anticipation, keeping his spyglass trained on the Petres as they traversed the meadow between our hideout and the village below. Time seemed to stand still.

The Petres were stopped by a sentry outside where the horses were hobbled for grazing. The encounter, from what Wyndham could see through his spyglass, was jovial and non-threatening. Withy Petre confirmed the safety of their encounter and conspicuously dropped her headscarf – which John Petre quickly bent over and picked up.

Wyndham, seeing the confirmation of safety, dispatched Charles… "William Jackson"… and me to amble down the hill to the village. Wyndham reminded the king that our roles were that of servants and that we should be at all times deferential to the Petres and the Roundhead officer in charge of the cavalry detachment. Our cover story was that we had stopped at the top of the hill to relieve ourselves, "out of the lady's sight." Men at arms were not given to such modesty in the field and generally just relieved themselves wherever and whenever they felt the need.

Reaching the Petres and the cavalry, we bowed respectfully to the commanding officer, made our excuses, and took the reins of the Petres' horses to lead them through to the other side of the village. I hoped that none of the Roundhead soldiers would recognize the man now known as William Jackson to be Charles II *incognito*. I did detect a glimmer of recognition from one of the servants, but no one in authority would be likely to take his report seriously.

Wyndham watched all of this through his spyglass and hoped that the cavalry would soon mount up and depart the village. As if they were responding to Wyndham's thoughts, the commanding officer instructed his horsemen to mount up. They were quickly on their way and passed us at a slow trot. With the Roundhead cavalry quickly out of sight, Wyndham followed with the rest of our entourage.

Lord Wilmot had also been observing the goings-on through his own spyglass. Once we were all safely together and the cavalry out of sight, Wilmot intimated to Charles that he was acquainted with the Roundhead officer and knew him to be a man of uncertain alliances, perhaps even a spy.

"I hope we never cross paths with that man again. He's not to be trusted," Wilmot said quietly, intending to be heard only by the inner circle around Charles, me included. "I am pretty sure our paths crossed at Dunbar while I was an advisor to Lord Newark just two years ago. When Edinburgh fell to Cromwell's forces, everything was in disarray, and it was hard to tell who was loyal to whom."

I suddenly felt like I was living inside a history book. Though I had briefly studied English history during my undergraduate days, it was in another time and another place and had no relevance to me in Michigan. Now I was in the thick of things, hearing raw first-hand accounts that were not already embellished by storytellers such as Samuel Pepys who interviewed Charles after he was reinstated to the throne in 1660 – nine years into my *current* future. It was certainly a mystifying situation. I hoped that the long-term effects of this bewilderment would not eventually drive me to insanity.

I still had no idea how I would get back to my own time. It was now clear to me that the round disk embossed with Hecate's Wheel had something to do with my presence in 1651. It could also be my gateway back to 2011.

*   *   *   *   *

Dawn broke over the cottage where the four White Ladies and Michelle were awakening. Michelle sniffed in disgust at the invisible miasma of chamberpot permeating the air. She hoped that, as a guest, she would not be expected to carry it outdoors to empty it. The other women seemed to be unaffected by the smell. This, Michelle thought, was living proof of people becoming "nose blind" to the odors of their environment.

Being the youngest of the four and the newest to their order, Alice was assigned most of the menial tasks in the cottage. It was her job to empty the chamberpot into the outdoor privy, then return to the cottage to rekindle the cooking fire.

Personal hygiene, Michelle noticed, was lacking; Alice did not avail herself of soap and water after emptying the filthy, smelly, disgusting chamberpot. Instead, she used cool ashes from the hearth as an abrasive, rubbing it first into the chamberpot as a cleanser and then between her palms in earnest, wiping both "clean" with an already soiled rag. Michelle almost retched in disgust and hoped that Alice would not be responsible for cooking any part of their breakfast.

While Alice was taking care of her chores, Mary invited Michelle to join her on a walk to the henhouse to gather eggs for their morning meal. Michelle was familiar with farms; her maternal grandparents had owned a successful farm in Southwestern Michigan when she was a child. She immediately noticed how immaculate the henhouse was, with each hen having its own cubicle, making it easy to gather the eggs.

"The henhouse is cleaner than Alice's hands and that chamberpot," Michelle thought to herself.

The hens were accustomed to Mary's daily intrusions and allowed her to retrieve the eggs – but Michelle was not someone the hens recognized, and they immediately went into protective "mother hen" mode. By the time she had cleared her twelve assigned cubicles of eggs, Michelle's right hand was a bloody mess of oozing puncture wounds, thanks to the hens' relentless pecking.

Mary stifled a chuckle as Michelle tried to hide her bloodied and now throbbing hand while at the same time applying pressure to staunch the flow of blood.

"Michelle, you're not the first one to fall victim to the beaks of our hens," Mary said as solemnly as she could.

"I forgot just how protective hens could be when someone or something was trying to take their eggs," Michelle responded as the memories from her childhood surfaced. They both erupted in raucous laughter. Internally, though, Michelle was concerned about the possibility of infection, as antibiotics were still about three centuries in the future.

"Let's return to the cottage for breakfast. Elizabeth will be ready to start our morning prayers… Lauds… before the cooking begins. It is Wednesday and we shall be baking bread throughout the morning," Mary explained. "It is our Michaelmas tradition to distribute bread to the less fortunate as we travel on the morrow to one of our smaller holdings to the south. Some will know we are Catholics, but others among the poor will think that we are nothing more than a group of generous women. We will be away for at least a fortnight. Katherine, because she is unable to walk for long distances, will remain behind to tend to the cottage, our gardens, and our hens. If we leave them to their own devices, the hens will flee in search of food and weeds will quickly overtake our wonderful, productive garden."

Michelle had noticed Katherine limping when they returned from the stream and wondered if there was some underlying medical cause. As part of her coursework, Michelle had studied forensic anthropology and had seen many skeletal remains with poorly healed fractures, joint displacements, or osteoporosis. She wondered which of those might be causing Katherine such discomfort, knowing that medical science and joint replacements in the 21st Century would likely have been able to restore Katherine to a pain-free and fully functioning existence. Michelle was saddened that the delightful Katherine was not living her fullest life.

After morning prayers and breakfast, the women went to work baking the small loaves of bread that they would distribute to the needy. Michelle was assigned the simplest task, that of shaping the leavened dough into round loaves. Once shaped, the loaves were placed on a baking stone and then into the oven.

The aroma of baking bread quickly filled the small cottage and evoked Michelle's memories of visiting her great-grandmother's farmhouse where it seemed like there was always something in or just out of the oven. It might be cookies one visit, bread the next, and pies the time after that. Michelle smiled at the happy memories and was momentarily distracted from her current situation and transported to the farms of Southwestern Michigan.

Mary interrupted Michelle's mental journey into her memories. "Our sojourn will take us about 50 miles to the south of here, to Stratford-upon-Avon, where we have a small holding. The caretaker there is a devout adherent to our faith. It usually takes us about four days to get there, even with our stops to distribute the bread. We have been doing this for many years and have yet to encounter any problems with the local villagers. They truly appreciate our efforts," Mary explained. "The wars have taken their toll on people's livelihoods. Children are starving and without some relief, many will die during the coming winter."

Michelle was curious about their mode of travel and asked, "Sister Mary, will we be on foot, horseback, or in a cart of some kind?"

Mary replied, "We go by whatever means God provides. If it is to be our feet, that it will be. If a gentleman offers us transport on horseback, we shall thank the Lord in our evening prayers. We will be most blessed if God Almighty provides us with a horse-drawn wagon so that we won't have to carry everything on our backs."

*   *   *   *   *

The Roundhead cavalry gone, we were once again on the move. Our next destination was to be Stratford-upon-Avon by way of Stratford Manor and other villages along the River Avon. Wyndham hoped that we would find a shallow draught rowboat in one of those villages that could easily be floated down the meandering Avon to its confluence with the River Severn. Finding a suitable vessel in Stratford-upon-Avon was a near certainty, Wyndham assured me, but also increased the chances of being recognized. He hoped that we would not have to wait that long. As he spoke, I vividly remembered how the previous sojourn to Bristol a few weeks earlier had been a total failure.

It had become habit for me to follow the directions of the men with military experience, most recently Colonel Wyndham. It was Wyndham's plan that kept us from being apprehended by the Roundhead cavalry at the last village and I hoped that he would be able to continue his success as we moved south. If it had been up to me, I would not have split the group up as he did – except for MacBride and Fraser and their Scottish brogues.

Wyndham also devised a plan for us to spread out along the route so that we were not traveling as an entourage, looking to the casual observer as if we were multiple groups. Though this left Charles and me more exposed and without armed escort at times, I agreed to the separation of as much as a mile between the lead group, the middle, and the end. I did suggest, however, that we not always keep the same group order, and that Charles and I be allowed to move to the front or rear during the day, when a reconnaissance for sleeping arrangements or a rear guard first thing in the morning were not necessary. Wyndham readily agreed to my suggestion.

We developed a daytime plan whereby the lead group would stop for a rest period and await the other two groups' passing. When the new lead group stopped, the other two would leapfrog ahead. In this manner, the lead group was always changing, and I was certain that we could make it to Stratford-upon-Avon without incident.

Regardless of the leapfrogging, our merry band could only move as fast as the slowest unmounted man. That limited us to between ten and fifteen miles per day, unlike the twenty or more we could accomplish if we were all on horseback and in a gentle canter, stopping as needed to rest and water the horses. Charles, thankfully, had developed enough physical stamina and fortitude that equine transportation was no longer essential.

We had been on the move for a little over two days and had just stopped for a rest period. Charles and I were in the lead group, resting as we waited for the rear group to catch up and pass us. Knowing that they were unmounted, I was surprised to hear the clatter of an approaching horse cart and... women's voices, one of which sounded strangely familiar in spite of the British accent.

Charles and MacBride both gave me a quizzical look. Because it was unlikely that the women were traveling without a potentially hostile male escort, MacBride quietly suggested that he and Fraser hide in the underbrush with their swords and daggers at the ready while Charles and I both kept our weapons sheathed. This way, at least half of us were prepared for immediate defensive action.

It was the young Charles who greeted the approaching cart with four women on board. We had decided earlier that Charles, in spite of his vertical stature, was the best one to meet unknowns because of his youthful appearance and non-threatening mannerisms.

"Good afternoon, ladies," Charles said in greeting, "I am William Jackson at your service. My master awaits your company just over there." There was not even the slightest glimmer of recognition from the women.

Ever chivalrous and polite, Charles helped each of the ladies down from the cart in turn and guided them over to where I was sitting. With a servile wave of his hand and a half-bow, Charles introduced me to our visitors.

"Ladies, may I present Mister Aaron Shepherd, my master?" Charles said in a syrupy yet common voice. He certainly was playing the part.

When he said my name, I heard a stifled squeal from one of the women. There was something familiar about that squeal.

"She's fainted!" the eldest of the party exclaimed. Carefully, the women lowered their unconscious companion to the ground and loosened the clothing around her neck.

"Mister Shepherd, do you perchance have some water or a draught of ale? It seems our friend is in dire need of liquid refreshment and a little more fresh air."

"Jackson, please see to the ladies' needs. It would be impolite of us to not be of assistance," I said with as much authority as I could muster; I hoped that the ladies would believe me to be the one in charge.

14: A Tense Reunion

Late September, 1651

After making sure the fainted woman was comfortable, Elizabeth introduced her group.

"I am Elizabeth Hastings. My three companions are Anne Eaton, Alice Deighton, and Miss Michelle Whitcomb." The two other conscious women nodded as Elizabeth spoke each of their names.

Elizabeth continued, "Miss Whitcomb is regaining her senses after her swoon."

It was my turn to be taken aback by the sudden appearance of a familiar name *and* a familiar face. Was it possible that this woman was indeed *the* Michelle Whitcomb from the Wroxeter dig? I would have to wait until she completely regained consciousness to find out.

A still groggy Michelle Whitcomb looked me in the eye. After a wide-eyed glimmer of recognition, she furrowed her brow. I could see the questions running through her mind, though they remained unspoken. I, too, had questions to ask the familiar face before me. I bobbed my head slightly and raised my eyebrows to let her know that it was up to her to open the conversation.

"Mister Shepherd, you seem vaguely familiar to me," Michelle said to open the conversation. "Where might I have seen you before?"

"I am not entirely sure, Miss Whitcomb, but you look familiar to me as well," I replied, raising my left eyebrow inquisitively.

Interrupting our tentative conversation, Elizabeth said, "We will leave you two alone for a bit so you can determine where your paths might have crossed previously."

"Ladies? Mr. Jackson? Shall we give these two a few moments alone?" Elizabeth's words were more of a command than they were a question, and in response the other two women, now accompanied by "William Jackson," walked about a hundred yards away, taking seats on a newly fallen tree. They tacitly understood that it was going to take some time for my discussion with Michelle.

After a few very uncomfortable moments, Michelle finally spoke. "Aaron, is that really you? We all thought you had abandoned us and were most probably dead."

"Miss Whitcomb," I began, keeping everything formal for the moment, "it is good to see you again. I am truly sorry our last parting was not on good terms."

"Aaron Shepherd! I am truly surprised by your behavior," Michelle Whitcomb snapped, in a tone that could only be described as a low growl. "We worked together for how long? Almost three years, was it? This is the thanks I get for covering your ass for as long as I did?"

"Do you know what year this is?" I asked, trying to deflect her burgeoning anger and about-to-explode temper.

"I know I'm sometime after Henry VIII and before George III," she replied.

"You are correct. We are in the Year of Our Lord 1651. The Battle of Worcester took place approximately one month ago," I informed her. "My man, William Jackson, is really King Charles II."

"My recollection of how I got here is very vague," said Michelle, "but I think it has something to do with that object we were working to uncover at the dig."

"I'm almost certain that's how I got here," I answered, "and I think I know how we could get back to 2011. We just have to find another Hecate's Wheel."

There was another awkward and tense silence before Michelle spoke, "Aaron… I was arrested for your suspected murder by the West Mercia Police and I am pretty sure that James Hudson has been arrested as a suspect in *my* disappearance. The female Detective Sergeant leading the investigations seemed to dislike Americans and was looking for a feather in her cap by making something stick. In my case, the American Consulate and the British equivalent of a public defender intervened to get my release from jail. I even had to surrender my passport to the Consulate."

She continued, leaning in conspiratorially, "Aaron, you need to know that I told these four ladies – who are actually Catholic nuns known as 'White Ladies' – that I was about to enter a convent in France but was called back home because of my parents' demise. I've also alluded to the possibility that I might have given my innocence to a man to add credence to my story of taking vows."

We spent the next several minutes explaining our current situations and what had transpired since our separate arrivals. When we both had said all we had to say, I tented my fingers under my chin, pondering how we should deal with our predicament.

"First, Michelle, we must not divulge our knowledge of how we got here to your three traveling companions," I said in a voice barely above a whisper. "Second, we have to maintain our cover stories: you, being a dishonored former virgin and me being a wealthy traveler with my manservant and two hired men-at-arms."

"Men-at-arms? What do you mean, Aaron? Why would you need a guard?" Michelle asked.

My answer was interrupted by Elizabeth clearing her throat to announce her approach. "Mister Shepherd and Miss Whitcomb, shall we be on our way? I am sure the two of you can discuss whatever it is you were discussing while we are on our way to our next village."

Michelle's deferential answer seemed appropriate to the situation. She clearly wanted Elizabeth to appear in control of our movements.

Meanwhile, I summoned MacBride and Fraser from the underbrush and sent them to the vanguard position with Charles after introducing them to the ladies. I did not want the men, Charles included, to overhear what Michelle and I would be discussing as we continued on our way. I was not concerned about the three women, assuming the clatter of their cart would obscure our conversation.

We were once again on the move and Michelle spent several minutes explaining the charitable mission she and the White Ladies were on. Her narrative explained the bakery aroma that was emanating from beneath the cloth covering the cart's cargo. As we so far had not eaten much during the day, I began salivating in anticipation of the fresh bread.

Michelle also told me about the hygiene practices she had observed when Alice emptied the chamber pot the previous morning. Aside from the story's nauseating undertones, we had a good laugh at how far we'd come from the days devoid of indoor plumbing and flush toilets. I did remind Michelle that one of the earliest flush toilets was installed in Richmond Palace during the reign of Elizabeth I. Regardless, I now found my appetite waning because of Michelle's story.

"Aaron Shepherd, would you please stop 'mansplaining' things to me? I think you remember that I have an undergraduate minor in English history," Michelle said with feigned indignation.

Our time together enabled the breakdown of some of the formal boundaries that existed between us in 2011. We were now more like lifelong friends than work colleagues.

I welcomed the subtle changes in our relationship, and I think that Michelle did as well.

"We are on our way to Long Marston, near Stratford-upon-Avon, where the White Ladies have a small holding. You and 'Mister Jackson' will be welcome there as well. Elizabeth has told me that the caretakers are sympathetic to the Royalist cause and practitioners of the Catholic faith," said Michelle, "and from Long Marston, we will turn back north for Chillington Hall and Elizabeth's leasehold there."

"You mean *the* Stratford-upon-Avon? That's where William Shakespeare lived!" It was difficult for me to hide my excitement at passing through a place of such historical significance. Shakespeare's works had always appealed to me.

"Again, Aaron, your willingness to restate the obvious is annoying," Michelle teased.

It must have been serendipity, as I had heard Lord Wilmot talking about Long Marston as a potential stopover for the royal entourage. Like the ladies, we would be spending at least two days there before continuing on our way. The stopover would provide me with an opportunity to speak with Michelle and potentially plan an exit from our current predicament.

In our initial discussion, I suggested to Michelle that we journey back to the north and try to find the places where we both arrived. We quickly discounted that as a viable possibility since we would have to separate from the safety of our now-combined groups. We were both concerned that our independent interactions with the local populace would reveal us as impostors.

I suggested that it would be best if I took Michelle into my protection and separated her from the White Ladies. We would then continue with Charles, ultimately crossing into France and hoping that we would find another Wheel that could transport us back to our own time. It was a longshot at best.

15: Wanderers

Still September, 1651

Autumn mornings in England were generally chilly, and this morning was no exception. The temperature was hovering a few degrees above freezing, and the exhalations of any breathing creature could be clearly seen. With a cloud of condensation, we set off on the next leg of our journey which we hoped would soon take us to Bristol and a ship bound for France.

With agreement from Elizabeth Hastings, Michelle Whitcomb was now under my protection. She would not be returning north with the three nuns. Because Elizabeth felt it was her duty to protect Michelle as a fallen woman, it was no small accomplishment to convince Elizabeth that I would safely transport Michelle to France and the convent she was to have entered.

Even with Michelle's companionship, I was emotionally at an all-time low and bordering on what would have been diagnosed in my own time as clinical depression. I felt like giving up, resigning myself to the possibility of remaining in 1651 as a servant to Charles II as there did not yet appear to be any viable or believable path back to the 21st Century. I perceived our situation was dire as memories of events in "our time" were fading from the forefront of my consciousness. Michelle Whitcomb notwithstanding, one thing I could remember was James Hudson's last report from his daily ground penetrating radar scan. Why that particular memory stuck with me was a mystery.

During our three-day stop, Charles – still using the alias Willam Jackson – had another close call with being recognized. One of the servants allegedly had been in the king's personal guard at Worcester, so Charles challenged the servant's memory.

"Good sir," Charles began, using a politeness not normally afforded the servants, "can you describe the man you saw as that scalawag, Charles?"

"He looked a little like you, but aye, a might bit shorter, perhaps by three finger or more," the servant answered. Over our evening meal, we all had a good laugh over the servant's identification.

As each day wore on, every one with a risk of discovery by Roundhead patrols, it seemed less and less likely that Charles would ever be able to leave England for the relative safety of France. That point was driven home when we arrived in Bristol and found out that there would not be another ship heading down the River Avon to the Severn estuary and then onward to France for at least another month.

Frustrated by this turn of events, we were now on our way to the home of Colonel Francis Wyndham in Trent, some 40 miles to the south. The Wyndham family was known to both Lord Wilmot and to Charles as staunch supporters of the Stuarts and the Royalist effort. That support and relationship went back to Charles's infancy.

While we were billeted in Trent, I was given the opportunity to participate in an evening patrol around the grounds. In one overgrown area – which some of the locals believed was haunted – I encountered a glow emanating from a small grove of oak trees. Thinking it might be a cooking fire of a forest-dweller or poacher, I crept as quietly as I could through the underbrush.

When I emerged into the clearing next to the oak grove, there was a familiar symbol carved into a large oak tree. It looked like it had been freshly carved, but at the same time weathered around the edges. The exposed wood seemed almost to glow in the dimming evening light.

My mind raced. *"I've seen this before!"*.

As I moved closer to the oak tree to investigate, I felt drawn to the symbol almost as if I had lost control of my own movements. The other two men assigned to the evening patrol, **James MacBride and Seumas Fraser – who were the sentries that discovered me naked in the woods after my time hop – watched** as I moved closer to the oak tree. I glanced back over my shoulder, and they appeared to be shrouded in mist and frozen in place.

My right hand involuntarily reached out for the carving. Fear of the unknown took hold of my emotions as my hand drew closer to the symbol, almost as if guided by another unseen hand over my own. My index finger extended and was drawn to the center of the circular symbol. It was then that I realized the symbol was the same one that appeared on the buried object at the Roman archaeological site back in 2011. *Was I about to make another jump in time, against my will?*

I didn't have to wait long to find out. I screamed in pain as my index finger touched the center of the circle maze. I felt like a swarm of mad hornets had just inhabited the entirety of my arm. It was a sensation I would never forget and never wanted to experience again.

Just as suddenly as it all started, I was released from the pull of the carving. The pain in my arm was subsiding through the pins-and-needles of blocked circulation and had become more of a nuisance than a discomfort. I turned around and saw that MacBride and Fraser were still standing in the same spots. They both had strange, puzzled looks on their faces.

"James, Seumas, did you see what just happened?" I asked.

"What do you mean, Mister Shepherd?" James MacBride responded, "I didn't see anything other than you touching that tree."

"You didn't see a glowing symbol carved into the tree?" I queried.

"No, sir. We was wondering why you wanted to touch that tree," Seumas Fraser answered.

"Was I dreaming that I was screaming in pain?"

"No, sir… we didn't hear a thing," the two men answered almost in unison.

Now I was even more confused. How had they not seen what had happened nor heard me screaming in pain? Had I been transported into a temporal void and left them behind for a few moments? Or… was I simply imagining things? I likely would never know.

When we left Colonel Wyndham's house, it was with instructions from Lord Wilmot that we were to return promptly after our patrol around the grounds. He had it from a good source, which I assumed to be a "lady" at one of the local public houses, that the Roundheads would not be in the area for at least the next few days. Wilmot shared the source of his information only with Charles and me. We both had a chuckle at Wilmot's admission of indiscretion with the so-called lady; he was, after all, a married man.

Reaching the Wyndham home, we set down our arms and I reported to Lord Wilmot and Charles that our patrol had been uneventful. In retrospect, I probably should have confided in at least Michelle about my strange, otherworldly experience. I was worried that she would not believe me and simply chalk it up to "too much drink" Regardless, I could not figure out why MacBride and Fraser had not shared any part of what had been, to me, a very real experience.

The Wyndhams regularly hosted banquets in their spacious dining room and I was invited to join them for the evening repast and surprisingly found myself seated at the head table next to Michelle, along with Lady Wyndham and her eldest son. Fraser and MacBride were seated to the rear of the dining room along with senior members of the household staff.

During the conversation, Lady Wyndham told me that her husband and Lord Wilmot had to leave on urgent business and could not attend the banquet. I wondered just what they might have been up to; perhaps it was to find us a vessel to transport us across the channel.

As the evening wore on, I saw Fraser and MacBride pointing repeatedly in my direction with their cutlery and erupting in laughter – which I assumed was at my expense. I could only imagine what they were saying about my mental state. Their guffaws and finger-pointing were so unsettling that I totally forgot that Michelle was sitting right next to me. What I would have given to be a fly on the wall, listening to their conversation.

The oak tree experience was very real to me, and I could not shake the image of the glowing carving from my consciousness. It haunted me even more vividly than some of the nightmares I had experienced as a young child. I knew it was going to be a long and largely sleepless night as I tried to mentally decipher what I had experienced at the oak tree. Once I made sense of it, I would have to recount it all to Michelle.

Several flasks of wine and mead later, everyone in the dining room was well on the road to intoxication, myself included. I justified my alcoholic excess as an attempt to blot out the patrol and to hopefully ensure that I would have uninterrupted sleep in the short hours until morning.

The banquet ended around midnight, and I returned to my quarters adjacent to Charles's. With a full belly and still buzzed, I quickly fell into a deep sleep – only to be awakened a couple of hours later by a visionary dream.

In the dream, I re-lived my journey back in time. I saw the collapse of the twin towers... Pearl Harbor... the Titanic... Lincoln's assassination... the Alamo... the Battle of Monmouth... George Washington fighting in the French and Indian War... slave ships unloading their human cargoes in New Haven... then a quick jump across the Atlantic to 1651 in the weeks after the Battle of Worcester – and my present situation. There was one problem, though: I had no memory of passing these waypoints in time when I jumped from 2011 to 1651. That hop backwards in time was seemingly instantaneous.

I awoke with a start after my dream sent me falling through the air only to crash land naked in the woods where I was discovered by the sentries. It was as if my mind was trying to make sense of it all and rationalize what had happened. New Haven, I remembered, was *my* connection to the past: it was a port of call for the *Hector* and its cargo of migrants from England in the 1630s.

"His wife... forthwith locked the doors upon him, and with the help of her two daughters kept him in by force, telling him that she and her children would not be undone for ever a landlord of them all; and threatened him that if he did offer to stir out of doors, she would go instantly to Lyme and give information against both him and his landlord to Captain Macy, who had then the command of a foot company there."

From the Alford Depositions, as included in Samuel Pepys' notes, 1684

16: New Beginnings
Late September, 1651

In our three evenings together at the Wyndham house in Trent, Michelle and I had reacquainted ourselves with each other. It was no longer necessary for us to maintain a professional relationship as we had during our time at Wroxeter but we were bound by the proprieties and moral standards of 1651. We both quickly realized we already shared feelings for each other.

As we sat at what would be our final banquet at the Wyndham house, Michelle surreptitiously reached to her left under the table and tenderly took my right hand in hers. I squeezed her hand firmly in mine to signal that I welcomed her touch. That single moment seemed to have stirred something in both of us.

Anticipating more interaction with Michelle after the banquet, I was careful about my further consumption of ale and spirits. The last thing I wanted was to be inebriated when an opportunity presented itself. I noticed that Michelle, too, limited her alcohol consumption.

With Lord Wilmot away, Lady Wilmot dismissed the musicians and the banquet was officially over. Many of the unencumbered male attendees simply fell asleep leaning against the outer walls of the banqueting hall or prostrating themselves on the floor. I had already learned that this was an accepted practice for large gatherings as the host did not generally provide beds for all of the guests.

It was only the unmarried women who were afforded barracks-style accommodation in the main house, sometimes four or more to a room. Married couples fared only slightly better, being assigned partitioned areas in their sleeping quarters. As Michelle and I were not married, she was expected to retire with the other unmarried or unaccompanied women. It was also not appropriate for the two of us to be unchaperoned for extended periods of time.

Michelle and I exited the banqueting hall into the cool moonlit night and took an outdoor path to the doorway leading to her assigned accommodations. In the shadows of a privet hedge, I could contain myself no longer and took Michelle Whitcomb into my arms, looked into her eyes, and kissed her passionately. She did not resist and seemed to welcome my ministrations.

"Aaron," Michelle whispered, "I've wanted this for a long time. Even that darned female Detective Sergeant knew I wanted more than a professional connection to you. She noticed that every time she mentioned your name, I would blush like a schoolgirl. I finally admitted to myself that I did indeed want more than a working relationship. Unfortunately, she used that against me and assumed that, because my affection was not overtly returned, I had taken the part of jilted potential lover and let anger control my actions. She could not have been further from the truth."

It was my turn to explain. "Michelle, you do understand that I could not afford for us to become romantically entangled at the dig. It would have compromised the integrity of our research. There were already rumors floating around the compound that I was giving you preferential treatment and I was not about to stoop to the level of James Hudson and his flagrant promiscuity. That barmaid was not his first conquest. There were several others before you arrived, all of them with... well... sluts."

"Yes, I know people were talking about us behind our backs," said Michelle, "but I discounted their gossip as jealousy. You, Doctor Shepherd, are quite a catch! You are intelligent, handsome, and polite."

Now it was my turn to blush. I was not accustomed to a woman giving me such high praise, especially about my status as an eligible bachelor.

After we declared our feelings for each other, we realized we had not been alone in the garden area. We had to stifle our giggles when we heard the sounds of at least one other couple engaged in... well... romantic activity. I clearly heard the brogue of Seumas Fraser encouraging his partner to keep going in the most graphic terms. I shuddered at the thought as I knew his personal hygiene practices were lacking.

Leaving Fraser's vulgar encouragements behind, we continued our leisurely stroll to the women's accommodation at the far end of the house. Outside that door, I gave Michelle a furtive and discrete kiss on the forehead and then on her lips. My left hand had been gently resting on her right hip; she took it in hers and guided it seductively to her breast before she eased it away. Her hand then slowly and teasingly slid from mine as she opened the door and stepped inside. Our fingertips were the last touchpoint to part. She smiled, turned into the room, and closed the door.

Back in the banqueting hall with the other unattached men, I was assaulted by the odors of flatulence, unwashed bodies, and a ripening chamber pot that the servants had conveniently "forgotten" to empty after the banquet. Had the night been just a little warmer, I would have opted for the opportunity to sleep outside in the fresh air. It certainly would have been healthier than sleeping in a room that constantly assaulted my olfactory nerve.

To mitigate the odors, I took a space as close as I could get to one of the drafty windows of the banqueting hall. Despite my exhaustion, sleep did not come easily as the events of the past few hours with Michelle remained fresh in my mind. I wished now that I had had more to drink and hoped that there might still be a partial bottle of wine somewhere in the hall. Unfortunately, the servants had done their jobs too well, removing anything stronger than ale for their own consumption. The only thing that was left was a jug of very flat and mostly tasteless inferior ale. Still, it was alcohol and just what I needed to fall asleep quickly; I would have to deal with the residual effects of its consumption on my urinary tract later.

Returning from the privy (I refused to use a chamber pot), I lay in my chosen spot for a few more moments in the semi-darkness before sunrise and was jolted fully wide awake by a call from Charles in the adjacent guest room.

"Mister Shepherd!" Charles bellowed, "we must be on our way forthwith. Lord Wilmot's messenger just reported that a Roundhead patrol has been sighted less than a half-day's ride west of here."

"Yes, sir," I answered, "I will pack our things." Charles was now treating me as his personal valet as well as his teacher.

"Sir, should I awaken MacBride and Fraser, too?" I asked.

"Yes, and that strumpet you call Michelle," Charles answered. His tone was icy.

"Yes, sir," I answered with no enthusiasm in my voice.

Strumpet? How dare he! I thought to myself, knowing that engaging Charles in a defense of Michelle's honor was almost certain to draw his ire. She was anything but a strumpet and had always been honorable in her dealings with anyone associated with Charles, me included. I wondered if he secretly feared that I would run off with Michelle and disappear from his service.

As I left Charles's bed chamber, I heard him bellowing for Colonel Wyndham and Lord Wilmot, who had just returned from their clandestine expedition. Their nonverbal cues told me that they had something to report to Charles that would determine the next leg of our journey. Lady Wyndham had already awakened the servants and the house was already bustling with early morning activity aimed at the singular goal of getting us on our way before the Roundhead patrol arrived.

I packed Charles's accoutrements, taking care to conceal his finer clothing. As I packed, I hoped that we would soon find passage to France. When we started, I was in awe of being a part of history; it had now become a tedious undertaking, and I now had the added distraction of Michelle Whitcomb.

Once we were on our way, Charles and Colonel Wyndham decided that we needed to emphasize speed in our movements more than concealment. So that we could move more quickly, they suspended the leapfrogging we had done before taking a respite in Trent. Unfortunately, that also meant I would be at Charles's side and not have the opportunity to talk to Michelle without a risk of being overheard except during our brief rest periods.

My continuing proximity to Charles afforded me the opportunity to overhear many of his discussions with Wyndham and Wilmot. Their clandestine jaunt in the days before we left Trent had taken them to Charmouth where they had allegedly contracted with a Captain Stephen Limbry to sail to Saint-Malo in a few days' time, leaving just after dawn.

Upon arriving in Charmouth, we took rooms in the Queen's Arms Inn. I shared a room with Charles while Wilmot and Wyndham shared another. Michelle was put in yet a third room along with Jane, Wyndham's cousin who was purported to be betrothed to and eloping with Lord Wilmot.

Early the next morning, we traveled to the beach where Captain Limbry was to have met our party. Limbry never appeared, leaving our small entourage stranded. Charles and Wyndham decided to investigate.

Taking Wilmot and Jane with them to maintain their cover story, they separated from the rest of us and headed for nearby Bridport. There, they hoped to find the missing Captain Limbry. Wilmot, however, had to remain in Charmouth to find a blacksmith after his horse lost a shoe.

While they were away, we learned that Limbry had been locked in his bedroom by his wife and daughters out of fear for his safety. Apparently, Limbry and his wife, Mary, had been the talk of the town for some time. Theirs was a rocky and tumultuous marriage, with the almost adult daughters generally making their arguments loud three-against-one affairs. Stephen was the laughingstock of the town's male population who considered him unable to control his wife, while the women felt emboldened by his wife's actions. In the 21st Century, Captain Stephen Limbry would likely have been diagnosed with maladaptive daydreaming, or "Walter Mitty Syndrome." He was fully functional only when he was out to sea; extended time on shore exacerbated his tendency to daydream.

Mary Limbry usually relented when Stephen recited and strongly emphasized a portion of their wedding vows, "… to love, honor, and *obey*…" If nothing else, Mary Limbry was a God-fearing Christian woman, baptized into the Church of England. She knew that women were supposed to accede to the demands of their husbands. When he presented her with a reminder of her vows, her temper abated somewhat.

In Bridport, Charles, Wyndham, and Jane discovered that the town was filled with Parliamentary troops preparing to head for Jersey. Undaunted, Charles walked through the encamped soldiers directly to the best inn in town and arranged for rooms. He was almost recognized by the proprietor but successfully talked his way out of the situation.

Wilmot later explained to me that a series of events allowed them to avoid capture by the local constabulary and Parliamentarian soldiers. They had narrowly escaped from Bridport on a small country lane, missing a military unit that was riding in from Charmouth. Wilmot also detailed how he and Charles had become disoriented after their rendezvous and elected to spend a night in the village of Broadwindsor at The George Inn where a contingent of soldiers was also to be billeted. According to Wilmot, serendipity prevailed once again when a camp follower went into labor; the combination of her birthing screams and a very vocal infant distracted the soldiers enough to allow Charles and Wilmot to quietly depart for their return to the Wyndham house in Trent.

Later, during a private moment, I shared with Michelle as much of Wilmot's tale as I could remember. I was not sure if it was embellished or if it was largely truthful. Michelle's response was something along the lines of "Holy shit!" and a short lecture on the fact that we were now living the history rather than just studying it from someone else's account. I was glad that no one had overheard her use of an expletive as the public use of vulgar language was considered unladylike, and she had done her best to present the persona of a lady, albeit without the formal title.

Michelle explained that her undergraduate studies had specifically covered this period in English history and that some of the hypotheses her professors espoused were now proven true. "If I could only jump forward... and backward... in time to tell them they were right," she mused.

17: Motivations

September – October, 2010

Gemma Royce-Smallworth was hired by the West Mercia Police Department a few months after her graduation from the University of Leeds in 2000 with a degree in criminology. West Mercia wasn't her first choice of employers. She had visions of being hired into the Metropolitan Police Service, euphemistically known as Scotland Yard.

She had interned there during the last months of her university coursework and found it to be a bastion of misogyny, arrogance, and male privilege. At times, it seemed to Gemma to be more like a gentlemen's club than a law enforcement agency. She was fully aware of the gender imbalance between male and female constables, which at the time was a ratio of four to one.

Gemma was elated when the courier delivered an official envelope bearing the MPS seal. That elation quickly turned to disgust when she read the offer letter: she would be hired into a position as a clerk typist rather than as a detective investigator. Not only did she feel this was an insult to her education and intelligence, but the proposed salary was barely enough to survive in central London. She declined the offer and instead chose to wait for another constabulary to reach out in response to her *curriculum vitae*.

Gemma didn't have to wait long before another envelope arrived with the seal of the West Mercia Police. All she had to do was complete the required two-year training course that focused on the operational aspects of police work. Though she had already been in school for four years to earn her degree, it was an opportunity she welcomed.

At the end of her first year of training, Gemma specialized as a detective – with a sub-specialization in firearms and weapons. She was ready to hit the ground running and quickly proved herself worthy. During her first year as a detective, she solved two murder cases and received a citation. One of those cases involved the extradition of an American servicemember who had been spirited out of the United Kingdom before he could be charged with murder.

Had Gemma been male, those two resolved cases on their own might have gotten her a conditional promotion to

Detective Sergeant. Instead, over the next seven years, she was assigned to over a dozen supposedly unsolvable cases. Using crucial evidence that was right under the noses of her self-important and arrogant male counterparts, she quickly solved each case – much to the amazement of her superiors.

The Wroxeter cases were perplexing. Gemma knew she was missing something and that the existing evidence against James Hudson was circumstantial. Hudson just did not seem like the type to have murdered two people and then disposed of their bodies. Then again, he was an alcoholic who seemed to be prone to blackouts and lapses in memory.

The Wroxeter dig was still an active crime scene, and all work there had stopped pending a release from the police investigators and the Magistrate's Court. Gemma had been designated as the "first police supervisor" for the scene and was responsible for overseeing and maintaining the integrity of the investigation. A team of three crime scene examiners had been assigned to her and she knew their work would be painstakingly thorough.

In the hole where the clothing of Aaron Shepherd and Michelle Whitcomb had been discovered, Gemma became curious about the nature of the round metal object at the bottom of the hole. To satisfy her curiosity, she instructed the crime scene examiners to photograph the object from as many angles as possible. She also reached out to a friend in the Archaeology Department at the University of Leeds and sent her a digital photograph of the object.

Less than twenty-four hours later, Gemma's friend, Saoirse Donoghue, was on a train from Leeds. Her text message back to Gemma was simple: "Don't touch anything! I'm on my way."

It took approximately four hours by bus and train for Saoirse Donoghue, PhD, to reach the Wroxeter dig. Walking onto the site, she immediately noticed Gemma and strode across the compound to greet her old friend.

"Gemma, it's good to see you again," Saoirse said with a genuine smile as they warmly embraced each other – perhaps a little longer and tighter than appropriate for just being friends.

"Thank you so much for coming," Gemma replied after a short and somewhat tense silence, "I've had two people disappear from this dig and a suspect in custody, but the evidence against him is circumstantial and I doubt I will get a conviction."

"What do you have to show me?" Saoirse asked. "Your picture was intriguing, to say the least."

"Well, it's easier to show you than to explain," Gemma replied as she pointed to the hole where the clothing of Aaron Shepherd and Michelle Whitcomb had been found after their alleged disappearances.

The two women walked to the edge of the hole and Saoirse peered over the edge. The metallic object at the bottom grabbed her attention immediately and she suggested that they climb down into the hole for a closer examination.

"Gemma, what you have here is what the ancient Greeks believed to be a symbol of Hecate, their goddess of crossroads, magic, and the Moon. The Romans, too, believed in Hecate as the daughter of the Titans Asteria and Perses. In both ancient Hellenic and Roman societies, Hecate was involved in nearly every aspect of life. It was almost as if she was the predecessor of the Abrahamic and Christian deities –"

"Thank you for the lecture, Professor Donoghue," Gemma interrupted somewhat sarcastically, "but I need to know why that symbol could be important to my investigations. I am running out of time to continue holding my main suspect, an American technician who had connections to both of my missing persons."

"Well, it's the idea of Hecate being 'the goddess of gateways' that perhaps has the greatest connection to your case. Neither Greek nor Roman mythology defined in any detail what this meant. Does that mean a gateway between realms such as life, the afterlife, or the underworld? Modern-day Wiccans believe that the wheel, *strophalos* in Greek, represents the cycle of life, death, and rebirth. Scholars have been debating the wheel's meaning for quite a while. Regardless, all of the beliefs about Hecate and her Wheel assume that there are mystical powers at play."

"Saoirse, when you say 'gateway,' could that have been what brought about the disappearance of the two American archaeologists?" Gemma asked.

"I'm agnostic about the idea that a symbol, icon, or talisman could have mystical powers that would cause people to disappear," the Professor answered with no emotion in her voice.

"Let's assume for a moment that the symbol does have a connection. Could it potentially transport someone across time and place?" Once again, Gemma's inquisitive nature was digging deep.

Saoirse answered, "Either is a possibility. Remember, the mythical powers of Hecate and the *strophalos* were never thoroughly defined in any meaningful way."

"I did have my Crime Scene Examiners look into the browsing history of Doctor Aaron Shepherd and his assistant, Michelle Whitcomb," Gemma explained.

"Wait… did you say Aaron Shepherd, from Michigan in the United States?" Saoirse asked in surprise.

"Yes. The very same. He was the chief archaeologist on this dig," Gemma responded. "When I interviewed his assistant, she was definitely suffering from a case of unrequited affection, and I thought that it could have been a motivator for her to kidnap or kill Shepherd."

"I've corresponded with Aaron Shepherd on and off for at least the past two decades," Saoirse offered, "and was surprised by the depth and breadth of his knowledge. He was with me on one of my many digs in Israel. The man was all business and did not seem to want any sort of romantic entanglement. Your assessment of unrequited affection is probably accurate."

"What is interesting in Shepherd's search histories is that he was researching Hecate and Hecate's Wheel," Gemma began, "and in one search, he accessed the archaeological database of the Michigan College of Mining and Technology, where he was a tenured professor. In another, he accessed a similar, yet more thorough, database at the College of William and Mary in Virginia. I believe Miss Whitcomb was a PhD candidate there and would have had unfettered access to their archaeological databases as part of her candidacy. In that database, we came across a vague reference to the possibility of Hecate's Wheel enabling time travel."

"H. G. Wells wrote about the concept of time travel in 1895," Saoirse added, "but that story was more allegorical than practical, focusing more on the societal issues than the mechanics of jumping across time."

There was a brief silence before Saoirse reopened the discussion. "Gemma, do you see anything unusual about the outer margins of the object?"

By this time, the two women were standing so close together that they could feel each other's body heat. The nearness was making it difficult for Gemma to concentrate. It took her a moment to collect her thoughts and respond to Saoirse's question.

"Wait... yes... there *is* something I didn't notice earlier. It looks like somebody traced around the outer edge with their finger, from the top center all the way around the circumference," Gemma noted.

"Do you notice anything else?" Saoirse asked.

"Two tracks of tracing, perhaps?" Gemma answered with a tone of uncertainty in her voice.

"Maybe we should make it three," Saoirse suggested with a wink as she impulsively reached out to touch the disk.

"Saoirse, stop!" Gemma said in her best police constable voice, "this is still an active crime scene, and I cannot allow you to touch *anything*. You could be compromising my evidence."

Saoirse didn't care. She knew the legends of Hecate's Wheel and could not resist the opportunity to test the validity of those legends.

Gemma reached out to stop her friend, grabbing Saoirse's hand; however, Saoirse was much stronger and able to resist Gemma's upward pull. At the same time, Gemma sensed her hand becoming one with her friend's as it traced the perimeter of the object in a counterclockwise direction.

Gemma was not sure if the melding of their hands was the result of the object or her own overpowering desire to rekindle her past relationship with Saoirse. As their joined hands traced through the south compass point and approached the east, their eyes locked. Saoirse's eyes made it clear that she was afraid of what was happening, after recognizing that it was now beyond any human control.

As their joined hands approached the north compass point once more after making a full circumferential trace around the object, Gemma finally sensed the reality of what was happening. Her vision became fuzzy, and she felt as if she was about to lose consciousness. The tympanic tremors beneath their feet intensified and crescendoed to *fortissimo* before there was an earsplitting crack – and total darkness.

18: Dazed and Confused

Beginning on October 6, 1651

It seemed like only an instant after the ear-splitting noise and darkness when the two women regained consciousness.

"Gemma, are you okay?" Saoirse whispered after regaining consciousness. Her head was spinning as if she had just awakened from a night of excessive drinking, and she felt as if she was going to vomit.

"I think so…" Gemma Royce-Smallworth answered, checking her body from head to toe for injuries as her police training had taught her. Gemma, too, was in considerable discomfort.

"Isn't this Stonehenge?" Saoirse asked rhetorically.

"Yes, it is!" Gemma readily agreed.

"How the hell did we get here?" Saoirse asked, emphasizing each word for effect.

"I don't know for sure," said Gemma, "but the last thing I remember was an irresistible urge to take your hand in mine as you traced the circumference of that… thing…

whatever it was. I hadn't felt that electricity since... well... I am sure you remember those days, Saoirse."

The archaeologist blushed a deep crimson at Gemma's suggestive recollection. She, too, remembered their days as a couple and the excitement they found in each other. Was this to be the rekindling of their own flame, they both wondered silently.

Adding to the strangeness of the situation, they both realized at the same moment that they were completely naked. Neither woman made any effort at modesty as they had previously been quite comfortable with each other's naked bodies.

"What happened to our clothes?" Gemma said as her investigative training took over. "Were we drugged, kidnapped and dropped here by some bad people?" It was the first thing that came to her mind after spending so much time and energy investigating the disappearances from Wroxeter.

"Shhh... Someone's coming!" Saoirse whispered as they ducked behind a clump of gorse – which offered little concealment this time of year.

Looking to the east, they saw two women coming towards them dressed in flowing robes and large hoods. Each of them carried a well-wrapped bundle.

"It looks like something out of a movie," Gemma observed.

"I think they know we are here," Saoirse whispered.

As if that was their cue, one of the approaching ladies spoke.

"Good morning, travelers! We've been expecting you. My name is Arwen and my friend is Cerys. Welcome to Stonehenge and the Salisbury Plain," said the taller of the two ladies. "We have gowns for you as it would not be appropriate for you to leave this place unclothed. Please, come out of hiding so we can be of assistance."

"May we have a moment, please?" Saoirse asked, then turned to Gemma. "I've read about things such as this in ancient texts we uncovered at several of our digs in Scotland, but I usually discounted their validity. It looks like I may have been wrong."

"You are the expert, Saoirse," Gemma said with an icy tone, suddenly remembering that their break-up had been caused by just this sort of thing and Saoirse always needing to be the smartest person in the room. *"Perhaps getting back together is not such a good idea, after all,"* Gemma thought.

"Gemma, just follow my lead and don't be ashamed of your body. If Arwen and Cerys are indeed expecting us, that means we probably aren't the first naked women they have helped," Saoirse said softly.

With that, Saoirse stood up and fully exposed herself to the two women. Gemma stood as well, but used her hands as defensive covers to protect her modesty. Arwen and Cerys both smiled.

"What do they call you, my dear?" Cerys asked.

"My name is Saoirse and my friend is Gemma," Saoirse replied. "Would you be so kind as to tell us what year this is?"

Arwen answered, "Why, it's the Year of Our Lord 1651."

Saoirse's eyes opened wide in amazement. "Gemma, do you realize that we are 360 years back in time?" As she turned to face Gemma, Saoirse realized she was talking to the air; Gemma had fainted and lay in a heap at Saoirse's feet.

Cerys quickly closed the distance between them, untied the bundle of clothing, and draped Gemma with a cloak. Reaching into a hidden pocket, Cerys also produced a small flask of what was probably mead or brandy. Tenderly, she lifted Gemma's head and allowed a few droplets of the liquid to fall into Gemma's mouth.

The alcoholic liquid brought an instant response from the unconscious Gemma. She sputtered and coughed as she quickly woke from her faint.

"Eww... that's awful!" Gemma exclaimed with a grimace. She normally did not drink anything more potent than beer or wine. Spirits were reserved for medicinal purposes, and then only when she was in the privacy of her own home.

"Gemma, you aren't the first person to swoon when they realize where and when they are. Our people have been dealing with travelers like you for many generations, going back to when the Romans occupied Britannia," Arwen explained, "and we even helped a soldier from the mysterious Ninth Legion during its time in York."

Saoirse suddenly realized that Arwen and Cerys were likely Druids, a mystical Celtic sect which, according to legend, was responsible for the construction of Stonehenge.

The legend remained a legend, as the ancient Druids kept no written records. They were, however, mentioned in Julius Caesar's *Commentarii de bello Gallico* (Commentary on the Gallic Wars), written five decades before the birth of Christ.

Based on Arwen's comment about Rome's Ninth Legion, which mysteriously disappeared during the Second Century, AD. Saoirse wondered if the Druids might have had something to do with the Roman Legion's fate.

The moment was interrupted by Gemma suddenly retching and voiding the contents of her stomach.

Cerys explained that the alcoholic draught she had administered to Gemma was a tincture of lobelia, an herbal concoction to induce vomiting.

"We've found that it helps travelers quickly adjust to their new surroundings if they arrive disoriented and nauseated," Cerys explained, "and it was quite obvious that Gemma was desperately in need."

Gemma glared at Cerys and grumbled, "Thank you for... well... nothing," Gemma groaned, "I hate throwing up."

As Gemma wiped her face, Cerys hushed the women.

"Someone's coming," Cerys whispered and pointed to the southeast.

"It's a man," Arwen observed, "a very tall man."

Both Gemma and Saoirse were focused on the man approaching them. Gemma, being used to observing body language, noticed that the man's gait was that of a laborer. Saoirse, on the other hand, furrowed her brow as she tried to understand why the man looked familiar.

"Good day, ladies," the man said as he was within a few yards, "William Jackson at your service!" He doffed his cap and bowed deferentially.

Saoirse suddenly realized that she and Gemma were alone; Arwen and Cerys had disappeared. They seemed to have vanished into thin air without a trace. Saoirse was completely baffled by their disappearance. *"Surely we would have heard them walking off through the gorse,"* she thought to herself.

When the man was about ten feet away, Saoirse made introductions. "My name is Saoirse and this is my friend, Gemma. We have become a bit disoriented and have lost our way."

"Then you shall accompany me to Heale House, about six miles away from here," Jackson replied.

Saoirse's mind was racing. There was something familiar about the man's name and a connection to history. She just couldn't put her finger on what it was – yet.

"Mister Jackson, we are desperately hungry," Saoirse noted, "as we have not eaten since yesterday."

"I assure you, Lady Saoirse, that there will be victuals aplenty at Heale House," Jackson replied.

"Mister Jackson, what brings you to Salisbury Plain this fine day?" Gemma asked.

"I merely wished to be alone with my thoughts and somehow walked a lot further away from Heale House than I had originally intended," he replied. "The wood we are about to enter is quiet and a good place for reflection."

Almost as if she had been struck by lightning, Saoirse realized whose company they were in. She discretely grabbed Gemma's hand, squeezed it tightly and pulsated twice. Gemma immediately recognized that it was a signal of something about to happen.

After they had walked a hundred yards or so into the trees, Saoirse spoke.

"Mister Jackson, would you be so kind as to allow my companion and me to avail ourselves of that thicket over there?"

"Of course, my lady. One must certainly heed the call of nature," Jackson answered with a smile, "and for your privacy, I shall be a few yards ahead on the path. You can rejoin me there."

Once in the thicket and after taking care of their needs, Saoirse rattled non-stop in a voice just above a whisper.

"Gemma, do you know who we are traveling with? I finally realized why he looked so familiar and why the name 'William Jackson' was so important."

"Slow down, Saoirse. At this rate, you're going to start hyperventilating," Gemma teased.

"William Jackson was the alias Charles II used after the Battle of Worcester," Saoirse explained, "and he wandered about the countryside for almost six weeks before he got on a boat to France."

"I know my history," said Gemma, "but I certainly don't have the depth of knowledge or the memory for very specific details that you do."

"Charles was also a very tall man, taller than most Englishmen of the period," Saoirse added, "and I believe the intent was to disguise him as a common man."

"So, we're now a part of history instead of just reading about it in a textbook," Gemma commented.

"Indeed, we are!" Saoirse exclaimed, "indeed, we are."

19: Sir, We Have a Problem

October 7, 2011

Detective Chief Superintendent Richard Mallory was deeply absorbed in the paperwork required by his position as Chief of the Criminal Investigations Division of the West Mercia Police Department. There were reports to read and critique, budget items to be reconciled, court appearances to be scheduled, and all the sundry tasks that kept administrators away from their chosen profession of police work. He was silently lamenting these inconveniences to himself when the telephone rang. The call was coming through on a line reserved for internal police communications.

"Mallory," he answered. Anyone calling him directly would already know he was the man in charge.

"Sir, this is Detective Chief Inspector Aberford. We have a situation on our hands in Wroxeter." Aberford's childhood stutter had suddenly resurfaced; all that was coming out of his mouth was a repeated sound of the letter 's': "S… S… S… S – " Normally, he was able to keep the stutter under control, but stress often exacerbated it.

"What is it, Aberford? Get on with it, man!" Mallory interrupted. He was, after all, a very busy man and the last thing he needed was a DCI groveling for attention. He had dealt with Aberford before.

Mallory clearly heard Aberford taking a deep breath before he regained his composure enough to continue.

"Sir, Detective Sergeant Royce-Smallworth has gone missing," Aberford said succinctly.

"Missing? What do you mean?" Mallory bellowed. "How does one of our best detectives go missing?"

"She was investigating the disappearances of a couple of the American archaeologists at the Roman digs here. We suspect foul play, sir," Aberford explained.

"Give me a run-down of the particulars," Mallory said; it was as much an order as it was a question.

Aberford began his report. "When DS Royce-Smallworth did not show up for the morning briefing, I sent one of the uniformed constables, PC Lambert, to her flat. He was well acquainted with her patterns of life and reported back that she was not there. Subsequently, I dispatched Lambert to her last crime scene, the Wroxeter digs. There, he found her official vehicle parked inside the compound. He checked the vehicle and determined that it probably had been sitting there overnight. The bonnet was cold and the entire vehicle was covered with morning dew."

"I trust that PC Lambert searched the grounds for signs of DS Royce-Smallworth engaged in some aspect of her investigation," Mallory commented in an effort to guide Aberford's report towards brevity.

"Sir, this is where it gets interesting…" Aberford paused for effect. "Lambert went to the active part of the dig, where the two Americans allegedly disappeared. At the bottom of a large hole, he discovered the clothing of not just one, but two women – including their… umm… underthings." Even as a career police officer, Aberford had never been entirely comfortable talking about women's anatomy or undergarments; he had been brought up in an ultra-conservative prudish home by his maternal grandmother after his parents were both killed in a motorway accident.

"A woman's underclothing is a private matter between her and her husband," Aberford could hear his grandmother saying.

"Okay, Aberford, I understand. What do you need from us here at HQ? You've had three people – "

"Four, sir," Aberford interrupted. "The two American archaeologists, DS Royce-Smallworth, and a professor from the University of Leeds, who was consulting at the request of DS Royce-Smallworth."

"Four people? What do you know about the missing professor?" Mallory asked.

"She arrived late yesterday afternoon, according to the access logs at the gate. Her name is Saoirse Donoghue, a PhD in archaeology. I don't have any other details, sir." Aberford explained.

"Is the area secure?" Mallory asked.

"Yes, sir. No one in or out, and all deliveries are inspected at the gate," Aberford noted. "Sir, I must tell you that keeping a guard on the site around the clock for an extended period will tax the resources of our precinct."

"I will send a team of Civil Enforcement Officers to assist with site security and an Evidence Collection Unit to process the scene. You need all hands on deck for the investigation. We also need to keep the tabloids away from the site as much as possible. Too much attention from the *paparazzi*, especially with the American connection, and we will likely hear from Number 10 and the Foreign Secretary, not to mention the American Embassy."

Mallory was already considering the possibility of a press debacle – or attention from the Prime Minister – that he really didn't need this late in his career. He was, after all, a mere two years away from full retirement and a possible knighthood. He just wanted to keep a low profile and stay within his budget. It was that simple.

"Thank you, sir," Aberford replied. "Should I have my own detectives stand down until the ECU arrives?"

"No. Just make sure they catalog and photograph everything," Mallory ordered, "and I don't need to remind you not to disturb any potential evidence."

"Yes, sir," Aberford acknowledged, "by your leave, sir?"

"Get on with it, man! Time is wasting," Mallory said just before slamming the phone's handset back into its cradle.

About 4 a clock in the morning, my selfe and the Company before named went towards Shoram, taking the Maister of the Shipp with us on horseback behinde one of our Company, and came to the Vessells side, which was not above 60 Tunn. But it being low Water and the Vessell lying dry, I and my Lord Wilmott gott up with a ladder into her and went and lay downe in the little Cabbin until the tide came to fetch us off."

As told to Samuel Pepys by Charles II, October 1680, twenty-nine years after the battle of Worcester. From the Trent University Library collection.

20: Disappearing Acts
Early October, 1651

After spending nearly a fortnight at the Wyndham estate, Charles and everyone in our entourage were becoming restless. The banquets were no longer celebratory nor entertaining; instead, they had morphed into simple communal meals with the concomitant lapses in manners and formalities. Sure, we still had a broad variety of meats, fish and late summer vegetables, but the fancy presentations and entertainment were gone. I confided in Michelle that I thought the cook had simply been worn out and no longer had the motivation to do anything beyond cooking and serving the meal.

Those participating in the meals, too, were worn out. Tempers often flared and fistfights broke out on a regular basis. Alcohol – or sometimes lack of it – was a contributing factor. Fortunately, none of the altercations had escalated to the point where Charles was involved.

Passage to France was finally arranged from Southampton and everything was made ready for Charles to be on the boat. Unfortunately, as we were getting ready to head for the coast, Wilmot received word that the boat had been commandeered to transport Parliamentarian troops to Jersey. Again, our plans had been foiled and Charles became despondent almost to the point of turning himself in to Cromwell's forces regardless of the consequences.

On October 6, I thought Charles had done exactly what he had suggested and turned himself in.

We had just moved from Wyndham's Trent estate to Heale House in Woodford. While we were settling the horses in the stables and unpacking, Charles somehow managed to spirit himself away and his disappearance was not discovered for a couple of hours. When Wyndham, Wilmot and I realized Charles was gone, we feared that it would not be long before we, too, would be taken into custody, put on trial, and remanded for execution. I knew that Charles was in deep despair: he was ready to give up completely and take the rest of us with him. Based on the broadsheet posted on the stable wall back in Worcester, it was likely that we would be hanged as accomplices once Charles was permanently out of the picture after losing his head on the chopping block, like his father.

By nightfall, Charles surprisingly returned to Heale House. He had managed to maintain his disguise and traveled as far away as Stonehenge, a little over six miles away, without being recognized by any of the locals. We watched his approach from lookouts on the upper floor of Heale House as Colonel Wyndham scanned the horizon with his spyglass to be sure that Charles had not been followed.

Wyndham did a double-take when he saw two women in threadbare garments following a few paces behind Charles. Wyndham handed me the spyglass so I could confirm what he was seeing. I noticed the women's clothing did little to preserve their modesty and I could clearly see some of their more womanly attributes in the bright sunshine.

"Colonel Wyndham, you were seeing exactly what you said you were seeing. Two women in desperate need of proper attire," I answered with a wry smile. There was something very familiar about one of the two women, but it was hard to see anything clearly through the spyglass. Optics in the 17th Century were anything but precise.

"We must go meet the king and be certain they are the only two people following him. Have Fraser and MacBride stand guard inside the door with their weapons at the ready," Wyndham ordered. I nodded in understanding.

A few moments later, Charles was at the top step of the portico.

"Colonel Wyndham and Mister Shepherd," Charles began, "I had to separate myself from our travels to clear my mind. It was my intent to quietly disappear for much of the day and Stonehenge was the perfect place for me to visit. It is so quiet and peaceful there and gave me time to ponder my future."

"Sir, what of these two ladies who followed you back here?" Wyndham asked.

"I found them at Stonehenge, hiding behind one of the stone pillars. I seem to have interrupted their ritual," Charles said with a wink. I was pretty sure he was talking about something other than a religious ceremony.

The two women averted their gaze towards the ground and kept their heads covered by the oversized hoods of their garments. They seemed to have been embarrassed by what Charles had just told us.

"Sir," Colonel Wyndham said, "are you sure you were not followed by any Roundhead patrols?"

"Of course not," Charles answered, "I did not encounter a single person other than these two women the entire day."

Wyndham turned back to the doorway and ordered, "Fraser, MacBride, you can stand down." The sound of the two guards sheathing their swords was unmistakeable.

Lady Hyde, the mistress of Heale House, stepped forward and welcomed the two ladies. "Please do come inside, my dears. It would be inhospitable of me not to offer you something to eat or drink."

As the two women passed, I sensed again that there was something familiar about one of them. When Michelle turned towards me, the look on her face was sheer terror. She, too, had seen something familiar – but about the second woman.

We remained outside the front entrance to Heale House until the rest of the people had left and could no longer overhear us. We would have to be quick, as it was not really appropriate for us to be left alone without a chaperone. I had learned quite some time ago that men of this era were "not to be left alone with a chaste woman." Only the Whiteladies knew of Michelle's contrived dalliance that had cost her her honor.

"Aaron," Michelle whispered, "I think one of the women was that Detective Sergeant who was investigating your disappearance. How the hell could she have gotten here?"

I replied, "I'm pretty sure the other woman was an archaeologist I worked with on a couple of digs in Jerusalem. I'm just as confused as you are, my dear."

"I don't think the Detective Sergeant recognized me. She looked disoriented, tired and hungry," Michelle noted.

"The same for the archaeologist. Her name is Saoirse Donoghue. She has a PhD from Leeds University," I explained, "and she was a pretty decent archaeologist, an expert on Greek and Roman mythology, and a walking encyclopedia of historical trivia."

"Aaron, what should we do?" Michelle asked.

"Let's wait until morning, when they should have recovered from the time travel disorientation and confront them," I suggested.

"I don't think we can wait that long," Michelle said emphatically. "We have to be careful how we engage them as it is not likely they have had time to realize where – and when – they are right now."

"Michelle, we have to go back inside before the servants start gossiping about our relationship and impugn your character," I said with a chuckle. Michelle simply smiled, quickly and covertly squeezed my hand, and led me back into the foyer of Heale House.

Once inside, I whispered, "Should we go to the kitchen and quietly confront our new guests? It might be safer there than in an uncontrolled setting with witnesses. I hope they would be able to stifle any verbal reaction to our presence."

"Aaron, I think that is an excellent approach," Michelle answered.

*　*　*　*　*

With the servants constantly coming and going "below stairs" (which I had learned was a euphemism for the servants' work areas), it was difficult to carry on a cohesive conversation with our two guests. From my own military days, I would have characterized our discussion as a debriefing as we were trying to gather information on their travels and how they ended up at Stonehenge. The only common thread between the four of us was that darned metal disk at the Wroxeter dig.

I did notice one dissimilarity between our travels through time. Michelle and I arrived in 1651 separately, while Gemma and Saoirse arrived at the same time. Eventually,

Gemma explained the circumstances of the two women being together at Wroxeter. She also apologized for a warrantless search of my browsing history but rationalized it as a discovery that could not be ignored – and the reason she had summoned Saoirse from Leeds. Royce-Smallworth, almost in tears, also apologized profusely to Michelle for the extended detention following my disappearance from 2011.

Saoirse, on the other hand, seemed to be a little more objective about their situation and certainly less emotional than Gemma. In fact, Saoirse attributed Gemma's hyperemotional state to the time travel – as if she had experienced the phenomenon before. She also explained and confirmed the connection between our current plights and Hecate's Wheel.

"Is there any way we can get back to 2011?" I asked once a group of scullery servants were out of hearing range.

"It depends…" Saoirse said quietly. "Did you notice any similar symbols near where you materialized here in 1651?"

Michelle shook her head negatively. "I was so concerned about being discovered naked in the bushes that I forgot to take stock of my surroundings. I completely ignored my training." She averted her gaze in embarrassment.

As another group of servants ambled past, my expression told Saoirse that I wanted to speak.

"I did have a strange experience while on patrol with Fraser and MacBride. It was as if I was frozen in time when I touched the center of a circular symbol carved into a tree. It was almost an exact duplicate of what we had discovered in Wroxeter," I explained. "When I touched it, I felt pain like I had never felt before and I am sure I was screaming in agony."

Saoirse smiled. "You went straight for the middle of the circle, yes?"

"Exactly," I answered.

"You are lucky you weren't stricken dead on the spot," Saoirse said with an ominous tone, "as the center of the circle is what the ancient Greeks called the 'death spot.' Did anyone around you notice what was happening?"

"No... neither Fraser nor MacBride saw or heard anything at. In fact, they questioned why I was so taken with the tree," I said with a chuckle.

About 4 a clock in the morning, my selfe and the Company before named went towards Shoram, taking the Maister of the Shipp with us on horseback behinde one of our Company, and came to the Vessells side, which was not above 60 Tunn. But it being low Water and the Vessell lying dry, I and my Lord Wilmott gott up with a ladder into her and went and lay downe in the little Cabbin until the tide came to fetch us off."

As told to Samuel Pepys by Charles II, October 1680, twenty-nine years after the battle of Worcester. From the Trent University Library collection.

21: Onward to France...

7-15 October 1651

The clock had just struck 2 a.m. when we heard Lord Wilmot bellowing for everyone to assemble in the courtyard of Heale House. He had finally secured a vessel for our passage to France, but it would take us the better part of two days to get there. An immediate (or as immediate as an entourage could make it) departure was necessary.

The night was cloudless as we departed from Heale House and the lack of moonlight slowed our pace until sunrise. However, once the sun was up and visibility improved, Wilmot increased our pace, keeping the horses at a gentle trot, but short of a canter, to conserve their energy. It was a relatively breakneck pace, allowing us to cover 10 to 12 miles every hour. Our only stops were to rest the horses and to relieve ourselves; we were expected to eat and drink on the move. Thankfully, the kitchen servants at Heale House had packed saddlebags with bread, smoked ox tongue, and flasks of beer for each traveler.

When we were separated from the main group, Wilmot confided to me that our destination was Shoreham, a little to the west of Brighthelmstone, a town I had never heard of. I took him at his word and assumed that he knew the lay of the land. Thankfully, during one of our comfort stops, Saoirse Donoghue quietly told me it was the old name for Brighton, a location I was familiar with and could picture on a 21st Century map.

Always full of facts, Saoirse spent several minutes explaining that Brighthelmstone was mentioned in the Domesday Book. She also explained that in 1514, during the reign of Henry VIII, the village was burned to the ground by the French in one of Europe's many wars. In the years following World War I, Brighton was transformed into a fashionable resort town for the wealthy and titled.

"Saoirse, your knowledge of arcane facts has never ceased to amaze me," I teased with a hint of sarcasm in my voice.

Though I was still responsible for his needs, Charles insisted on riding with either Lord Wilmot or Colonel Gunter, who had just joined us as our local guide. Conversations with Wilmot and Gunter consumed the king's attention, so it gave me more of an opportunity to talk to Michelle, Gemma, and Saoirse about our next steps. Coherent conversation, however, was impeded by the noise and clatter of our mode of transportation; so many horses trotting together was anything but peaceful and quiet.

"Will we be crossing the Channel to France with the king?" Michelle asked.

"At this point, I am not entirely certain. He may balk at anyone other than me joining the party," I answered, "and even though we have established a connection, he is more inclined, I think, to leave me behind in favor of someone like Lord Wilmot."

"Is there a chance we could cross the Channel separately?" Saoirse asked.

"This crossing has been difficult enough to arrange, and I doubt that one for the four of us will be any easier," I said dejectedly.

Gemma had been pensively observing the proceedings and suddenly chimed in, "His Majesty wants to maintain anonymity, something we do not have to do. We only need a believable cover story for our reason to travel to France. I believe Michelle has already given us that in the story she told to the White Ladies."

"Excellent point," I agreed, "but we also do not have any cash to offer as payment."

"Maybe you should ask the king for a stipend," Saoirse suggested.

"Hmm… that's not a bad idea," I agreed.

Arriving at the beach, we found out that only the king and Lord Wilmot would be crossing on the *Surprise*, a coaler displacing approximately 60 tonnes. Its master was a Captain Nicholas Tettersell who appeared to support the king – for a price. Tettersell's obsequiousness towards Charles was nauseating.

Still under the cover of darkness, the king and Wilmot said their goodbyes and boarded the *Surprise*, which lay aground and listing slightly to port on the low tide. It would be at least two more hours before the vessel could float free on the rising tide. The king was exhausted from our travels and quickly fell asleep in the small forward cabin despite the list. Tettersell and his lone crew member stayed nearby but did not intend to board the *Surprise* until the tide began to rise.

In spite of Colonel Gunter's arrival, Colonel Wyndham had remained with us as our guide since departing Heale House. Waiting for the rising tide would give me an opportunity to speak to him privately; I had discovered that he was the keeper of the king's purse and had access to a significant amount of money, enough to cover several channel crossings in much nicer accommodations than those available on the *Surprise*.

It took me less than half an hour to get a small allocation of cash from Colonel Wyndham. Tettersell, on the other hand, was less than forthcoming with information about other vessels' upcoming crossings to France. He even suggested that there would not be an available vessel any time soon, and possibly not even until the spring – but also offered to take me and the three women across the Channel to France himself for a price that I was not willing to pay. Tettersell's exorbitant price quote left me with no choice than to return to Shoreham and try to arrange passage on my own.

Our predicament was compounded by the fact that I was traveling with three women, none of whom was my wife nor a close relation. In the Puritanical climate of England under Cromwell, I could be accused of immorality and potentially sent to prison. I could see only one way to prevent that from ever happening.

"Michelle… Miss Whitcomb… could I have a private word with you, please?" Gemma and Saoirse took the hint and removed themselves from the area. At the same time, Michelle Whitcomb and I stepped back towards the dunes adjacent to the beach.

"Yes, Aaron? What is it?" Michelle teased. "I hope you have good news for us all."

"Actually, Michelle, it's extremely important to me right now that you listen carefully. Tettersell has offered to take us to France, but at a price I believe is more than twice the going rate. He also claims that there might not be another ship available until spring. I highly doubt this, as I can clearly see vessels of all shapes and sizes on the open waters of the English Channel.

"After the king, Lord Wilmot, and the rest of the entourage leave us, we will be on our own," I continued, "and our best option looks to be a return to Shoreham to find passage from there. I understand the moral code of this period in history would frown on me traveling alone with three women who are neither my wife, my betrothed, nor any sort of kin."

Michelle blushed to an almost crimson hue as I dropped to one knee and took both of her hands in mine.

"Michelle Whitcomb, will you do me the honor of becoming my wife? We can be married in the nearest church with Gemma and Saoirse as witnesses."

Michelle thought for a moment before responding. "Aaron Shepherd, after all we have been through together and separately, it only makes sense for us to be married. I accept your proposal. Now will you get up off your knee and kiss me properly?" Her tone told me she meant business.

What followed was probably the most passionate kiss of my entire life. I didn't want the moment to end but knew that we had to be on our way as soon as the *Surprise* was afloat and her sails unfurled. That would also be the appropriate time to give our good news to Gemma and Saoirse.

About an hour later, the rising tide was lapping around the hull of the *Surprise* and it would not be much longer before she was once again afloat. As Tettersell and his crewman prepared to board, I told Tettersell that I was declining his original offer of conveyance.

"Mister Shepherd, the king speaks very highly of you. Perhaps we can negotiate a better price for you and your… ladies… to cross the channel into France," Tettersell suggested condescendingly. He had every intention of extorting a fare of passage from us, but I would have nothing to do with his manipulations.

"Captain Tettersell," I countered, "we will be seeking passage out of another port. We no longer desire to engage your services."

A few minutes later the *Surprise* was afloat and under sail. I turned my back on the scene and left the beach with Michelle, Gemma, and Saoirse close behind.

Reaching a suitable place and certain that we were alone, I stopped the group and pulled Michelle close to me. She was smiling from ear to ear.

"Gemma, Saoirse… we have some important news," I stammered. "Michelle and I are getting married."

Gemma in particular glowered at Michelle, which I believed was a result of their previous entanglements with each other following my disappearance from Wroxeter. Unbeknown to me, during their previous relationship, Gemma had suggested to Saoirse that they enter into a civil partnership as same sex marriage was not legal in England, Wales, or Scotland until 2014.

Saoirse was pragmatic and launched into one of her academic lectures. "You know, under English common law of the 17th Century, a church wedding is not required. You don't even need witnesses. All you have to do is declare yourselves to be husband and wife and it has the legality of a formal church ceremony. In Scotland, the practice is known as 'handfasting.' It wasn't until the middle of the 18th Century that England required more formal documentation and witnesses."

"Is it really that simple?" Michelle asked excitedly.

"Yes, that's all there is to it," Saoirse replied.

There was a pregnant pause before Gemma spoke up.

"Michelle," Gemma said meekly, "I apologize for the inconvenience you encountered back in our time and I congratulate you on finally –"

"Shh…" Michelle interjected, "what we discussed in the police interview room is going to stay there."

"I agree," said Gemma with a wink. "It wouldn't be fair to either you or Aaron."

I had the general gist of what had just transpired between Michelle and Gemma: there were details of the 2011 police investigation that Michelle did not want shared with me. I was fine with that, knowing that Michelle had nothing to do with my disappearance. I had also figured out several days ago that Michelle had strong feelings for me that might have clouded the police investigation with presumed motive and opportunity as a jilted lover.

22: Dead Ends

October, 2011

Detective Chief Superintendent Mallory hadn't even hung up his suit jacket before the telephone jarred the morning silence. Abigail, his long-time assistant, normally held all of his calls until he had had a chance to read through the intradepartmental messages over a cup of Earl Grey tea. Mallory was more than a little angry that his assistant had actually let a call come through.

"If she keeps this up, she won't be my assistant much longer," Mallory muttered to the empty office as he strode from the coat closet to his desk.

"Mallory." His tone was as gruff as he could make it and appropriate for what normally would have been his "quiet hour."

"Sir, this is Detective Chief Inspector Aberford. A moment of your time, sir, if I may?"

"Go ahead, Aberford," Mallory replied.

"Sir, the ECU is at a dead end. They have found nothing that wasn't already in DS Royce-Smallworth's handwritten notes which they found under the pile of women's clothing at the bottom of the dig," Aberford explained.

"What do you recommend, Aberford?" Mallory prodded.

"Sir, I think that it would be the best use of resources to recall the ECU back to Shrewsbury and release the Civil Enforcement Officers," offered Aberford, "that way, the dig team could resume operations – albeit without any of their leadership. But… I do think that we should call in our cyber experts to do a deep dive into the online profiles of our four missing people, DS Royce-Smallworth included."

"Are there any other solid leads?" Mallory queried.

"None, sir," Aberford answered.

"I will take your recommendations under advisement and ring you back after lunch," Mallory directed.

"Yes, sir. Very good, sir," Aberford confirmed.

Mallory slammed the phone back into the cradle and went back to his tea and messages. It was going to be a long day, and he worried that he would be forced to once again cancel his evening plans. *"My poor wife… she's been a saint all the way through my career and never a cross word,"* he thought silently.

"Smith!" Mallory bellowed, "please come in here for a moment."

"Yes, sir?" Abigail Smith said as she entered Mallory's inner sanctum. Smith was a fully-qualified constable but had been relegated to the role of clerk by a chauvinistic hierarchy, much like what could have happened to Gemma Royce-Smallworth if she had not completed the two cold cases early in her career. Smith resented everything about Gemma and had a strong dislike for her superior, Detective Chief Superintendent Mallory. But a job was a job and a single mother needed every penny.

"Please ring the florist and have them deliver a dozen roses to my wife. You can fill in the sappy details for the card, please," he instructed. "*Maybe that will appease her somewhat,*" he mused.

"Yes, sir. I'll sort it, sir," Smith replied with absolutely no enthusiasm. "*This is 2011 and I thought stuff like this was a thing of the past,*" she muttered to herself as she left Mallory's office.

In Wroxeter, Aberford was already assuming that Mallory would accede to his recommendations. He knew from experience that his superior normally did not issue decisions on-the-spot and that the delay until the second half of the day was Mallory's *modus operandi.*

Even with the knowledge that Mallory was likely to agree with his recommendations, Aberford was still uneasy. There was something about this case, made even stranger by the disappearance of a Detective Sergeant, that just didn't make sense. People simply did not disappear without a trace.

"PC Lambert, a word, please?" Aberford called out from the command post that had been set up in the center of the Wroxeter compound. Lambert always seemed to be within earshot of his superior, something that Aberford made a mental note of.

"Yes, sir?" PC Lambert said as he stepped into the command post.

"I've just been on the blower with DCS Mallory and I recommended that we pull back from our investigation here. We've not turned up any new evidence since your discovery of DS Royce-Smallworth's official vehicle and that pile of... umm... clothing at the bottom of the dig. Instead of waiting for the DCS to ring me back with new orders, I am taking it upon myself to release the Civil

Enforcement Officers at lunch time, followed by the ECU after a final debrief over lunch," Aberford explained.

"Are we completely ending the investigation, sir?" Lambert asked. The constable had experienced enough boredom during this case to last two careers. He wanted nothing more than for his superiors to order an end to the investigation.

"Not entirely, Lambert. Not entirely. I've also asked for a forensic cyber team to take a look at the online activities of our four missing persons. There has to be something in their electronic footprints that will shed some light on their combined disappearances. It is starting to look like a conspiracy of some kind," said Aberford.

"So far, sir, we've stuck to the physical evidence," Lambert acknowledged, "but you are correct that the electronic evidence – assuming there is any – should tell us *something*," Lambert said as if he were thinking out loud.

"We will naturally have to wait for a warrant," said Aberford, "and I am already working on the application to file in accordance with the Police and Criminal Evidence Act. We have to tread carefully and be absolutely certain we stay within the bounds of our authorities and the terms of the warrant once it is approved. With a bit of luck, I should be able to present the application to the Magistrate's Court by end of day."

"Sir, we also have the small matter of Mister Hudson to consider. We're reaching the limits on our ability to hold him as a suspect," Lambert noted.

"You can release him immediately," Aberford ordered. "We have no further reason to hold him as there is no evidence to support his involvement. I would, however, recommend to Mister Hudson that he consider returning to the United States forthwith."

"Yes, sir. I will handle his release myself," Lambert acknowledged.

23: From Shoreham to Le Havre

Later in October, 1651

Tettersell had been correct after all: finding a captain willing to cross the channel with winter approaching was a dubious notion at best. Our situation was deteriorating as rapidly as the daylight in London's smog, so I felt we needed to conserve our cash to pay for the Channel crossing.

Surrounded by that uncertainty, we bartered with a farmer's widow for our food and lodging, offering hard labor in exchange for her hospitality. As her husband had been recently killed in a cart accident, Widow Compton needed all the help she could get to keep the leasehold farm running and not have it taken from her. Our contribution of labor, even for a short time, probably kept her from losing the farm.

Every other day, I made the short trek from the Compton farm to Shoreham and inquired about the possibility of passage to France. The weather fears notwithstanding, it seemed that no captain wanted to take on passengers of questionable morality, and certainly not a man traveling with three women – despite assurances that Michelle and I were married and that Gemma and Saoirse were our servants. I guessed that our "strange" foreign accents made us untrustworthy. My level of frustration with our current predicament was rising to the point of hopelessness.

We had choices to make: give up and remain here in the 17th Century, return to Wroxeter and try to locate the buried Hecate's Wheel without the aid of 21st Century technology, or find a place where there *might* be another Wheel that could transport us forward in time.

Finding the *strophalos* in 1651 Wroxeter without James Hudson's 2011 ground penetrating radar would be difficult. There was also Stonehenge, where Gemma and Saoirse appeared. They had told me about their encounter with Arwen and Cerys and how the two ladies of mystery disappeared into thin air when Charles approached. It was my hypothesis that there was a time gateway of some kind at Stonehenge, a site that had always been surrounded by inscrutable mysticism and legend.

Another long shot was the place where I saw the tree carving and where time seemed to have stood still. I doubted I would be able to find that place again as it was just a fleeting moment in my consciousness. With

MacBride and Fraser's help, I might have been able to locate it once again – but they had been released back to Colonel Giffard's command several weeks earlier.

Saoirse remembered that there were Roman ruins in Rouen and wondered if they might hold an artifact similar to the one we had uncovered in Wroxeter. "It will be like finding a needle in the proverbial haystack, without knowing for sure that the needle is even there," she said with a shake of her head. "Serious excavations won't start for about another two hundred years – which will be during the heyday of archaeological awakening in Britain and mainland Europe." Her ability to regurgitate factual minutiae never ceased to amaze me.

Getting from Le Havre to Rouen could be problematic. Rouen lay approximately 75 winding miles upstream on the *Seine maritime*. The river was deep enough for most vessels of the day, but going upstream on the winding waterway was all but impossible against its very strong and often unpredictable current. Overland, it was a distance of around 50 miles.

Any way I looked at it, we were well and truly screwed. The best course of action I could recommend to the ladies was to go ahead with our plans to cross the Channel and make our way to Rouen, on foot if necessary. If we were unable to find the Roman ruins and a *strophalos* there, we would continue on to Paris, where I hoped we would be able to meet up with Charles and his mother, Queen Henrietta Maria. I hoped that Charles would not be indifferent to our plight and help us as a *quid pro quo* for helping him escape from England.

"Ladies," I began, "we need to cross the Channel at the first opportunity and not be too picky about the type of vessel or price. Le Havre is reachable in a little over a day of sailing, depending on the prevailing winds and currents."

Despite Saoirse's suggestion of Roman ruins at Rouen, Michelle was worried that if we did cross the Channel, we would be locked in this timeline with no possibility of returning to 2011. I hoped her defeatist attitude would not be contagious.

Gemma was more pragmatic. She recognized that we would probably have to accept remaining in 1651 for now, and that a return to our own time would be a matter of luck. I had to agree with her point of view more than I did with my own wife's.

We ended up remaining on the south coast of England at Widow Compton's farm for almost another fortnight before we were able to secure passage across the Channel. Charles's crossing in a small private cabin on the *Surprise* was quite luxurious by comparison. Our vessel, the *Hope*, under the command of Captain Richard Pettigrew, was nothing more than an open fishing boat with a single mast reminiscent of the skipjacks I had seen on Chesapeake Bay during an archaeological project on the Delmarva Peninsula to document the locations of alleged slave cemeteries.

We boarded the *Hope* at midday. Unlike the *Surprise*, our vessel was anchored in a sheltered deepwater cove and not aground at low water. We would be rowed out to its anchorage on the 17th Century equivalent of a water taxi. Thankfully, the water in the cove was calm; I did not trust the seaworthiness of the dory serving as the water taxi as there was very little freeboard once we were all aboard. The dory certainly had seen better days; thankfully, our trip out to the anchorage passed without incident.

Once we were aboard the *Hope*, Pettigrew and his crew of five made ready to sail. As a condition of carriage at a discounted price, I had to sign on as the sixth member of the crew and was expected to assist with the line handling under the tutelage of the First Mate, James Fisher. I quickly realized how much work it was and earned the rope burns on my hands to prove it. Michelle, who was now my acknowledged wife, treated my injuries with tenderness and sympathy.

We were fortunate that the breeze out of the north continued as the sun set to our west. With our spinnaker unfurled as the daylight faded, we were propelled downwind on our way across the channel.

With the sun setting to our right, we watched the coast of England disappear below the horizon behind us. For safety, whale oil lamps had been hung on both sides of the bow outside and below the rail to let other boats see us. I could only hope that other boats had extended the same courtesy. An open-water collision would spell disaster.

By the time I was relieved by the night watch, the darkness was so complete that the stars overhead glowed in the moonless sky. It was the epitome of romantic settings, but I was too exhausted to enjoy the ambience. Instead, I curled up under a heavy wool blanket that I shared with Michelle and was lulled to sleep by the boat's gentle fore-and-aft porpoising on its downwind tack

On the other side of the boat, Gemma and Saoirse were intertwined under their own blanket. I could hear them talking quietly to each other in a friendly tone interspersed with the occasional girlish giggle. I was still puzzled by the nature of their relationship and at times sensed some tension between them.

Michelle and I were awakened by First Mate Fisher around 3 a.m., when it was time for the change of watch. Once I was awake and out from under our shared blanket, she fell quickly back to sleep, now wrapped in two layers of wool to preserve her own body heat. After relieving myself and before assuming my watch as lookout, I visited the rations crate. There, I drew a portion of jerky and hardtack after taking a swig of diluted rum. I was slowly chewing the jerky when I reported for my watch.

"Mister Shepherd," the off-going crewman began, "everything is as it was when you were relieved six hours ago. The spinnaker lines are fast and our course has been steady. Good luck to you, sir."

"Thank you, Mister Cooper," I acknowledged and watched him go to his chosen sleeping location outside the Captain's meager quarters near the stern.

About halfway through my watch, I had the pleasure of watching a glorious sunrise to the east. The clouds changed from gray to red to orange to gold. I felt lucky to be alive in this moment and felt at peace with myself and my situation – especially now that I was married to Michelle.

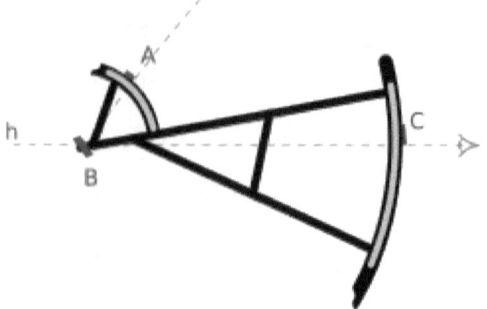

24: Le Havre

Late October, 1651

At the end of my watch around 9 a.m., Captain Pettigrew suggested that we could arrive in Le Havre before midday. He had plotted our approximate position with a quadrant staff; the more accurate sextant was still about eight decades into the future. With the knowledge that landfall was imminent, I was too excited to sleep.

Michelle noticed my excited agitation as she stood beside me, taking my hand in hers.

"Aaron, you have to relax. When we are ashore, we will all need our wits about us. We will be in a strange country, with a different language and unusual customs," she said in a reassuring tone.

Our touching, private moment was interrupted by the bellowing of a lookout, "Land, Ho! Land Ho! Land Ho!" and it was all hands to their stations. I dropped Michelle's hand and hurried to my assigned post as port side lookout.

The closer we got to Le Havre, the more our vigilance would be needed as all manner of craft came and went from the harbor. Ship and small boat traffic generally increased on calmer days with a wind out of the east-northeast like today. This sheltered the mouth of the Seine and the waters adjacent to the port, making it safer for small, open fishing boats to ply their trade.

Michelle offered an observation from her knowledge of British history. "Aaron, the modern maritime 'Rules of the Road' are still at least two centuries in the future. Ship traffic is governed by the Law of the Sea, based on the Roll of Oberon that was created by Eleanor of Aquitaine in the Twelfth Century. Queen Eleanor was the wife of both Louis VII of France and later Henry II of England. She was quite an interesting character…"

My wife, like Saoirse Donoghue, could be a walking encyclopedia at times. I did appreciate how Michelle did not lord her knowledge over us like Saoirse did: Michelle explained the history rather than regurgitating mere facts. I could see that the two women were likely to butt heads in the future. Getting caught in the middle of that potential disagreement was not something I relished. Michelle was loving and patient when she was around me, but with other women, the claws could easily come out. That was the last thing we needed in our current situation.

Captain Pettigrew was a skilled seaman and ably guided our small vessel to an anchorage about half a mile out from the mouth of the Seine. Dropping anchor, even for a small vessel like the *Hope*, was a dangerous undertaking. Most anchor rodes were made of heavy ropes or forged chains, and men engaged in dropping anchors could easily lose limbs or digits. Knowing my inexperience, First Mate Fisher excused me from anchor duties.

Pettigrew maneuvered the Hope across the outflow of the Seine and into quieter waters. As we crossed the outflow, I sensed its pull on our hull at about the same time First Mate Fisher instructed me to lower the spinnaker and bring the remaining sails into a close reach.

It took us the better part of an hour to anchor and another hour or so for a tender to be rowed out to us. There were nine souls aboard the *Hope*, so there was no way all of us could be ferried ashore in a single trip. Thankfully, Captain Pettigrew allowed me and the three women to disembark first, along with our small bundles of belongings. The tender would then return to the Hope and take the rest of the crew ashore.

"Captain Pettigrew, do you have any recommendations for reputable establishments where we could rest for a couple of days before heading to our destination in Rouen?" I asked as the tender approached.

"As you are traveling with the gentler sex, Mr. Shepherd, I would not recommend taking lodging within sight of the wharves. Most of them are frequented by ruffians and thieves, not to mention ladies of the evening," Pettigrew explained, "and your ladies could easily be taken into service; I hope you understand what that entails."

"I will consider your recommendation, sir, and I thank you for your hospitality and seamanship," I said with a handshake as I turned to assist the three ladies over the rail and into the tender.

Once ashore, we made our way into Le Havre, seeking out affordable lodging. Thanks to our no-cost barter arrangement with Widow Compton and my willingness to sign the *Hope*'s manifest as a temporary crew member, we still had more than half of our cash available for food, lodging, and transportation to Rouen.

We could easily save on room and board with all four of us in the same room, but Michelle and I had not enjoyed more than a couple of nights' privacy since we declared ourselves married. I suspected that Gemma and Saoirse had plenty of things to discuss privately as well. It would use up our funds faster than I would like, but there really wasn't another alternative, knowing that we still had to get ourselves to Rouen.

The establishments nearest the port were, as Pettigrew explained, anything but reputable and catered to a transient maritime crowd like sailors and fishermen. Prostitutes were also clearly in evidence.

"Aaron, we can't stay anywhere near the port," Michelle said matter-of-factly. Gemma and Saoirse nodded their agreement.

"My darling," *(did I really just call her that?)* "if we move a short distance away from the wharves, we should find an environment more suited to businessmen and a genteel clientele. It will certainly be more expensive, but I really don't want to sleep at night with a weapon within easy reach. We won't be here for more than a night or two."

We walked the streets towards the business district and hopefully more upscale lodging. As it was mid-day and too late to begin our onward journey to Rouen, we made it a leisurely stroll to take in the sights – and smells – of a 17th Century port city in France. Along the way, I noticed several livery stables and wainwright shops where we could purchase a horse and a wagon. I made a mental note of their locations.

We took two rooms at the *Auberge du Roi* (King's Inn) and settled in for the evening. Thankfully, Gemma was fluent in French and handled the negotiations on our behalf: we would receive dinner and breakfast as part of our rate. On the *Hope*, we had eaten nothing other than hardtack and jerky, so the thought of a proper meal was making our collective mouths water. We were all famished.

When the church clock struck 6 p.m., we headed down to the dining room. The landlady seated us at a private table in a secluded corner of the room and promptly set down a bottle of table wine with four glasses, then handed each of us a menu slate – which Gemma quietly translated:

"*Poisson du jour*, fish of the day."

"*Filet mignon*, no translation necessary."

"*Soupe à l'oignon*, onion soup."

"*Poulet rôti*, roasted chicken."

"*Légumes rôtis,* roasted vegetables. "

"*Navets et carottes bouillis,* boiled turnips and carrots. "

Saoirse jumped in, "Gemma, it all sounds wonderful, even the turnips. I am so hungry I could eat a horse – but please don't tell her that!"

Turning to the landlady, who seemed to be getting impatient, Gemma told her what we wanted.

"*Madame, tout, s'il vous plaît. Style familial. Plus de vin, s'il vous plait!*"

"*Oi, merci!*" the landlady responded as she turned and hurried back to the kitchen.

"What did you tell her?" Michelle asked.

"Everything… family style, and more wine!" Gemma beamed, "My A-level in French finally paid off. I just hope my pronunciation wasn't too far off."

It turned out to be an absolutely wonderful meal, better than what we likely would have gotten in a wharfside rooming house. All I could think of as we passed some of those establishments was the "Master of the House" from *Les Miserables*, and I gave those seedy establishments a wide berth.

When our meal was served, it was clear to all of us that the French love affair with food was the same in 1651 as it was in 2011. Every dish was an event unto itself, to be shared, enjoyed and savored without hurry.

Sated, we retired to our sleeping quarters as midnight approached.

Once inside our corner room, Michelle made a big deal of closing and locking the door. With an impish grin and a twinkle in her eye, she put her right index finger to her lips, suggesting I should be quiet.

"Sit down, Aaron," she said softly, "we're alone for the entire night and you belong to me now…"

25: On the Front Page

THE Sun

October 27, 2011

FOUR MISSING FROM ROMAN DIGS
Foul Play Suspected

A Detective Sergeant from the West Mercia Police Department and an Archaeology lecturer from the University of Leeds have gone missing from the Roman digs at Wroxter. They were researching the disappearance of two American archaeologists who were on fellowships from the University of Cambridge.

The missing individuals are Detective Sergeant Gemma Royce-Smallworth and Dr. Saoirse Donoghue. Also missing are Americans Dr. Aaron Shepherd and his assistant, Miss Michelle Whitcomb.

A spokesman for the West Mercia Police, Detective Superintendent Richard Mallory, has told the Sun that the disappearances appear to be the result of foul play. He is "pulling out all the stops" to hopefully rescue the missing individuals and arrest their kidnappers. "Because this is an ongoing investigation of suspicious circumstances," DS Mallory said, "I can only release the names of the missing individuals at this time." When pressed for additional details about any evidence discovered at the scene, DS Mallory declined to comment.

The Sun had the opportunity to interview another American, a Mr. James Hudson, about the disappearances. He suggested that this was a case of unrequited love gone bad, claiming that Miss Whitcomb was romantically interested in Dr. Shepherd. Hudson also commented that the romantic interest appeared to be one-sided.

Hudson also suggested that DS Royce-Smallworth and Dr. Donoghue were more than just colleagues, adding a new dimension to the suspicious circumstances.

26: On the Road to Rouen, Part I

Late October, 1651

The sun was already up when I woke up the next morning with Michelle sleeping contentedly on my shoulder. I desperately needed to use the chamber pot, but did not want to awaken my wife after the fulfilling and exhausting night we had just spent together. The numbness in my right arm added additional urgency to my predicament. One way or another, I had to get out from under Michelle's sleeping embrace.

I stirred slightly by gently flexing the muscles in my upper arm, hoping that Michelle would awaken on her own. The movements offered a suggestion of waking up, rather than an all-out assault on her unconsciousness. It wasn't more than a couple of minutes before she was propped up next to me on one elbow, smiling sweetly and looking into my eyes.

"Good morning, husband," she cooed, "I've been waiting for a night like that for a long time."

"My darling, I really need to use the chamber pot. I hope you will be here when I get back," I teased, knowing she would still be there. I also hoped that she would, after using the chamber pot herself, be willing to pick up where we left off in the wee hours of the morning.

Michelle took care of her own needs and, still naked, opened the shuttered window before hollering in French, *"Prenez garde à l'eau!"* (Mind the water!) and emptying the fetid chamber pot down to the street three floors below. The situation left me laughing uncontrollably.

"Aaron, I didn't tell you yesterday that I, too, speak a little French. I thought having Gemma as interpreter was enough," she said, grinning almost seductively as she playfully turned her naked body back towards me. That was enough to distract me for the next couple of hours.

When the church clock struck noon, we realized we were famished. We dressed quickly, fully anticipating the knowing giggles from Gemma and Saoirse at our late arrival to the dining room. Before we headed downstairs, we stopped by their room across the hall and knocked on the door. It turned out that the two women were themselves just getting up.

"Aaron, Michelle," Gemma said as she peeked from behind the door, "please go downstairs without us. We shall be along shortly."

I peered into the room and saw that Saoirse was still in bed, sitting upright with the covers gathered around her. There was little left to my imagination and their behavior confirmed what I had already suspected.

Michelle and I went downstairs and took the same seats we had occupied for dinner the evening before. Lunch consisted of a selection of charcuterie and pastries – and the ever-present bottles of red wine. We slowly ate our fill, hoping that the other two ladies would soon be joining us.

We had been there about half an hour before Gemma and Saoirse arrived. After they had the opportunity to eat, I explained to them what my afternoon would entail. It ended up being more of a lecture than an explanation:

"I will go back towards the port to where I saw a livery stable next to a wainwright's shop. We could certainly walk to Rouen for next to no cost, but it is over 50 miles from here and it would take us the better part of three long days to get there on foot. In a horse and wagon, we can cut that time in half. I have to balance the cost of a horse and wagon against what it could cost us for lodging on the way, as well as the implied danger of highwaymen. I would be no match for an armed assault, and the longer we are on the road, the more likely a robbery – or worse – becomes."

Gemma replied first. "I think we should remain here overnight again and set out first thing in the morning, as long as Aaron is able to procure a horse and wagon this afternoon."

Michelle and Saoirse readily agreed, with Michelle adding that she wanted to be someplace where she could have a proper bath, even if it was in a flowing stream along our route. She did not want to wait until we reached Paris and the relative luxury of the palace.

"I'm so tired of smelling *eau de toilette* to cover up body odor," she said with a chuckle and a wrinkle of her nose, "I really need a bath – and so do you, Aaron."

"Maybe I should wait until I am back from the stables," I retorted. "Even a simple sponge bath in clean water would be better than smelling of hay and horse manure."

The food we had eaten since our arrival in Le Havre was probably the tastiest since arriving in 1651 a little over a month before. Though the English farmhouse fare had been delicious in its own right, the French certainly knew *la nourriture* (French for 'food,' as Michelle had explained to me) and how to use one dish to complement another. They also took meat curing to a new level far beyond the smokehouse and root cellar approach of the British. Today's charcuterie was a good example.

"Ladies, while I am gone, can you try to convince the proprietors to provide us with a suitable charcuterie to eat on the road?" I asked.

Gemma readily agreed to handle the request. Of the two women who spoke French, she was the most proficient in the classical language and less likely to be embarrassed by a misplaced 21st Century usage. That also meant I could take Michelle with me to serve as translator – though I anticipated that merchants in a port city, even in a country as linguistically centric as France – would speak enough English to complete basic business transactions. I also detected a subtle look exchanged between Gemma and Saoirse that suggested they would be enjoying their time alone during the afternoon.

When we left the inn, Michelle quickly took my left arm. She had noticed early in our travels that in France it was customary for a woman under a man's protection to take his left arm while they were strolling in public. This ensured the escort's right arm would remain free to draw a weapon if necessary and made it clear to everyone that she was not alone.

The only weapon I carried was a concealed dagger suspended in a sheath under my left armpit. Most men openly carried a sword or pistol – or both – as deterrents against being held up. I preferred to keep my weapon concealed as I believed the element of surprise would be to our advantage. I hoped I would not have to prove my theory along our route to Rouen and Paris.

I had memorized the landmarks to find our way back to the livery stable and wainwright shop I had identified after we arrived. It took us less than half an hour to find them and another hour or so to negotiate a price for a horse and wagon. Another little tidbit I learned about Michelle was that she was raised on a farm and was familiar with working horses.

It was Michelle who kept me from accepting the lowest-priced mare to be our trusty steed. She checked the animal over from nose to tail and found things that would not have been obvious to the uninitiated.

"Aaron, two of the mare's shoes are loose and will probably cause problems for us along the way," Michelle whispered to me, "and she also appears to be malnourished. Look how thin she is. Her ribcage is so prominent that I wonder if it is not an indication of a deeper issue."

Michelle took that opportunity to run her hand down the mare's flank. Her muscles rippled in response and she took a tentative sidestep and shied away from Michelle.

"Did you see that when I touched her flank?" Michelle asked. "It is a good sign that this horse is in pain. I suggest we look at another animal."

Turning to the proprietor of the stable, I was firm and direct. "This horse is not healthy, and her shoes are about to fall off. We shall take our custom elsewhere if you cannot offer us a different animal." His expression told me he understood my concern.

"*Mais oui, monsieur*," the stabler replied, before switching to English, "I have another animal, but the price will be much, much higher."

He was back a few minutes later with a strong and healthy gelding, which Michelle checked over. It was freshly shod and there was no pain response when she patted the animal's flanks.

Turning away from the stabler, Michelle leaned in to quietly convey her assessment.

"Aaron, this animal is strong and will serve us well. I suggest you offer the stabler the same price he wanted for the mare and accept a price between that and what he unrealistically wants for the gelding." Ten minutes later, we had a contract.

The wagon was a little easier to evaluate. I gave everything a good shake. It felt solid. The axles were intact and well-lubricated, and the hardware (what little there was in 1651) was newly forged.

I made a deposit of half the negotiated amount and got a written receipt with a contract for 9 a.m. the next morning. Wanting to be absolutely sure we would not be duped as foreigners, Michelle cornered a passing priest to witness the transaction. She knew how devoutly Catholic the French were in the 17th Century and that lying to a priest was a venal sin. My wife was making me proud.

We returned to the *Auberge du Roi* around 4 p.m. Michelle reminded me once again that we both needed to wash before dinner, so she sought out the landlady for a washbasin, a bucket of warm water, soap, and washing cloths. She returned to our room a few minutes later; the soap smelled of lavender and the water appeared clean, but the washcloths were nothing more than coarse threadbare rags. I cringed at the thought of their abrasiveness and where they might have been before being offered to us for our ablutions..

I was pleasantly surprised that our traveling clothes had been washed and dried in the sun while we were on our foray into town. There was nothing better than the feel of clean clothes against a clean body and we both luxuriated in the experience.

"I forgot how good it could feel to be clean," I teased Michelle, "and there are only a couple of things in this world that are more enjoyable."

"Aaron, you smell so wonderful – even if it is lavender – and that could be enough to… well… you know…" she teased reciprocally. It was all I could do to contain my urge to take her up on her suggestion right then and there.

Clean, refreshed and dressed, we ventured down to the dining room a little after six p.m. to find Gemma and Saoirse already seated at our usual table. They, too, had bathed and were now dressed in clean attire. We looked and felt like new people.

"Ladies," I said to open the conversation, "we will get our horse and cart at 9 a.m. tomorrow."

Gemma expressed some concern that the merchants could easily stiff us for the goods; she could not turn off her police training to evaluate ulterior motives. Saoirse was more congratulatory and seemed anxious to leave Le Havre behind as quickly as possible. I shared her desire to be on the road sooner rather than later. Even in 1651, Le Havre attracted the more unsavory and violent members of society. In the areas immediately adjacent to the harbor, hardly a night went by without some sort of fatal altercation, usually involving a misunderstanding between transient seamen.

* * * * *

The next morning, after a wonderful breakfast of pastries and tea, Michelle and I set out for the livery to collect our gelding and cart. When we were ready to pay the remaining balance for our purchase, the proprietor had added an additional day of stable fees to the balance. I was livid and viewed it as an attempt to recover the difference between the price I agreed to and the price he originally offered.

"But *monsieur*, it is a cost to me to keep your horse in my stables overnight. I had to feed him and shovel his *merde*. I think you British call it shite. Somebody has to pay," the stabler said with an open palmed shrug.

Michelle had seen enough. Her temper suddenly boiled over and I was glad it wasn't me she was targeting. She was in high dudgeon and her eyes were shooting daggers at the poor man.

"*Écoute, espèce de menteur,*" she began, "*nous avions un accord et signé un contrat. Vous ne pouvez pas changer cela sur un coup de tête. Vous honorerez notre accord sans frais supplémentaires ou je vous dénoncerai à votre prêtre.*"

I turned to Michelle and away from the stabler. "What did you just tell him, my dear?"

"It was a simple commentary," she beamed, "After calling him a liar, I told him he could not change the contract on a whim and that we were not paying any more than the agreed price. Then I threatened to report him to the village priest."

The stabler's demeanor had changed dramatically after Michelle's short diatribe and the animal was quickly brought from its stall. I paid the balance due, insisted he sign the contract as paid in full, and watched attentively as the stable boy hitched the gelding to our wagon. I knew I would eventually have to do that myself, so learning the process was of paramount importance.

I had never driven a horse-drawn cart before, so I needed quite a bit of coaching from Michelle, who I just found out had been a competitive carriage driver in high school. *"Was there anything this woman could not do?"* I wondered to myself.

"Be gentle, Aaron. Louis is still getting used to your style. Too much direction and he is likely to bolt," Michelle explained, "and if he does suddenly break into anything more than a gentle walk, gently pull back in the reins. He will stop from the pressure the bit puts on his mouth."

The streets going back to the *Auberge du Roi* had become quite crowded. Thanks to the wagon and horse traffic, the combined smell of last night's chamberpots and fresh animal manure was nauseatingly overpowering.

"How did people live like this?" I asked Michelle, not expecting an answer. "I will be glad when we are back in the countryside."

27: On the Road to Rouen, Part II

Late October, 1651

When we arrived in France, we really had nothing more than the clothes on our backs. The lack of possessions made it easier for us to load the wagon and depart for Rouen. It was Michelle and me sitting on the driver's bench at the front of the cart. Gemma and Saoirse were seated behind us, on a makeshift bench over the axle and facing to the rear. The load was well-balanced, taking some of the strain off our trusty steed, Louis.

Thanks to Gemma's diligence and food-focused language skills, we had a basket full of cured meats, cheese and breads plus another filled with a combined cache of wine and ale. If we carefully monitored our consumption, I was pretty sure the food would last us until we reached Rouen.

Gemma also found out from the hotel's proprietor that a part of our route would take us through the *Trait Maulévrier* Forest. I knew from our travels in England that wooded areas could be dangerous for travelers, especially second-growth areas where underbrush provided concealment for potential attackers. We would have to be on our guard passing through that area. Our concern appeared to have been misplaced; we didn't encounter a single person as we passed through the forest.

The remainder of the route took us through farmland on public rights of way. I would not call them roads in any sense of the word; rather, they were deeply rutted pathways that jarred us to our bones. I decided that accelerating our pace would not be a good idea.

We spent our first night in the bucolic village of Caudebec-en-Caux on the bank of the Seine. The local inn there was a step up from our accommodation in Le Havre and the food was even better. An added benefit was the opportunity for all of us to take a hot bath – for an additional fee, of course. As a married couple, Michelle and I were expected to share the bathwater.

After a good meal and the hot bath, Michelle and I were so relaxed that all we could think about was sleep, which came quickly once we were cuddled naked under the duvet in the overstuffed feather bed.

The next morning, we once again feasted on fresh pastries and tea before setting out on our way to Rouen. The boredom of plodding 17th Century travel was taking its toll on our patience. Paris was still at least three days away.

Eventually, the time came for us to find lodging for our second night after leaving Le Havre. Roadside inns were few and far between in this part of France, leaving us with little choice but to find an abbey or manor house which would accept weary travelers. On the recommendation of two monks we encountered on the road, we would head for the *Manoir de l'Aumônerie*, an abbey just west of Rouen that the monks said had once belonged to the Knights Templar from the Crusades.

As the monks' story unfolded, Saoirse and I exchanged anticipatory glances with each other and with Michelle. France was literally covered with abbeys and in our time, preserved abbeys were treasure troves for archaeologists, with many artifacts being uncovered in carefully excavated trash piles or outdoor privies. Most also had an elaborate feretory to house alleged relics of departed saints.

Gemma did not share our passion for history or archaeology and reminded us that we should stick to our original plan, waiting until the monks had left us before telling us what she was really thinking.

"I wish the three of you would focus on getting us back home," Gemma declared. "There could be a portal in Rouen like Saoirse suggested and the abbey could be a distraction. If we do not find a Hecate's Wheel in the Roman ruins at Rouen, we should continue on to Paris as soon as possible."

Saoirse chimed in, "If the layout of the ruins in Rouen is like those in Wroxeter, we should be able to approximate the location of the *strophalos*. We will have about 400 years less detritus to dig through – but will surely draw suspicion from the locals. The abbey where we are staying is just a mile or two outside of Rouen and convincing the monks there to allow us to stay for more than one night in return for a little hard work should be easy. Staying will let us be a little more cautious with our digging."

Gemma's pragmatic nature reared its head once again as she with a profanity-laced tirade directed at no one in particular. In her tirade, Gemma confirmed what I had suspected all along: that she and Saoirse were once romantically involved.

"… and another thing, Saoirse Donoghue, P-H-fucking-D, if you think we can go back to the way things were, you are mistaken. I've had enough of your fixation on antiquities and your blindness to our current situation! You haven't changed one bit."

After pausing to catch her breath, the normally composed and thoughtful Gemma Royce-Smallworth broke down into tears. Saoirse tried to console her but was physically rebuffed. The stress of our predicament and little possibility of resolution had taken its toll on her ability to remain calm and composed.

The sudden outburst of hysterics discomfited Michelle as well. The tears welled up in her eyes as she took my hand and said softly, "Aaron, we should give them some privacy."

I pulled Louis and our cart off into a small grassy meadow and dismounted with Michelle, giving the horse a chance to graze for a little while. Gemma had already started to regain her composure, but there were plenty of things the two ladies needed to work out before we reached the abbey and what likely was to be an enforced solemn and thoughtful environment. Tirades like we had just heard would not be acceptable in the cloisters of the abbey and could result in our immediate expulsion.

It was late afternoon when we reached the *Manoir de l'Aumônerie.* Entering through the austere foyer, we were greeted by an elderly monk, Brother Tomas, who spoke excellent English.

"I studied in England at Oxford University before taking my vows here in France now thirty years ago, when His Majesty, King James, dissolved Parliament," the monk explained. "Until then, I practiced my faith in secret, though I took an Oath of Allegiance to the Crown. James tolerated this arrangement with Catholics, understanding that he might some day need our support."

Michelle, with her undergraduate work in English history, was completely spellbound by the monk's tale. As she had told me not long after her arrival in 1651, she was living history and not just reading about it. Regardless, she was concerned that any actions on our part could have implications a century or more into the future.

Brother Tomas led us to our rooms. Michelle and I would be getting one of two rooms the monks had set aside for married guests. I had already quietly explained to him that Gemma and Saoirse should be housed together as our servants and not afforded special privileges of privacy. With a wink and a smile, Saoirse acknowledged what I had done on their behalf.

"Guests of *Manoir de l'Aumônerie,*" Brother Tomas declared, "dinner is at 6 in the evening. If you desire, you may join us for Vespers in the chapel when the clock chimes the half hour before that."

"Brother Tomas, how do you conduct mealtimes here? I hope they are not silent affairs and will be filled with conversation. My husband and I – and our servant ladies – do enjoy mealtime conversations," Michelle explained sincerely. I just hoped that Gemma and Saoirse would be on their best behavior and not embarrass us with a continuation of their earlier imbroglio.

"Mistress Shepherd, during the day while going about their chores, brothers remain silent for long periods. When we are not working, like mealtimes, ours is a boisterous abbey where free discussion of religion and secular happenings are expected and encouraged," Brother Tomas replied.

"We look forward to joining you for dinner," I replied, extending my hand for a handshake.

"Certainly," Brother Tomas answered, "and we do believe that 'cleanliness is next to Godliness,' so your rooms have washing basins and cloths for your use." With those instructions, the monk left us to enjoy our surroundings.

Closing the door behind us, Michelle said, "Aaron, I think we should participate in Vespers as a show of our good intentions. I know you weren't raised Catholic like I was, but it's pretty easy to follow along and at least go through the motions. If you remember the other women who accompanied me on the road when we first met, it was my knowledge of Catholic practices that kept me in their good graces."

"As usual," I replied, "you are correct, my darling. But what do we do about Gemma and Saoirse? We can't force them to attend Vespers, can we?"

"If we are to maintain the ruse of them being our servants, we should at least make that suggestion to them," Michelle said with a nod.

*   *   *   *   *

Seated around the massive dining table were the four of us and a dozen monks. Brother Tomas had explained to me that there were no distinctions between master and servant in their abbey and that Gemma and Saoirse would be seated with everyone else. I personally had not given the issue much thought but recognized that the social construct of the day would normally have kept us separate at mealtimes. The other two ladies would have consumed their meal "below stairs" with the household servants. The pecking order in a monastery was much different than that of an English manor house.

Approaching the head of the table was Abbot Bernard, the overseeing monk. I observed that no one sat down until Bernard invited them to do so and that conversation was kept to a minimum before the attendees genuflected and Abbot Bernard said grace, switching from French to English for our benefit:

"Bless us, O Lord, and these thy gifts which we are about to receive from thy bounty, through Christ, our Lord, Amen."

With the "Amen," everyone genuflected once more, our traveling party included.

Abbot Bernard gave the sign for everyone to be seated, after which the meal was promptly served by the three youngest monks. The meal was a fine combination of root vegetables, bread, roast pork, and chicken. Our libations were a choice of either some very fine ale, barley wine, or brandy – all of which were potent enough to knock over a horse. I only hoped that inhibitions would not fall to the alcohol and present us with yet another embarrassing situation involving Gemma and Saoirse.

Conversation around the table was quite lively. Michelle and I were opposite each other, at either side of Abbot Bernard. To my right was Brother Matis, who I would quickly discover shared my interest in historical artifacts. To Michelle's left was Brother Gervais. He was an antiquarian who had spent time studying the few texts preserved from the Catholic abbeys in England.

"Worcester?" I hear Michelle ask excitedly.

"Yes, Mistress Shepherd, the very same," Brother Gervais replied.

"I thought most religious libraries held by Catholics were destroyed after Henry VIII," Michelle commented as she tilted her head and raised an eyebrow.

"Some cathedrals... minsters in England... managed to hide ancient texts in their undercrofts, where scholars toiled day and night transcribing the texts to preserve them for the future. I was one of those scholars and fortunate that my adherence to Catholicism was never discovered," Brother Gervais explained.

Michelle looked across the table and caught my eye. She was up to something, and I was trying to focus on both her and my interesting conversation with Brother Matis.

"Mister Shepherd, I understand from your servants that you wish to see the Roman ruins in Rouen," Matis said, "and I am the person you want for your guide."

Eavesdropping on Michelle's conversation would just have to wait.

"Brother Matis, I would like that very much. We are particularly interested in any indications that there were postern gates in the Roman walls and what might lay buried in the ground nearby." I paused, hoping that what I had just said would not be viewed as the ramblings of a crazy person.

"Mister Shepherd, I know exactly what you are talking about," Brother Matis replied, "and in my studies here, I have found drawings from earlier times that depict the layout of the Roman fort at Rouen."

I decided I should take my inquisition a bit further.

"Did you ever see a drawing of a circle with what looked like a maze on it?" I asked.

"Yes," the monk replied, "and it was what the ancient Greeks would call a *strophalos*."

His comments hit me like I had just run into a brick wall at full speed. This monk knew a little (maybe a lot?) about what we were looking for. The unanswered question was if he knew *why* we were looking for it. I wouldn't have long to wait before finding out. I could tell the brandy was having an effect on Brother Matis and he was becoming quite talkative. Rather than trying to guide the conversation, I elected to remain silent and let him speak.

"You see, Mister Shepherd, the ancient Greeks and even the Romans believed in a goddess named Hecate. She was one of the most poorly defined deities in either of their mythologies. It seemed that she was everywhere – and yet nowhere – all the time, kind of like our own God," Matis explained. "Hecate was also the guardian of gateways. What that meant remains unclear even to this day. Was she the goddess of entrances to homes, businesses, and temples – or were those gateways between worlds? Some mystics and even the Jew's Kabbalah would agree that to be the case."

Brother Matis was surprising me with his grasp of this concept, talking to me in almost 21st Century terms. Was Rouen ultimately going to be our ticket back to 2011, or would we have to wait until we got all the way to Paris?

"I think I should show you the postern gate in the Roman wall in the morning after breakfast. I do not have any assigned chores tomorrow," Brother Matis said with a smile, "so I am free to engage in what we call 'learned pursuits' and it would be my honor to escort you, your wife, and your two servant women to Rouen."

I could hardly contain my excitement over what I had just been told; I just hoped it wasn't misplaced or premature. Regardless, based on Brother Matis's tale, there was a good chance a *strophalos* existed in Rouen…

We could be going home!

28: Another Brick in the Wall

Early November, 1651

After the evening meal, I gathered our group together to tell them about my conversation with Brother Matis. As I expected, Michelle and Saoirse were hopeful while Gemma was pragmatic. It would take a leap of faith to believe that an artifact as large as a *strophalos* was buried in or near the remains of the Roman fort in Rouen.

"Brother Matis asked that we meet him in the dining room after Matins tomorrow morning, have our breakfast, and be ready to walk the short distance to the remains of the Roman wall," I explained. What I didn't tell them was that I had a suspicion that Brother Matis might himself be a time traveler. There was just something about him that told me he was not of this century.

After their disagreement before our arrival at *Manoir de l'Aumônerie*, Gemma still seemed a little on edge. I was afraid that any enthusiasm and hopefulness I showed would be a trigger for her – and Saoirse would be the one taking the brunt of Gemma's temper. I could see that Saoirse was excited about tomorrow's possibilities and didn't want to light the fuse for another one of her tempestuous explosions.

Saoirse told us goodnight, took Gemma's hand and led her back to their small chamber. They still had a lot to work out between the two of them, but I could definitely see progress towards resolution, at least for now.

At dinner, Michelle had experienced something quite profound, having been seated between Abbot Bernard and Brother Gervais. She could not easily explain it, but her Catholic faith had been rekindled over the past few weeks, starting with her arrival in England and her involvement with the White Ladies.

Michelle explained, "I used to just go through the mechanics of being Catholic when I was younger. My mother was devout almost to a fault and attended Mass every day except Monday. My father was faithful as well, but was not as rigid about Mass. Here, I feel safe… special… in the presence of true believers."

There was a long silence before Michelle continued, "Brother Gervais asked me to attend Matins with him tomorrow morning at sunrise. He said he would knock on our door when it was time. I intend to join the monks and will see you later at breakfast – unless you feel you should join me."

I responded, "Michelle, my darling, if that is what you feel called to do, I will support you and appreciate your faith. Myself, I am agnostic about the existence of a deity – any deity – who is characterized as benevolent, yet allows bad things to happen to believers. So much harm has been caused to others in the name of faith."

"Aaron, I appreciate your perspective, and I thank you for accepting mine," Michelle said as she pulled me close and wrapped her arms around me. The kisses that followed were some of the most passionate we had shared in our short marriage.

As promised, Brother Gervais knocked on our door a little before sunrise. Michelle awoke with a start. She took very little time to make herself presentable, gave me a quick kiss, and headed into the corridor for Brother Gervais to escort her to Matins.

Because I was already awake, I elected to take a solitary stroll around the abbey grounds. It was peaceful in the crisp morning air. As I walked, I realized that I had been in this time for nearly two months – trying to remember my life before touching Hecate's Wheel at the Wroxeter dig for the first time. The details were becoming more and more fuzzy with each passing day, and I wondered if I would be able to reassimilate into the 21st Century if our time in 1651 became protracted and took us into 1652 or beyond.

I tried not to dwell on that thought, choosing instead to focus on the here-and-now. I was in a good place. I'd hobnobbed with royalty, participated in a fugitive's adventure, gained a wife, and reestablished contact with an old colleague. It was certainly less monotonous than the day-to-day drudgery at an active dig. Most of them were months of boredom broken only by minutes of euphoria when a significant artifact was unearthed.

On the eastern edge of the grounds, I paused for a moment to marvel at the sun as it rose over Rouen and the inverted "u" bend in the Seine to the east. It was one of those mornings where the clouds glowed in the rising sun. I felt at peace with my situation and really wanted our adventure in 1651 to continue.

The quiet was interrupted by a combination of a rooster crowing and the chapel bell tolling the end of Matins. I knew it was time to head towards the dining hall to meet Michelle, Brother Gervais, Saoirse, and Gemma for breakfast. Despite my excitement after dinner yesterday at the prospect of unearthing a *strophalos*, I really was in no hurry to do so.

Breakfast in the abbey was more solemn than dinner as it was the start of the monks' workday. As we were told by Brother Tomas, during working hours the monks spoke little and performed their chores as silently and as efficiently as possible. Out of politeness, we kept our own conversation to a minimum, waiting instead for the meal to finish and for Brother Matis to escort us to the Roman ruins in the old city.

Gemma seemed to be in high spirits this morning and I nodded to her with a smile. I wondered if she and Saoirse had reconciled overnight. My curiosity was laid to rest when Saoirse caught my eye and winked. I nodded, lips pursed and my left eyebrow upraised. Perhaps their lovers' quarrel was now behind us…

The end of the meal was marked by Abbot Bernard rising to give a benediction:

"*Vade in pace et servies Deo… In nomini Patri, et Filii, et Spiritus Sancti…* Go in peace and serve God, in the name of the Father, Son, and Holy Spirit," the abbot pronounced as he made the sign of the cross, adding the English for our benefit.

In unison, the monks rose and filed silently out of the dining hall, heading directly for their chores. Some would be working in the barns tending the livestock. Others would be in the impressive gardens cultivating the late-season vegetables and preparing the ground for winter. Only about half a dozen monks, the oldest of the lot, remained inside and tended to the scullery following our meal. It was also their job to prepare a light mid-day meal, the French equivalent of a ploughman's lunch, for the other monks.

We joined up with Brother Matis outside the main entrance to the abbey. He had loaded a donkey with several shovels and our food for the day.

"Ladies and Mister Shepherd, Rouen is a very old city, known to the Romans as *Rotomagus*. The old city and the remains of the Roman settlement are on the north bank of the Seine – so we will not have to cross the river at the stone bridge built by Mathilde the Empress in 1160. It is the same bridge where the ashes of *Jean d'Arc*… Joan of Arc… were scattered over the Seine two centuries ago."

"Do you know where the postern gate is in the Roman wall?" Saoirse asked.

"Yes, I believe so, Matis replied, "and it leads into a concealed passageway."

"We should start there," I suggested.

"Of course, Mister Shepherd," Brother Matis agreed.

Along the way, we had to stop a couple of times as Michelle was overcome by nausea and needed to sit down. I wondered if it was something she had eaten for breakfast – but if that were the case, it should have affected all of us as we had all eaten the same pastries, the same potatoes, the same eggs, and the same meats. It was highly unlikely that only her portions were causing her distress. After the third stop, she began vomiting violently.

I was at a complete loss how to assist my wife, leaving her to the ministrations of the other two women and Brother Matis. I stood idly by, hoping that I would not devolve into an episode of sympathetic vomiting. I could spend an entire day at a site digging through decomposed remains and the offal of a privy – but the sight, sound and smell of someone else vomiting had always triggered me to do the same. I could not hear Michelle's conversation with Matis and the other women.

"Brother Matis," Michelle said between heaves, "are any of the other monks qualified as physicians?"

"Yes, Mistress Shepherd. In fact, two of the brothers trained in the Paracelsian disciplines," Matis replied. "One is Brother Jacques and the other is Brother Guillaume."

"Which one would be the most comfortable dealing with a woman as a patient?" Michelle asked.

Brother Matis thought for a moment before recommending Brother Guillaume as the preferred choice and offering that "Brother Guillaume assisted with the delivery of many babies in Rouen when the midwives took ill with consumption."

"You can forget any idea that I may be with child. For now, I would like a few sips of brandy if you are carrying a flask," Michelle suggested.

"I have just the thing," Matis responded with a wry smile.

The remainder of our trip was without incident and Michelle needed no further stops. At the Roman ruins, Brother Matis took us directly to the postern gate, which surprisingly was nearly intact, complete with the hidden passageway immediately behind the main wall as he had described.

The gate itself was concealed by a semicircular evergreen hedge several yards out from the base of the wall. We would be concealed from prying eyes; the last thing we wanted was an inquisitive citizen reporting us to the civil authorities. The environment was totally different than what we experienced in the 21st Century where everything related to a dig was out in the open and surrounding vegetation stripped down to bare dirt.

Michelle, Saoirse, and I dug where we expected the *strophalos* to be buried, Brother Matis took Gemma inside the concealed passageway. It was only a matter of minutes before Gemma returned, white as a sheet and trembling. She stumbled to where we were digging, leaving Matis at the postern.

"I... I... felt like Fortunato in Poe's 'The Cask of Amontillado,' waiting for that last brick to seal the alcove, I've never felt so claustrophobic in my life," Gemma whispered to the rest of us, "I had to get out of there before I completely lost it." I could see from her hyperventilation and the way the veins were pulsing in her neck that Gemma was close to a full-blown panic attack. Back out in the fresh air, she quickly regained her composure and appeared to be interested in what we were doing.

By lunchtime, we had dug down approximately three feet and had uncovered no artifacts at all. I was beginning to doubt the existence of the Wheel at this location, wondering if we should abandon the effort, return to the abbey, and prepare to head for Paris.

"Aaron, we can't stop now," Saoirse said firmly. "We have to see this through. If my calculations are correct, we have only another foot or so left to dig."

"We'll keep going until the village clock strikes 3," I reluctantly agreed, "and if we don't encounter *something* by then, even if it is not the *strophalos*, we will return to the abbey and get ready to leave for Paris after breakfast tomorrow morning."

The hopeful mood we all shared when we arrived was turning darker with every shovel of dirt we removed from the hole. We had not encountered so much as a pottery shard, much less anything metallic. It didn't help anyone's disposition to have Gemma pacing back and forth next to the hole, not really contributing anything to the effort. Brother Matis was outside the hedge as our lookout, sitting on stump and pretending to be reading his Bible. He was to exclaim something – anything – in Latin if anybody approached us.

The village clock tolled 2:45. Still nothing. Michelle, usually our rock of stability, was on the verge of tears.

With only five minutes to spare, Saoirse's shovel hit something solid, with a metal-on-metal "clank!"

"Did you hear that, Aaron?" she asked.

"Everyone did, Saoirse. You're the expert of the bleedin' obvious," I answered sarcastically.

There was just enough room in the hole for one of us to kneel and begin the tedious process of using our hands to uncover whatever Saoirse's shovel had struck. Michelle had the best feel for such things, so we helped her down into the hole.

For the next several minutes – which seemed to all of us like hours – Michelle carefully and painstakingly used her hands to brush away the dirt from the object Saoirse hit with her shovel. As the object became clearer, it was obvious that it was not what we were looking for. It looked like the lid to a strongbox of some kind, and with gentle puffs of air from her pursed lips, Michelle blew the dirt away. On top of the lid, the words "*Imperium Negotium*" appeared.

"Empire business?" Saoirse asked, as she translated the words from Latin.

"I think we've stumbled upon what the British Government would call a despatch box. In our time, they were used to carry classified papers between government departments. Their use goes back to the reign of Elizabeth I," Michelle explained, drawing from her extensive knowledge of English history.

"I wonder if the ancient Romans used boxes for similar purposes. To the best of my knowledge, nothing of the kind had been discovered in Britannia... England... even through our time in the 2020s," Saoirse added.

"My guess is that the box will be locked," I added as an afterthought.

"Of course it will be locked," Gemma interjected, finally joining the conversation.

It was nearly 4 p.m. by the time Michelle uncovered enough of the box to expose the entire lid, the hinges, and the lock. It looked to be made of brass and easily breakable with a modern steel shovel.

"Brother Matis, could you join us, please?" I called out. "We have something here that may interest you."

Matis took one look at the box and immediately translated it aloud, "Government Business... hmm... I wonder what could be inside."

It took me two strikes with the blade of the shovel to break the badly corroded padlock. I carefully removed it to preserve its parts, then knelt beside the box to open the lid. Because the hinges were even more corroded than the padlock, I used the blade of a flat spade as a lever between the lid and main box.

The hinges creaked like a teacher's fingernails on a chalkboard as I slowly levered the lid open. The other four crowded around the edge of our hole to catch their first glimpse of what was inside as I widened the opening. The first thing we saw was a stiff leather binder with "*Documenta Officialis Militaris*" embossed on the cover.

"Official military documents," Brother Matis translated.

I knelt beside the box and carefully lifted the binder to open it on its hinge made of leather cord, which was surprisingly intact. A single document was contained in the binder. It read:

"*Ad Legio IX Hispana in Eboracum: statim Rothomagum in Gallia explicant et contra Gallicos rebelles praesidia muniunt. Omnibus modis tene usquc ad mortem. Hadrian, Imperator.*"

Brother Matis translated, "To the Ninth Legion in York: deploy at once to Rouen in France and take up defensive positions against the Gallic rebels. Hold at all costs, even unto death. It's signed by Emperor Hadrian himself!"

Saoirse's eyes lit up like she had just seen a ghost. Michelle, too, had a look of awe on her face. Both seemed to be aware of Rome's mysterious Ninth Legion and the fact that it disappeared without a trace sometime during the Second Century AD. Here was apparent proof that it had been transferred from *Eboracum*… York… to France. This document alone would dispel any speculative theories on the legion's disappearance.

29: *Retardé en cours de route*

(Delayed Along the Way)

November 1651

While Brother Matis took the strongbox into Abbot Bernard's office, I called the three ladies together in the abbey courtyard. I gave them an overview of what had just transpired.

"Our dig was unsuccessful from our perspective as we had not uncovered what we had hoped to find. Instead, we found a military despatch box from the time of Emperor Hadrian. Beneath the binder with the military order for the mysterious Ninth Legion were several soft leather drawstring bags, filled with gemstones and coins of the realm, which should have deteriorated in the fifteen centuries since Hadrian's reign," I said, once again sounding like the Professor of Archaeology that I was.

Gemma provided us with a forensic explanation. "The strongbox was well engineered and possibly self-sealing. With repeated cycles of heating and cooling, that seal became almost as durable as a vacuum container."

Saoirse added, "The location did not appear to be susceptible to flooding from the Seine, at least up to this point in time, as the surrounding soil seemed to be devoid of any organic matter."

Giving an open palm signal, I stopped our conversation as Abbot Bernard and Brother Matis approached.

"Mister Shepherd, Mistress Shepherd, and ladies," Bernard began, "on behalf of my brothers here at the abbey, I thank you for turning over your discovery to us. The contents of the pouches will keep this abbey solvent for many years, and I remain eternally grateful. In recognition of your contributions, the debt for your stay here has been discharged."

"Abbot Bernard, we will be departing for Paris in the morning. Could we impose on you for a basket or two of food for our journey?" I asked on behalf of our group.

"Mister Shepherd, we would be honored if you would remain with us for two more nights and delay your departure. We would like to have a proper feast before you leave and there has not been enough time for Brother Antoine and his kitchen boys to prepare anything more than a routine evening meal," Abbot Bernard said with a smile.

"Another day or two will not matter. It would be discourteous for us to depart in such haste," I replied.

"This will also give Brother Antoine to assemble a proper travel basket for you," Bernard answered, "it is the least we can do. Now if you will excuse me, I must return to my studies."

Michelle seemed relieved that we were delaying our departure, in contrast to Gemma's overwhelming impatience. When the abbot was back inside, Michelle explained why she was reluctant to rush away from the safety of the abbey.

"Aaron, earlier today, I think you noticed that I was taken ill. I had hoped it was something we had eaten, but when none of the rest of you became sick, I ruled out that possibility. Besides, the nausea subsided by the time we reached the Roman wall, and I thought nothing of it."

"Will you be okay to continue our travels, my darling?" I asked.

"Before we leave, I think I should see one of the brothers who were physicians in their former lives just to make sure there is nothing amiss," she answered. "Brother Matis suggested that I see Brother Guillaume before the evening meal. Now that you have agreed for us to stay for two more nights, I can wait to see Brother Guillaume until tomorrow morning."

"I think it would be appropriate for you to take either Gemma or Saoirse with you," I suggested.

"Yes, that is a very good idea," Michelle answered with a smile, "but I know what you are thinking… that I may be with child."

I didn't say a word; instead, I raised an eyebrow and cocked my head inquisitively, as if to suggest that she was not telling the truth.

"Aaron Shepherd, if you must know, we haven't been together in that way long enough for me to get pregnant – and it's been less than a month since the last time I bled, which was just before we accepted each other as husband and wife," Michelle explained as unemotionally as she could. "I want to see a physician to be sure there is not something else going on, like an infection. Lord knows, this place is a petri dish waiting for its next victim."

"Yes, dear…" I replied sheepishly.

The next morning, Michelle and Saoirse sought out Brother Guillaume just after Matins and before breakfast. They found him in the abbey's infirmary, sorting out the potions and powders he kept on hand to treat a variety of maladies.

"Brother Guillaume," Michelle called out as she entered the infirmary, "do you have any men under your care at the moment?"

"No, my lady," he replied, "we are blessed that none of the brothers has taken ill for quite some time."

"On our way to Rouen yesterday, I was taken ill," Michelle explained, "and it quickly passed. My husband suspected I could be with child, but that is not possible as we have been married less than month."

"Mistress Shepherd, may I examine you?" Brother Guillaume asked.

"Please…" Michelle replied, "and I would like my servant, Saoirse, to remain in the room with us."

"As you wish," he confirmed.

Brother Guillaume spent the next several minutes palpating and prodding Michelle from head to toe. Everything seemed in order – until he prodded over her right kidney. She winced in pain.

"I am sorry if that pains you, Mistress Shepherd. I believe you may have an inflammation of your kidneys. Are you able to give me a sample of your water?" Guillaume asked as he handed her a glass collection flask. "There is a chamber pot behind that screen in the corner.

A few moments later, Michelle returned with the sample. Guillaume held it up to the light and noted that it was cloudy with the occasional hint of pink – a sign of a potential kidney stone, which Brother Guillaume quickly confirmed.

"Mistress Shepherd, you should consume as much liquid as you can and avoid cured meats for the next several days. As the stone begins moving its way to its… uhh… exit from your body, you will be very uncomfortable, even in pain. You should have someone with you whenever you make water as some women have been known to swoon from the pain."

"Brother Guillaume, I have had stones before. I know what to expect," Michelle answered, "and I will have Gemma and Saoirse at my side."

After our breakfast, Michelle took me aside to convey what Brother Guillaume had told her.

"Aaron, he thinks I have a kidney stone. Brother Guillaume also warned me that passing it would be painful and could cause me to faint. I'm no stranger to that pain as I have had a problem with kidney stones all my life."

"How do we take care of it?" I asked.

"I have to drink plenty of liquids and avoid cured meats for the next few days while we wait for it to pass," Michelle explained. "He also said that until the stone passes, I should not be left alone when I pee – which will be a lot if I drink as much as he said I should."

I almost laughed out loud at the suggestion of a need for frequent stops on the way to Paris.

Gemma did not stop fidgeting the entire time Michelle and Saoirse were visiting the infirmary. For some reason, she was once again on pins and needles. I'd noticed since her arrival in 1651 that she was prone to periods of extreme agitation followed by times when she was completely calm. Her behavior was so erratic that I wondered if she would have been eventually labeled as bipolar in 2011 and placed on medication.

With guidance from the elderly Brother Tomas, we spent the rest of the day working alongside the monks in whatever capacity they needed us. Michelle, being familiar equine care, was sent to the stables once again. Gemma needed both mental and physical distraction, so I volunteered her to work with the abbey's tailors to repair the monks' cassocks and scapulars. Saoirse worked in the garden plots to help get them ready for the coming winter, harvesting root vegetables like carrots, turnips, and potatoes. I ended up with the most arduous of work, helping one of the newest monks, Brother Remy, excavate for a new privy in the grove downhill from the main abbey building.

It all seemed like we were fitting into our roles as citizens of 1651. When… *if* was probably more accurate… we returned to 2011, would we look at our lives in the same way we had before our departure, taking our technology for granted?

30: Making Headlines - Again

November, 2011

THE Sun on Sunday

November 13, 2011

WROXETER FOUR STILL MISSING
Suspect In Custody of West Mercia Police

Mister James Hudson, an American allegedly from Connecticut, was released from the custody of the West Mercia Police. He was suspected of being involved in the disappearance of four individuals from the digs at the Roman ruins in Wroxeter, which we reported nearly a fortnight ago.

Still missing are Detective Sergeant Gemma Royce-Smallworth, Saoirse Donoghue, PhD, from Leeds University, and two Americans, Aaron Shepherde, PhD, along with his assistant, Miss Michelle Whitcomb.

According to police sources, Mister Hudson had no alibi as to his whereabouts during the times when the four went missing. Local sources with knowledge of Hudson's routines assert that he is prone to violent outbursts, especially after binges of excessive drinking.

277

Hudson's jilted lover, Miss Lucy Penderel (a barmaid at a local public house), was less than complimentary of Mister Hudson's behaviour. She went as far as to suggest that Hudson was jealous of Shepherd's relationship with Miss Whitcomb. "He only used me to get their attention," Penderel claimed.

31: April in France

April, 1652

We spent the winter as guests of King Charles II and his mother, Queen Henrietta Maria, at *Chateau-Neuf de Saint-Germain-en-Laye* a few miles west of Paris. It was at Queen Henrietta Maria's insistence that we remained through the winter. She asserted that it would be less than hospitable and certainly un-Christian to send us away during the coldest part of the year.

I discovered that Charles and his mother were guests of the boy-king, Louis XIV – not quite 14 years old – and receiving a monthly stipend from the Bourbon family coffers. Among the royal entourage was Lord Wilmot – who instantly recognized us from our adventure of helping Charles escape from England almost seven months earlier.

It was Wilmot who crossed the Channel with Charles on the *Surprise* and held the exalted position of "gentleman of the bedchamber." This meant that Wilmot was one of Charles's closest confidantes, fully aware of the strained relationships within the royal household. Charles didn't go to the privy without Wilmot knowing about it.

Once we were in the privacy of his chambers, Wilmot felt it necessary to confide in me that the situation at *Saint-Germain* was dire and that the British coffers needed a quick infusion of cash if they were ever to have a hope of reinstating the Stuart family on the British throne.

With the financial situation at the forefront, Charles II had created Wilmot as the Earl of Rochester, giving credibility to his position to negotiate on behalf of the exiled king. As the Earl of Rochester, Wilmot would be envoy to the Holy Roman Emperor, Ferdinand III, in hopes of negotiating an agreement for substantial financial support.

"Mister Shepherd, I believe the time has come for you to depart from our good graces and seek out your fortunes in the New World. Spring is now upon us and passage across the ocean will soon be available from both England and France. I suggest that you make haste downriver to Le Havre forthwith and decide your future from there," Wilmot explained.

I found his tone condescending and sanctimonious, much more so than I had ever experienced before. He was clearly enamored with his own importance to Charles.

"Your Lordship," I began, deciding the time was appropriate for formality, "it was not our intention to remain any longer than necessary. My wife and our two servants will do as you suggest, leaving here the day after tomorrow."

Wilmot did not even give me the politeness of a verbal response. Instead, he harrumphed and waved me away dismissively with his left hand before resuming a scratchy scrawl across the page in front of him with the quill he held in his right. The theatrics continued through his folding the stiff paper and affixing a wax seal.

From his exaggerated actions, I knew that if we did not leave on our own, we would soon become *personas non grata*, no matter how much Charles got involved in our situation. I bowed from the neck, pivoted on my heel, and left Wilmot's chambers. Again, there was no acknowledgement from the pompous ass.

I quickly located Michelle and the other two women after my encounter with Wilmot, telling them that our time in France had to come to an end.

"I don't know what our best option is, but I think we should head for the Colonies. Charles will not be reinstated to the throne for another nine years and there is just too much turmoil in England to remain there under Cromwell. We are already out of the good graces of Charles's most trusted advisor, and it is unlikely that we will get any support from the French crown, even with intervention from Charles or his mother," I rambled in explanation.

Michelle broke the silence. "We probably don't want to sail from France as their ships go to the French Colonies, known as 'New France' – we know it as Montreal and Quebec. Sailing from an English port will get us to the British Colonies. We're about a decade beyond the end of what is known as the 'great migration' when people were leaving England to escape the civil wars and to avoid religious persecution. I think we should use our knowledge of the future to our own advantage in this case."

Saoirse added, "I have no idea where we could begin searching in Paris for a *strophalos*. I've seen that most of the remnants of Roman civilization in the city have been obliterated, so we would be in worse shape than we were at Rouen."

Gemma remained silent as the rest of us discussed our options. Her moods had been pensive at best for the past several days and I hoped that she was not teetering on the edge of an emotional abyss. Even her normally loquacious conversations with Saoirse had become taciturn and I sensed that they were at an inflection point in their relationship. I didn't want to lose Gemma entirely as it was her keen analytic mind that saw data points the rest of us didn't.

I was surprised when Gemma suddenly and unexpectedly spoke up.

"If there is any money or gold left from the strongbox we found in Rouen, we could use it and the proceeds from selling Louis and our wagon to book passage back to England. There we would decide what our best option is. The rest of you are only seeing the big picture, not its component parts," Gemma explained. "In England, we have more options than we do here in France, even with the Roundheads remaining in charge."

"What are you saying, Gemma?" Saoirse asked.

"Think about it for a moment. We know where the Wheel should be in Wroxeter. If we can make it back there, all we have to do is dig," Gemma said with growing enthusiasm. "There's also Stonehenge, where Saoirse and I had our encounter with the mysterious Arwen and Cerys after our engagement with the *strophalos* in Wroxeter."

"Michelle, Saoirse, what do you think of going back to Wroxeter instead of simply sailing across the ocean from the southern coast of England?" I asked, trying to guide the discussion in the direction Gemma suggested.

"Staying here – in either England or France – is not a good idea," said Michelle, "as the British monarchy won't be restored for another nine years. There will also be numerous wars here in Europe, most notably the imminent Anglo-Dutch wars. The North American Colonies are probably our best option – though I do like the suggestion that Wroxeter or Stonehenge are possible gateways back to our time."

Saoirse added, "After giving it a little more thought, I agree with Michelle. Staying in England is probably not our best option."

"Are you suggesting we stay in this time?" Gemma asked.

"If we don't make it to Stonehenge or Wroxeter, we are accepting our fate here in 1652," I said dejectedly.

"If that is the case," Michelle added, "I vote for the Colonies."

32: More Headlines

April, 2012

THE Sun

April 15, 2012

WROXETER FOUR PRESUMED DEAD
No New Leads After Six Months

The West Mercia Police have suspended their investigation into the disappearance of four individuals missing from the archaeological digs at Wroxeter since September of last year. No new leads have been uncovered since the untimely death of the prime suspect, Mr. James Hudson, in an alcohol-related traffic accident early last November.

The four missing individuals are now presumed dead. They are West Mercia's own Detective Sergeant Gemma Royce-Smallworth, Professor Saoirse Donoghue from the University of Leeds, Professor Aaron Shepherd from Michigan Technological University and Miss Michelle Whitcomb, from Western Michigan University in Kalamazoo, Michigan.

A memorial service will be held for Detective Sergeant Royce-Smallworth at an unspecified date in the future. Because she was an alumna of the University of Leeds and because Professor Donoghue was a tenured lecturer there, the Chancellor has offered the University chapel as a potential venue.

33: On Board the *Hector*
June, 1652

We had been aboard the *Hector* for about six weeks and had been absolutely miserable since departing Portsmouth. Our quarters were so cramped that privacy was non-existent and the odors of unwashed bodies, human waste, and deteriorating provisions permeated everything. Weather permitting, we elected to remain on the main deck as much as possible; this, we hoped, would preserve our health until we landed in New England. I decided I would never again complain about sleeping rough in the great outdoors as we had done during Charles's escape to France.

With our connection to Greek and Roman mythology through Hecate's Wheel, it wasn't lost on us that we were on board a ship named for another character from Greek mythology who had been central to Homer's *Iliad* and Virgil's *Aeneid.*

The captain of the *Hector* was none other than Nicholas Tettersell, previously captain of the *Surprise*, which had transported Charles and Wilmot across the English Channel a little more than six months earlier. He was knowledgeable of the sea and certainly well-suited to be captain for a transoceanic voyage, but for some reason I did not trust the man. Money was always on his mind.

The three women shared my concern that Tettersell would impose a surcharge on his passengers before allowing them to disembark. We had paid up front for our crossing, thanks to the sale of Louis and our cart and what we had surreptitiously withheld from the Rouen strongbox before turning it over to Abbot Bernard.

We had also stopped at the *Manoir de l'Aumônerie* for a couple of days on our way back to Le Havre and were pleasantly surprised when Abbot Bernard provided an additional infusion of cash.

"It is the least I can do, *Monsieur* Shepherd. The Roman antiquities in the strongbox have proven to be quite valuable and marketable for cash. You have made us solvent for probably the rest of my earthly days," the abbot explained.

We decided that it was best to conceal our cache of funds from Tettersell and his crew. If they – or our fellow passengers – were to discover we were carrying a large sum of money, it was not beyond the realm of possibility for us to be thrown overboard and our cash taken.

The craftsmen at the abbey understood our plight and had provided us with four valises, each with false bottoms to conceal a single layer of coins. We all agreed that the money would not be revealed or used until we were in the New World and safely ashore. I trusted Michelle and Saoirse implicitly but was still somewhat nervous about Gemma's vacillating states of mind. I still sensed that she was just one stressor away from an overload situation.

We were sailing on a west-southwesterly course with a following wind and tolerable seas. The seasickness that had beset the crew and most of the four dozen passengers had abated over the past week or two, something I attributed to almost everyone "getting their sea legs." I found out that Captain Tettersell had factored the seasickness into his ration calculations, intentionally shorting the ship's stores of food in favor of taking on additional quantities of "fresh" water and rum. In the long run, it appeared to have been a masterstroke of genius as dehydration was a known consequence of prolonged seasickness.

On our 45th day at sea, the watchman in the crow's nest called out, "Ship ho, ten points off the larboard bow!"

Captain Tettersell brought out his spyglass and went to the bow to scan the other vessel. His evaluation was succinct and direct.

"We will avoid that vessel at all costs. It is a slaver known as the *Desire*. Captain Palmer runs a tight ship, doing his best to keep his human cargo alive and in line. During the day, a portion of them is allowed on deck for exercise. Like any master of a slaver, Palmer will be worried that his cargo will revolt upon sighting another vessel and attempt to escape. We cannot allow that to happen," Tettersell lectured – more for the benefit of his crew than the paying passengers.

"Captain," the lookout bellowed, "they are dumping their dead overboard."

I noticed that the bodies were not given the same treatment that would have been afforded a white seaman or passenger. The bodies were neither wrapped in sailcloth nor weighted, providing easy pickings for the ever-present sharks. Hollywood in the 20th Century didn't come even close to the carnage of a shark feeding frenzy.

"Helmsman, adjust course to starboard and give the *Desire* a wide berth," Tettersell ordered.

"Aye, sir. Adjusting course," the helmsman acknowledged.

Tettersell turned to the passengers and explained what the lookout had observed.

"The conditions on board slavers are some of the most abhorrent known to mankind. Much of the cargo dies on the crossing from Africa, sometimes by half," he said. "Regardless, the captain of a slaver receives a bounty for each head delivered alive to the slave market holding pens," Tettersell continued, "and this is in addition to the fees charged for the vessel and crew. I have been told it can be quite lucrative. In fact, the previous master of the *Hector*, Captain Richard Bentley, gave up transporting paying passengers from England in favor of the slave trade. I will follow in his footsteps once we reach New Haven."

As Tettersell droned on and on, my revulsion grew. I looked over to Michelle; she was wide-eyed and white as a sheet. Same for Saoirse and Gemma. Most of the other passengers took the situation in stride as if it were perfectly normal.

After one of Tettersell's more graphic descriptions about the treatment of the slaves on board most ships, Michelle, Gemma and Saoirse ran together to the rail and voided their stomachs over the side. We never in a million years expected that we would be exposed to slavery in real time.

Because the crew of the *Desire's* was engaged in exercising its cargo, only half of its sails were unfurled, allowing us, under full sail, easy passage to her starboard side. Eventually, we were directly downwind and the vile odors from the *Desire* were quickly noticeable. Once again, the three ladies paid a visit to the rail to retch. It was all I could do to suppress the same urge, knowing full well that I would be viewed by the crew and the other male passengers as being less than a man if I were overcome by the odors.

Three days after our encounter with the *Desire*, the lookout bellowed "Land ho! Dead Ahead!"

Everyone, passengers and crew alike, came up to the main deck to catch their first glimpse of *terra firma* since leaving Portsmouth a day short of seven weeks ago. One of the other passengers was a Presbyterian minister and he gathered everyone for a prayer.

"Lord God Almighty, Thou hast delivered us to our destination and for that we are thankful, Grant, we beseech Thee, divine guidance to Captain Tettersell and his crew that we mayest be seen safely ashore in the coming days. In Thy Holy Name, Amen."

Captain Tettersell immediately summoned his First Officer to calculate our position using his quadrant staff. A few minutes later, he indicated that we were heading straight for the northeastern end of Long Island Sound.

"Captain," the First Officer said quietly, "I must remind you that New Haven harbor presents challenges for vessels such as ours. I recommend we prepare for anchorage until we are certain we can safely approach the quay."

Having overheard the exchange between the Captain and First Officer, I was apprehensive. What were the challenges of New Haven harbor? The First Officer's conspiratorial tone suggested something unusually dangerous that was common knowledge among seafarers – and likely to cause panic in paying passengers. I felt it was my duty to inquire on behalf of my group.

"Captain Tettersell, I could not help but overhear what the First Officer told you about anchoring until it was safe to approach New Haven harbor. Why is he so concerned?" I asked.

"Mister Shepherd, there are obstacles on our way into the harbor known as 'the Devil's Steppingstones' that have split the hulls of many a vessel. We need near perfect conditions to make our approach to the harbor," Tettersell explained, "and I ask that you keep the treacherous conditions to yourself and not cause a panic amongst the ladies," he said as he leaned in conspiratorially. "The last thing we need are a bunch of swooning women, eh?"

"What a condescending prick," I thought to myself. If he only knew what women would be doing in my time, the 21st Century... These were simpler times and women were considered the 'weaker sex,' relegated to bearing children and caring for their husbands – including the ones like Tettersell, who were absent for months or even years at a time.

At dawn the next morning, we rounded the northeastern end of Long Island and headed towards the mouth of New Haven harbor. The wind was not as brisk as it had been on the open waters of the Atlantic, but still strong enough to keep us moving at a graceful speed. It was the idyllic times like this that I almost enjoyed being at sea.

About a mile offshore of the harbor, Captain Tettersell ordered the sails to be furled and the crew to prepare for dropping anchor. He also cautioned the paying passengers, me included, to stay out of the way, preferably belowdecks.

"This is no time for landlubbers to get in the way," Tettersell told me brusquely, "we still have to get past the Devil's Steppingstones without holing the ship."

My time aboard the *Hope* as we crossed the English Channel to France was irrelevant as I had been assigned menial tasks and lookout duties not involving the dangers of line or anchor chain handling or climbing aloft in the rigging, three aspects of sailing vessels that had high rates of injury.

An injury was the last thing I wanted on board this vessel, and especially not with our destination in sight. I did not trust the *Hector*'s so-called surgeon, having seen first-hand the way he handled the many injuries among the crew. His suturing technique was almost barbarian, and he wore a bloody apron like a badge of honor. I had also heard rumors that he was very quick to resort to the bone saw; it was fortunate that he had not been forced into that situation on this crossing.

The nervous energy aboard the *Hector* was electric. Everyone was impatient to finally be heading for dry land. The fact that we were dropping anchor and waiting until the next afternoon's onshore breeze to proceed into the harbor was met with grumbling from the passengers, some of whom even suggested commandeering the dories and rowing ashore without permission from Tettersell.

"Captain Tettersell, a word if I may?" I asked as soon as I could find a private moment.

"Yes, Mister Shepherd? Please step into my quarters for a moment," Tettersell responded.

"Captain, the male passengers are angry that you are not proceeding into the harbor with haste. They are anxious to be ashore and have even suggested taking the dories to go ashore on their own," I explained quietly. I did not want to be overheard by any of my fellow passengers.

"I will post an overnight watch, armed with muskets and pistols, to prevent any such action from the passengers," said the captain.

I agreed, telling Tettersell, "That, sir, is a reasonable and prudent course of action."

34: *Terra Firma*, Connecticut Style
June, 1652

What was to be our last night aboard the *Hector* passed without incident. Seeing armed guards posted at every one of the lowering stanchions was enough of an incentive for the male passengers to rethink their plans. It also helped that the wives among the passengers insisted that their husbands not make widows out of them this close to their destination. All of the men were farmers or shopkeepers and despite their proximity to the battles of the last civil war, none had any military experience or nautical skills aside from what they had gained on this voyage.

When we were out of hearing range of the other passengers and standing against the rail in the bow of the ship, Michelle asked, "Aaron, you weren't planning on joining the other men, were you?" She was dead serious.

"No, my darling. I was the one who encouraged Tettersell to set armed guards around the dories. He had already explained to me how treacherous the approach to New Haven harbor is and that we needed to be much closer to the quay," I told Michelle with a wry smile. "I wanted to keep the men from committing suicide. Commandeering the dories without any knowledge of the local waters made death by drowning a near certainty."

"Aaron, I am proud of you for thinking about the other passengers," Michelle said as she beamed from ear to ear, "and I am even more proud that I can call you my husband."

Michelle wrapped her arms around me and held me close. We had been aboard the *Hector* for over six weeks and had had little time or privacy for marital intimacy during the entire voyage. Her touch sent shivers of anticipation through my body, and I knew full well what lay ahead once we were ashore.

*   *   *   *   *

After a tense night and uneventful morning, the Hector was moored at the quay rather than riding at anchor as we were expecting. Thanks to the seamanship of Captain Tettersell and his crew, we were all able to disembark together. No dinghies. No separation of parties. All personal effects unloaded by the dock hands as we watched.

While I supervised the unloading of our baggage, Michelle and the other two women hired a wagon to transport us to a highly recommended inn on the north side of town. It was supposedly near the city green that I knew

298

would eventually become part of Yale University. It was also near what was then the slave market, complete with its holding pens where slaves were kept to recover from the rigors of the ocean crossing before being auctioned to the highest bidder.

New Haven of 1652 was an eclectic mix of European and Native American cultures. The English-speaking colony was growing rapidly, while the Quinnipiac were being displaced and moved further away from the sea. Everywhere we turned, we could see connections to England, and especially the Puritan culture that was supported by the Cromwell protectorate. The monarchy was despised almost as much in 1652 as it was when the Colonies would be in the throes of revolution over a century later.

"Aaron, we still need to find our way back to our own time," Michelle said to that evening after dinner. "I don't know how much longer I can continue in these primitive conditions. I know I've been on archaeological expeditions, but they always had some of the comforts of home. Here, we have nothing much other than the clothes on our back – which, I remind you, are in desperate need of washing. And… Doctor Shepherd, if you ever intend to be a father, do you know what the childbirth mortality rate was in the 17th Century? I'll answer that for you: it's more than 50 percent."

"My darling," I replied, "I am just as anxious to return home as you are. I know that Gemma and Saoirse are, too. I just don't have any ideas or suggestions where to start."

*　　*　　*　　*　　*

We had been in New Haven for a little over a week when news of the *Desire*'s arrival spread through the town. Captain Tettersell was correct in his prediction that the slaver would arrive about a week behind us. Meanwhile, the locals knew that it would only be a matter of time before there would be an auction on the village green.

We soon saw evidence of the *Desire*'s cargo when Captain Palmer led a coffle of black men and women to the holding pens adjacent to the village green.

The men's modesty was preserved only by a loincloth of rags, while the women were naked from the waist up. The four of us were, for the moment, speechless. The crowd, especially the men, were quite vocal about what they were observing, commenting openly about the female bodies being paraded before them.

After the shock of the situation wore off, Saoirse finally spoke. "I can't believe we ever did this to other human beings. Such cruel, inhumane, and inhospitable conditions… and just look at how undernourished they are."

Gemma added more to the conversation. "We're only seeing the new arrivals. There is another group of pens behind this one, where slaves ready for auction are held. Their physical condition seems to be much better, probably because the more fit specimens draw higher prices."

"Ladies, I'm at a complete loss for how to return us to our time. I am not aware of any archaeological digs in this area that uncovered much more than pottery shards, primitive implements like arrowheads, or bones."

At that moment, I felt a tug at my sleeve. I turned to my left and saw a young Native girl, maybe 12 or 13 years old. She was smiling as if she understood what we were discussing.

In broken English, the girl said, "My name Aiyana. You come with me. Grandmother Chepi want to see you in village."

We were all intrigued – especially about the perception that this young girl knew something that we didn't. We would just have to wait and find out.

"Come," Aiyana said, "village not far. Dark soon."

As we moved to the southwest, it was obvious that the trail between the town and the nearby Quinnipiac village was well-traveled. Apparently, the relations between them and the European settlers had not yet soured. Along the way, we passed several groups of Quinnipiac women carrying baskets of vegetables towards the town and assumed that they would be sold in the village markets.

We entered the Quinnipiac village, which looked just like what our ancestors had documented in drawings and other artwork. In the center of the village was a communal cooking area. There, several women were busy roasting meat and cooking vegetables in iron pots that had obviously been made by the European settlers.

One older woman seemed to be in charge of everything we were seeing. When she saw Aiyana, she beamed. It was obvious there was some connection between the girl and this older woman.

"Grandmother Chepi," Aiyana said in greeting, "these people need your help." I was puzzled why Aiyana was speaking English to her grandmother.

"Sir, ladies, please come sit down with me," Chepi said. "We know why you are here." The old woman's English was flawless and nearly unaccented.

"Where did this woman learn English? Settlers had been here only since about 1634," Michelle whispered to me.

Chepi was seated on a bench and waved us to sit on the ground in front of her. We were all nervously curious about what was happening.

"Please, tell me your names," Chepi said with authority, "and you may call me either Grandmother or Chepi – or both, if you prefer."

Being unsure of gender roles in Quinnipiac society, I decided to speak first and make introductions.

"My name is Aaron Shepherd."

I pointed to each woman in turn. "This is my wife, Michelle, and our good friends, Gemma and Saoirse."

"Mister Shepherd," Chepi began, "you do not belong in this time nor this place. We have helped other people like you to find their way back home." She stopped to let us absorb the importance of what she had just said.

The four of us exchanged curious glances. Collectively, I think our thoughts were all the same: "Is *this woman going to help us get back to 2011?*" I could see goosebumps rising on everyone's bare forearms.

Chepi continued, "In the forest not far from here, there is a symbol carved in a tree. Once you see it, I think you will recognize it."

Gemma, always the impatient one, could not contain herself. "Can we go now? I want to go home." She was near tears as she spoke.

"Patience, child," Chepi said in a voice meant to calm Gemma down, "the portal only has powers on moonless nights, which will not be for another two weeks. You will have to wait until then."

"Grandmother Chepi, how is it that you speak English almost like one of us?" Saoirse asked.

Chepi answered, "When the first English came nearly twenty summers ago, before Aiyana was born, we chose to learn their ways and accept their religion. I was baptized a Christian as soon as I could recite the Lord's Prayer and Psalm Twenty-Three." It was clear to all of us that Chepi had told this story before – and probably would do so again.

She continued, "Aiyana is my only true granddaughter so far, and she was raised speaking both English and what I assumed to be Quinnipiac. When she was old enough, she went to the Christian school under Reverend Eaton. She is used to having visitors such as yourselves."

Gemma had been fidgeting since we arrived in the village and even more so after taking our seats. I knew she was uncomfortable whenever we had to wait for something, and this situation was no different. I hoped that she would not have one of her episodes that only Saoirse could calm down.

"Grandmother Chepi," Gemma began, "you said the next moonless night is in two weeks. What are we supposed to do until then?"

"You are welcome to remain here with us as our guests. You will be comfortable and away from the influences of New Haven," Chepi said. "However, I do suggest that you attend the slave market on Saturday just to observe how the settlers treat our African arrivals."

Michelle looked at me, aghast at the suggestion. Her eyes were wide as dinner plates. Like any student of history, she had studied the conditions of slavery in the United States during the 19th Century – but we were now two centuries earlier and in a *northern* colony. Surely the conditions would be quite different than those in the agricultural southern colonies.

In contrast, our two English companions had no concept of slavery as an institution in America. The closest exposure they had was the complicated history of India as a colonial entity of the British Empire. They seemed to be intrigued by the notion of a slave auction.

"Grandmother Chepi, we will be honored to remain here as your guest," I acknowledged, "but not until we retrieve our belongings from the inn. Our room and board are paid in advance through tomorrow morning, so we will return here tomorrow afternoon. We would like it very much if Aiyana could guide us to town and back to your village once more."

"Yes, that can be arranged," Chepi acknowledged before continuing, "Mister Shepherd, I must speak with your wife privately before you return to New Haven."

"Yes, of course..." I replied, nodding to Gemma and Saoirse that we should leave the area.

35: An Interesting Development
June, 1652

"Mistress Shepherd," Chepi began, "I have lived for a long time and have the gift of foresight. I can see things in the future."

"Is that why you have asked to speak with me privately?" Michelle asked.

"Yes. Your future is a happy one if you leave this time and place at the next opportunity," Chepi said with a smile.

"Please tell me more," Michelle teased.

"I am hardly ever wrong in matters such as this…" Chepi paused for effect. "You are with child, Mistress Shepherd, and will be delivered of a baby six or seven moons from now."

"How can you be sure? My husband and I have not had the time or the privacy since our last night in England nearly two months…" Michelle's voice trailed off into silence before she exclaimed, "Oh, my God! I thought it was just seasickness and stress!"

"Mistress Shepherd –" Chepi began but was interrupted by Michelle.

"Grandmother Chepi, I would be honored if you would call me by my Christian name, Michelle."

Chepi resumed her speech without missing a beat. "Michelle, please come closer so I can touch you."

Michelle did as Chepi asked. When she was within reach, Chepi placed a hand on Michelle's lower abdomen.

"Michelle, you and your baby are both healthy, even though you have not yet felt movement," Chepi explained, "and you must leave here before the child is born or you will remain here, starting in the Year of Our Lord 1652, for the rest of your days."

"Grandmother Chepi, this seems like a simpler time than my own, 360 years in the future. I would like to remain –"

Chepi interrupted, "You must know that mothers frequently die in childbirth in this time. My own daughter, Aiyana's mother, was one of them. Please consider your choice carefully and discuss it with your husband. Make your choice wisely and I will help you however I can. If you remain, you will be adopted as our own and separated from the English in the town. I see struggles in their future that you need not be part of." Michelle was puzzled by this comment but recognized that her own knowledge of American History was woefully inadequate in the early Colonial period. Though intensely curious about what Chepi was referring to, Michelle decided not to press the issue.

In Chepi's visions. she had foreseen King Philip's War a little more than two decades into the future. That war would take the lives of ten percent of the European men of military service age. Aaron Shepherd would probably be called to fight in that war if they remained and the odds of him being killed or wounded were extremely high. Grandmother Chepi wanted to spare her new friend the agony of burying a husband if she lived through childbirth.

What Chepi left unsaid was the imminent decline of the Quinnipiac as a viable tribe. They fought alongside the English colonists, losing many warriors in the Great Swamp Massacre in December of 1675. Chepi saw that battle in vivid detail in one of her dreams.

Michelle explained, "Aaron has already told me he wants to return to our time, as has Gemma. I am not sure yet about what Saoirse wants to do."

"Remember, child, it will be another two weeks before there is a moonless night," Chepi explained. "Even if clouds block the sky, we know when there is no moon behind them. My people since long before my own grandmother's time have observed and recorded the moon. The moon guides our plantings, our hunting and fishing seasons, our harvests, and even when women should go into seclusion."

"I will talk to Aaron and our other two companions as soon as I can," Michelle said with a smile, "and I am sure they will be delighted by my news."

36: An Idyllic Time

Late June, 1652

When Michelle emerged from her audience with Grandmother Chepi, she was laughing and crying at the same time. I had never seen her emotions so conflicted, even when we were engaged in our archaeological efforts back in Wroxeter. On top of the emotions, she was, as my own grandmother used to say, "as nervous as a long-tailed cat in a room full of rocking chairs." I had come to expect constant nervous fidgeting from Gemma, but Michelle had always been the epitome of calm. It was one of the many things I loved about her.

In Chepi's village, mealtimes were communal events often filled with boisterous adult conversation and the joyful laughter of children. Most of the adults spoke passable English. The children made their best efforts to communicate in our tongue, switching back and forth between English and Quinnipiac whenever it was necessary. The setting was completely different from the staid formality of 17th Century English mealtimes, where the children and obsequious servants were to be "seen and not heard."

The idyllic setting reminded me of the communal meal after an Amish barn raising. As an undergraduate student, I studied Amish society during one summer semester and a barn raising is something that you never forget, and certainly not the feast afterwards!

One thing that I noticed was that parenting responsibilities seemed to be shared across all the women of the village, with Grandmother Chepi being at the top of the matriarchy. The younger unmarried women of childbearing age engaged in hands-on supervision of toddlers who were mobile and weaned from their mothers' milk, while older married women focused on children who in the 21st Century would have been elementary school aged. I was intrigued by the social dynamics and how the men of the village focused on teaching hunting and fighting skills to the boys, almost completely ignoring the girls.

Michelle remained silent throughout most of the meal despite us being seated at a position of honor near Chepi. I knew instinctively that something was bothering her but did not want to risk a meltdown in front of our hosts. Whatever it was, it would have to wait until we had a private moment.

Our meal consisted of smoked fish, roasted wild boar, root vegetables from the previous year's harvest, and fresh early vegetables such as peas and beans. Cornbread was readily available, as was a very weak and unfiltered wheat ale that the men proudly shared with us. It was tasty, despite its low alcohol content, and did more to ensure proper bladder function than to cause inebriation.

At the end of the evening, Michelle and I finally had a private moment as we casually strolled back to the guest lodge. About halfway there, Michelle took my right hand in her left and abruptly stopped, encouraging me to turn and face her directly. The moon was full and I could see her eyes glistening with imminent tears.

"Aaron, my darling," Michelle began, trying to control her emotions, "Grandmother Chepi knows we are not from this time. Her people are the keepers of the gateway that allows travel from one time to another. She also knows… that… I'm… we're… we're going to have a baby."

"That's wonderful news. You know I've always wanted children, but I was missing one important ingredient: a loving woman as my wife," I answered, full of emotion myself. However, my elation was short-lived thanks to the ever-pragmatic Michelle.

"Aaron, there's one thing Chepi told me that really has me worried. She confirmed that mothers often die in childbirth here, and she said that we must leave before my time is more than halfway gone or I will be stuck here to have the baby. Until she told me about the maternal mortality rate, I was convinced that staying here would be good for our family. It's certainly a simpler time than what we have in 2012. Just imagine raising a child in a technology-free environment!"

"So, you're saying that Chepi can help us get back to our time?"

"Well, she didn't cite a specific year – but did say we could jump to the future with her help."

"What about Gemma and Saoirse?"

"They will have to make a choice. They can either stay here in 1652 or come with us to the future, whenever that might be."

"Michelle, this is an awful lot to take in all at once. First, we were expelled from France, then we had a nasty sea crossing. Now you're pregnant and we have to leave this welcoming and safe environment or risk your own death in childbirth. It's your body and your choice, so if you really want us to jump to the future, we will. If it were entirely up to me, I would remain here in this simpler time and hope for the best."

Michelle's mood had changed from elation to anger in the blink of an eye – and I was the target of her growing rage. She quickly turned to face me and emphatically placed her hands on her hips as she started to speak.

"Aaron Shepherd! I am surprised at your selfishness. How can you let this so-called 'simpler time' interfere with your judgment about what is best for your wife and baby? It really should not be a choice at all, as long as we are transported into a time where maternal mortality is much less of a factor than it is right now."

Here we were, in 1652, having a very 21st Century disagreement. It was the first time I had ever seen Michelle this upset over anything. Instead of continuing the discussion, I elected to remain silent for a bit, hoping that she would quickly calm down. I couldn't have been more wrong.

Through clenched teeth, Michelle growled, "Aaron, would you please answer me? Will you be coming into the future with me or not?" Her frustration with my silence was evident.

By this time, I had broken out in a cold sweat. She was putting me on the spot, though there was only one correct answer, and I knew it.

"Michelle, darling, you shouldn't even have to be asking that question. Of course, I will be coming with you wherever... whenever... you go. We are a team, and I would not have married you if I didn't have every intention of us being together through whatever comes our way. Before we married, I might have made a different decision – but those days are in my past, and I can no longer let my professional interests cloud my personal judgment."

Tears were now streaming down Michelle's cheeks. I think she already knew what my answer was going to be, what my answer *had to* be. She just needed to hear it from me first-hand and not simply take it for granted. I also needed to hear myself giving her the answer just to reinforce my own conviction that my now-growing family had to come first before everything else.

I accepted that Grandmother Chepi was going to help us travel across time, but I still had more questions than answers. When? How? Would we be going back to 2012 or some other year? My mind was racing.

Michelle sensed my trepidation and confusion and offered an explanation. "Aaron, Grandmother Chepi told me that in two weeks, we would have a moonless night, making it possible for us to leave this time. She did not offer any more details than that, and I suspect that she was intentionally vague to keep us from getting impatient and trying to find the portal ourselves."

"Chepi is a wise woman," I replied with a smile. "She has read us like a book. How are we going to explain this to Gemma and Saoirse?"

"We'll just have to do the best that we can. Who knows… they may actually want to stay here," Michelle answered with a wink.

"Let's talk to them in the morning when we go back to Newhaven to collect our things from the inn," I suggested, "but Aiyana will be guiding us and we might have to watch what we say."

"We don't have to hide anything from Aiyana. She knows all about people coming from other times," Michelle added, "Chepi was very clear on that."

We walked back to our lodge hand-in-hand. It was going to be a long night and an even longer two weeks.

When Saoirse and Gemma joined us in our lodge, it was well after midnight. Michelle took the lead in explaining to the couple what was afoot. Their excitement and impatience were palpable, re-confirming Chepi's reasoning for not telling us where the time gateway was located. We had to wait for the next moonless night. It was not negotiable.

Gemma and Saoirse were aware of their unique circumstances. They knew the English settlers would not tolerate their relationship and likely would accuse them of witchcraft. Michelle knew of witch trials and executions in both Hartford and Wethersfield in this time, much earlier than the Salem Witch Trials in Massachusetts. We could not let the two ladies get caught up in the mass hysteria if and when it spread to New Haven.

The Quinnipiac, on the other hand, seemed to tolerate unusual pairings and polyamory, even as an extension of established families of husband, wife, and children. As much as they seemed interested in staying here, they asserted their need to return to some point in the future where society was more tolerant. The question we needed answered was if all four of us could pass through the gateway together or if we would have to each go separately or perhaps in pairs.

*   *   *   *   *

After an early breakfast the next morning, we were on our way to New Haven and our rooming house to collect our personal effects. As we left the Quinnipiac village, Chepi reminded us that it was Saturday and that the slave market

318

would be held on the village green. She re-emphasized that it was an experience not to be missed.

With Aiyana as our guide and with two pack horses in tow, we arrived in New Haven around 10 a.m. It was more than enough time to clear out of the inn before the start of the slave market at noon.

The inn's proprietors, Jethro and Miriam Alden, were wonderful people. When we announced our imminent departure, they went out of their way to help us pack our few things and had even washed our dirty laundry while we were away. To show our appreciation for their help, I paid them an additional half-day's lodging as a gratuity.

While we were loading up our pack horses, I told Mr. Alden that we were moving to the Quinnipiac village as the guest of Grandmother Chepi and that we would be attending the slave auction at noon.

"Mister Shepherd," Alden began, "if you plan on spending time with those savages, mind how you go. You never can trust a savage."

"I have no reason to doubt the sincerity of Grandmother Chepi's invitation and our exposure thus far has been completely aboveboard. I have been given no reason not to trust her or anyone in her village. I am insulted by your casting aspersions on their character just because they are different. You, sir, have insulted my judgment because of your own narrow-minded views. Good day to you, sir!"

Alden's jaw dropped; he apparently had some influence over the town and people's perceptions of the Quinnipiac. Here I was, an outsider, putting him in his place. He was speechless and I left him mouthing silently like a fresh-caught trout.

Michelle, Gemma, and Saoirse had observed the entire exchange from the doorway of the inn. I looked over and could see all three of them beaming with pride. As I tied the final bindings for our load, they pushed past Jethro Alden, with their heads held high and noses disdainfully in the air. As far as I was concerned, we couldn't leave New Haven quickly enough.

37: The Auction

Late June, 1652

We approached the village green, near what I recognized as what would become the campus of Yale University some five decades in the future. At the corner of Chapel and Church Streets, we read a broadsheet:

Slave Auction

On the Village Green

Noon Every Saturday

All Manner of Africans

Ready for Sale

To

The Highest Bidder

It was just past 11 a.m. and the area was filling rapidly. A carnival atmosphere prevailed. There were games of chance for the men, plenty of pickled and smoked food to purchase, and activities intended to prevent the myriads of children from running helter-skelter through the crowd. It was an unsuccessful effort.

Leaving Aiyana at a predetermined spot outside the assembly area, we took a place as near to the slave pens as we could while remaining within sight of Aiyana. We all knew she could take care of herself – she always carried a well-honed knife on her belt. Regardless, I felt a responsibility for her protection and would not want to face Grandmother Chepi with unpleasant news.

From our vantage point, we could see the current "ready for sale" pen and the other holding areas further into the yard. Michelle pointed out to me that the holding areas further away from the green appeared to be where the newly arrived chattel were held to recover from their sea voyage and to fatten them up for sale. Any way you looked at it, the smell emanating from the pens complex was worse than anything we had ever experienced, including the decomposing bodies on the Worcester battlefield.

Promptly at noon, the auctioneer rapped his gavel on the podium to note the start of the auction. A young black man was promptly marched front and center, being led by a rope that was loosely looped around his neck, almost as if he were on a leash. He was clothed in loose linen trousers and a similar linen shirt, open to the waist. His sculpted musculature was on display for all to see.

"Gentlemen, feast your eyes on this young specimen ready for a day's work in your fields, warehouses, or sawmills. Guessed to be nearing twenty years of age, young Goliath is learning English and the ways of Our Lord. We will open the bidding at one hundred shillings."

As the bidding progressed past two hundred shillings, one potential buyer shouted a request to see the young man's back. With a nod from the auctioneer, one of the attendants turned the black man around and lowered the shirt. A gasp went up from the crowd and at least one woman fainted when the evidence of several floggings, some stripes still fresh, became visually obvious.

I heard the two men next to me discussing the importance of the scars.

"James, I tell you that one will be trouble if he's already been whipped to an inch of his life."

"Aye, I'll not bid on one that's been whipped. Already damaged goods and probably headstrong as well. He might make good breeding stock, though." Both men laughed conspiratorially.

The crowd satisfied, the linen shirt was pulled back up over the man's shoulders. At a final bid of two hundred and fifty shillings, the young man was led to the sales desk where a clerk made an entry in the ledger. With the rope still around the young man's neck, we was handed over to his new owner, much like a piece of livestock. I fought back tears of embarrassment.

Michelle, Gemma and Saoirse remained silent throughout the entire process. I was pretty sure what they were thinking, and I knew that we would not be staying much longer than the first couple of sales. The icing on the cake was when the next slave, a young girl developing into womanhood, was marched out to the dais.

Female slaves were treated slightly different than the males: instead of a rope around their necks, it was tied loosely about their waist. Their clothing was a little more modest than the males', but not much.

The two men nearest me were once again full of lewd comments.

"James, I tell ya', she'll make a fine bedwarmer once she's broke of African stubbornness."

"No doubt," James replied.

I did my best to ignore their continued locker room repartee and tried to keep my focus on the auctioneer.

"Gentlemen, this young woman will be fine breeding stock. She already knows how to cook and sew. We will start the bidding at seventy-five shillings." That bid was quickly topped by an unsolicited offer of one hundred shillings.

As with the first male, the young woman seemed to be in the prime of health. It wasn't long before the men in the crowd were demanding to see more of her… attributes.

As the linen shift was forcibly removed from the young woman's shoulders, she raised her chin in defiance and steeled her expression of hate.

The lewd comments about the young woman's now-exposed breasts were more than we could take. As we were already on the fringe of the crowd, it wasn't difficult for us to extricate ourselves from the marketplace and rejoin Aiyana.

When we were out of the market area, Michelle dropped to her knees, in tears and overwhelmed by what she had just seen. Her face was drained of all color and she was ghostly white.

"Aaron, how could one human being mistreat another one like that? Those poor Africans were treated no better than barnyard animals. I think I am going to be sick…"

As Michelle retched up the contents of her stomach, I held her hair back and out of the way. Gemma and Saoirse, too, were affected by what they had seen – but they did not have pregnancy hormones affecting their bodies. I probably would have vomited sympathetically if the other two women had joined my wife.

Once Michelle regained her composure, we rejoined Aiyana and began our return to the Quinnipiac village. I hoped to never visit New Haven again on a slave market day. It was definitely a once in a lifetime experience.

When we got to the village, it was early evening; the smell of cooking fires was overwhelming. None of us had eaten anything substantial since departing just after breakfast. The disagreement with Alden at the inn precluded any chance of purchasing a mid-day meal in that establishment and the events at the slave market had temporarily taken our appetites away. We were now ravenous.

Grandmother Chepi seemed glad to see us and got straight to the point.

"Did you go to the slave auction as I suggested?"

Michelle answered before I could even open my mouth.

"Grandmother, it was disgusting. How can one human being do that to another?"

"The English treat the Africans no better than livestock," Chepi agreed. "We, too, have slaves through conquest but it is our responsibility to see that they are taken care of. They may have been our enemies at one point, but once they are vanquished, they become one of us. We never buy or sell our slaves."

"Grandmother, in our future, slavery in all forms is abolished," Michelle explained, "and in about 200 years there will be a great war fought between the white settlers over slavery. Brothers will fight against brothers."

Chepi thought for a moment before responding. "Michelle, do you know what happens to my people and the other nations who were here before the English arrived?"

"Yes, Grandmother, I do. The future is pretty bleak. Your lands will be sold or taken away and those that survive the many battles will be herded onto lands called reservations," Michelle explained. Chepi nodded silently in understanding.

After a short contemplative silence, Chepi took Michelle's hand in her own. "I think that is enough of the future for one day. Our meal is ready. Will you join me for dinner?"

"Of course we will," Michelle answered, "it will be our honor to join you and to remain in your company until… well… when the time comes for us to leave. After what we saw today in New Haven, I don't think any of us have a desire to go back there unless it is absolutely necessary. The slave market was disgusting and offensive."

"That is why I wanted you to see it for yourselves," Chepi said solemnly.

We sat down in places of honor at either side of Grandmother Chepi in the communal dining lodge. Michelle and Saoirse were to her right; Gemma and I were to her left. When everyone was seated. Chepi stood and made an announcement to her people, first in Quinnipiac for the ones who were still learning English, and again in English for our benefit.

"My brothers, sisters, and children: our four English visitors will remain with us for another two weeks. Then, they will be sent on their way towards Fairfield. I ask you to treat them as you would my own family."

In affirmation of Chepi's edict, the men whooped and the women trilled their tongues. We all smiled and nodded in response. We felt welcomed.

Once again, the meal was a sumptuous feast. This time, there was more fish than before. The plentiful striped bass, slow-roasted whole on woven mats of wet green willow and sprinkled with native herbs, was better than any I had ever eaten in 21st Century restaurants. Oysters, roasted in the shell, and a communal tom turkey filled out the meat choices. Potatoes, carrots, onions and another unidentified root vegetable seemed to have come from the winter stores. The variety and complexity of the Quinnipiac diet amazed me.

For the first time in several days, Gemma and I had a chance to engage in private conversation. The Quinnipiac elder seated to her right did not understand much English, so were probably safe from his eavesdropping.

"Gemma, are you ready to jump across time?" I asked.

"Aaron, I can't leave this time soon enough. I've been at wit's end since we left Wroxeter and long for all the modcons we had taken for granted. This primitive lifestyle just isn't for me."

"That's understandable," I replied, "but look at the interest Saoirse has taken in these people and this time."

"I want our… whatever it is… to work out this time," Gemma said with tears welling up in her eyes.

"That's all the more reason for the two of you to come with us. English society in this age is very intolerant," I said with a raised eyebrow.

"If it were completely up to Saoirse, we probably would stay here in 1652, regardless of the consequences," Gemma said dejectedly.

"You could possibly assimilate into the Quinnipiac. I am sure that Grandmother Chepi could make that happen. If you hadn't already noticed, this band is tolerant of unique relationships and polyamory that transcends our vision of a husband-wife-child family structure," I explained.

"Thank you very effing much, professor," Gemma said sarcastically. Her reply made me realize that I had suddenly jumped back into an academic mindset totally inappropriate for the situation.

"Gemma, I am so sorry for being insensitive. It's something that plagues me from time to time. When I am faced with a challenging situation like yours, my normal response is exactly what you encountered – like something out of a graduate textbook."

For her part, Michelle was engaged in a heady conversation with Saoirse, probably similar to the one I was having with Gemma. As with our side of the table, they were insulated from eavesdropping, thanks to what I deduced was Chepi's wisdom: she had intentionally seated people next to us who understood very little English. I could tell the older man sitting next to Saoirse was unsuccessfully trying to keep up with their conversation. His furrowed brow and pursed lips told me everything I needed to know.

Once dinner was over, the four of us huddled near the guest lodge. Gemma originally looked worried that Saoirse would decide to remain here in 1652. Her nervous fidgeting told me that she was expecting the worst. Michelle and I had already made our decision and communicated that to the other two women separately during dinner. We wondered what they would decide.

There was a pregnant pause of several minutes as Saoirse and Gemma stared into each other's eyes, neither of them sure who should speak first. The tension between them was palpable. It seemed as if the entire Quinnipiac village was waiting for their answer. There were no babies crying, no crickets chirping nor tree frogs trilling their songs. There was just dead silence as we waited... and waited.

Everyone was startled when an owl and its mate began calling out to each other in the darkness, almost as if it was a cue for the ladies to speak.

"Gemma," Saoirse began, "we have been on this adventure together and I have realized that you mean more to me than my academic desire to remain here and experience history first-hand. My love, I will follow you wherever you go, even across time."

38: The Waiting Game

Late June – Early July, 1652

The next two weeks were a heady mix of anticipation and camaraderie with each other and with our Quinnipiac hosts.

I spent most of my time working with the younger males of the village to improve their English language skills. They had not had a proper teacher in the village since the previous summer, and my young charges soaked up my teaching like sun-dried sponges in a thunderstorm. It was refreshing to see a lust for learning and deferential respect for a teacher, unlike what I had experienced during my last stint as a lecturer before leaving the classroom for archaeological field work.

My three female traveling companions were assimilated into the agricultural work supporting the village. In the fields, the women removed weeds from the crops, tilled the soil, and harvested the fruits and vegetables that were ready for consumption. Michelle, because of her pregnancy, was assigned less intense work in the shade, shelling peas and snapping beans for the upcoming evening meal. She thought it was somewhat amusing that when they were working in the fields, the Quinnipiac women lost most of their modesty, removing their tunics and working shirtless. In the field, Gemma and Saoirse were quite conspicuous with their white cotton shifts and much lighter skin.

The more we engaged with our hosts, the harder it was becoming to accept that our departure was imminent. It was only Michelle's pregnancy that provided motivation for us to keep moving forward towards our jump, hopefully back to our own time. Each of us knew full well the medical implications of remaining here, and I was not prepared to raise a child on my own, even with the implicit support of Chepi's village.

Based on my calculations and Chepi's assertions, I expected the next moonless night, or what we would call a "new moon," would fall on July 5. Chepi still had not informed us of the details of our time hop. She remained adamant that we not be provided with too much information, as we would become impatient and take matters into our own hands.

Chepi somehow knew that our 21st Century lives had conditioned us for immediate gratification and response.

"Mister Shepherd, our people believe that good things come to those who wait," Chepi explained, "and there is no way to hurry the natural course of events. You must be patient. I know from other travelers that your world is very different from ours and that we can not even imagine some of the things that are possible in your time. Trying to leave us before the moonless night will just cause heartache for everyone."

Chepi had just confirmed that there had been other travelers. I was immediately curious but opted not to press the issue. How long the gateway had been here was anybody's guess as knowledge of it seemed to have been passed on from generation to generation. I wondered if Aiyana, too, would become a wise Grandmother in the future after spending her life under Chepi's tutelage.

When the day finally came for is to leave, it was a tearful occasion. Michelle, Gemma and Saoirse had developed strong bonds with the Quinnipiac women. Their bond was strongest with Grandmother Chepi and Aiyana.

After the evening meal and just before we set off to the portal, Michell took Chepi's hands in hers.

"Grandmother Chepi, we thank you for being our host and friend since we arrived here. We will never forget you."

Chepi pulled Michelle close and offered a blessing in both English and Quinnipiac, "Go with God, my child. Go with God and may Mother Earth take you home."

The rest of us joined Michelle and Chepi in a group hug, then turned to Aiyana and embraced her as well. We didn't want to leave – but had to if we were going to have any chance of returning somewhere close to our original timeline.

As we turned to leave the village, we were treated to a well-orchestrated light show. The male members of Chepi's band stood along the sides of a woodland path, alternating sides at 10-to-15-foot intervals. Chepi touched her torch to the first man's torch, and the fire was passed from man to man until it seemed to disappear into the woods. I wondered if the visual would be as amazing in the winter as it was right now, with no foliage on the trees and the torchlight reflecting off of the snow.

With Chepi and Aiyana in the lead, we slowly and solemnly walked into the woods. The anticipation of what we knew was about to happen had us all in goosebumps and made the walk into the woods seem longer than it really was. It was truly an eerie situation.

After passing the second bend in the path's "s" curve, I detected a glow emanating from one of the trees. I understood the concept of natural bioluminescence but had never encountered the phenomenon away from swampland and decomposing vegetation.

As we got closer to the source of the glow, more of the Quinnipiac men began softly beating deer hide drums and chanting in low voices. Grandmother Chepi told me that this is what her people had done for as long as she could remember when they were sending travelers on their way.

"It is our ceremony to wish travelers well in the past or future, wherever they go," Chepi explained.

We entered a clearing and circled around a very thick oak tree. On the side hidden from our approach, I instantly recognized the glow was coming from a carved Hecate's Wheel about four feet off the ground. Michelle and I gave each other a puzzled look but remained speechless. Saoirse and Gemma did the same as they, too, recognized what they were seeing.

With a quick and authoritative raise of her right hand, Grandmother Chepi stopped the chanting and drumming. Michelle took my hand in hers as the torches were extinguished in the reverse of how they were lit, leaving only the glow from the tree carving. It was the strangest example of bioluminescence I had ever seen – if it was not something completely otherworldly.

Grandmother Chepi stood between and slightly behind Michelle and me. She whispered softly in our ears that it was now time for us to go. Guiding us to the tree, Chepi had our hands in hers.

"Aaron, Michelle… you must continue touching each other, no matter what happens," Chepi explained, her tone more solemn than a minister conducting a funeral. "Miss Gemma and Miss Saoirse will follow shortly."

"Yes, Grandmother," Michelle and I responded in unison. Our voices sounded as if we were in a trance.

As we approached the oak tree, a deep humming reverberated under our feet, almost as if we were experiencing an earthquake. It was very similar to the sensation I had experienced when I left 2012 from the Wroxeter digs. I was sure that Michelle felt it, too. Her expression as we got closer to the glowing tree confirmed my assumption.

The top of the circle appeared to be outside Chepi's reach because of her diminutive stature, yet she was able to reach it with no problem. It was almost as if she was standing on a pillar of air. Slowly and deliberately, Chepi guided our joined hands to top dead center of the carving.

Just like my experience at the Wroxeter dig, my hand felt as if it were being pulled in and compelled to touch the carving. Once I was within a foot of the emblem, there was nothing I could do to stop its pull on our hands. I also discovered that my hand and Michelle's had become as one.

Touching what would have been north on a compass rose, our joined hands began a slow circle clockwise – a direction that I knew indicated a move towards the future. When our joined hands passed the south point at 180 degrees of arc, a purple aura seemed to surround Michelle and me, reaching its peak intensity when our hands approached west, or 270 degrees of arc. The ground vibrations, too, seemed to reach their peak.

In a blinding flash of purple, Chepi suddenly disappeared from the picture, and we were plunged into total darkness. The only connection to reality was the one Michelle and I shared through the touch of our hands. I didn't want to, nor could I, let go of her hand. Having been raised in a religious home and having attended many church weddings before going afield, I was reminded of a Bible passage: "What therefore God has joined together, let not man put asunder."

My last thoughts before becoming completely disoriented were for the welfare of our unborn child. Chepi had assured us that he or she could endure time travel while in the protection of Michelle's womb, but I was still worried. It gnawed at me until I momentarily blacked out.

39: *When* Are We?

Early July, Somewhere in Time

The next several minutes – which really could have been any measurable chronological increment – were a blur. Michelle was by my side and our hands remained joined as we moved forward through time. I was aware of events as we passed along the continuum of time and even some of the details surrounding those events, but we did not linger in any of them.

I saw New Haven merging with the Connecticut Colony, the founding of Yale University, the French and Indian War, Jonathan Edwards documenting native languages, Captain Benedict Arnold breaking into the powder house, the *Amistad* trial, Harriet Beecher Stowe causing an uproar with her book, *Uncle Tom's Cabin*, the 14th Connecticut Infantry marching off for Gettysburg, New Haven ceding its joint capital status entirely to Hartford, the calls for military enlistments before the draft was established near the end of World War I, and the first Frisbee being thrown on the New Haven Green.

Our journey through time ended abruptly when we were unceremoniously deposited in a wooded glen that resembled the place where we had left Chepi and the Quinnipiac villagers behind. Dazed and confused, neither Michelle nor I had any concept of time. Barely conscious, we clung to each other as if our lives depended on it.

As we slowly regained awareness of our surroundings and our nakedness, Michelle covered herself as best she could before calling out quietly to Gemma and Saoirse, hoping that they had joined us in our time travel. After several minutes of calling out their names in a progressively louder voice, I suggested to Michelle that it was time to give up and focus on our own survival and not draw unwanted attention to ourselves just yet. Until we knew *when* we were, maintaining a low profile was essential to our survival.

"Michelle, did any of the events we passed indicate where we might be in time?" I asked.

"I think we might be in the 1920s," Michelle suggested, "because I seem to remember the origin of the Frisbee somewhere around 1920. I was a huge Ultimate Frisbee participant during my undergrad days and even took a course on the evolution of unusual competitive sports that included Ultimate Frisbee."

"We have to accept that Gemma and Saoirse will not be joining us," Michelle said with tears welling in her eyes, "but I... we... have to focus on my health and that of our baby. Even in the 1920s, childbirth was still largely at home, including the cities, and the maternal mortality rate was only slightly better than it was at the start of the 18th Century."

I was amazed by Michelle's knowledge of obscure historical facts and statistics like the maternal mortality rate for a particular period in time. Like her, I was concerned that we would not have the medical support to which we had become accustomed in 2012 – but decided that I could not fixate on it as I needed to ensure our own survival. That of our unborn child would naturally follow.

Still slightly dizzy, I looked more carefully at our surroundings. The remains of a path like the one we walked down with Chepi just a few moments ago were clearly visible. Where it entered the clearing, there was now a small cabin that looked unoccupied. It wasn't much larger than an outhouse, but at least it could provide some shelter until we figured out our predicament.

* * * * *

Back in 1652, Gemma and Saoirse approached the tree carving, but it was Aiyana as their guide, not Chepi. Chepi had trained Aiyana for this very moment, and Aiyana was trembling with anticipation.

"Grandmother, I am not afraid. I will do everything you taught me to do," Aiyana said with a smile.

Gemma was puzzled by Aiyana's comment. Though she had been in this time for nearly nine months, she was still a detective at heart and detected a nuance in the young girl's comment. Gemma wondered what was really about to happen.

"Saoirse, something just isn't right with what's happening now. I think Chepi and Aiyana are up to something," Gemma whispered.

Saoirse pursed her lips pensively and took Gemma's hand in hers.

"Gemma, once again your fear of the unknown is getting the best of you," Saoirse said as she pulled her lover closer. "I will be by your side, whatever happens. I told you this before and I meant it with all my heart."

After saying their goodbyes to Grandmother Chepi, Aiyana stepped between the two ladies and took each of their hands in hers. It was now Aiyana who guided the travelers to the tree carving. Chepi remained unobtrusively in the background.

When the trio was within about twenty feet of the tree, a loud humming became obvious, and the ground seemed to tremble under their feet. Gemma thought it might have been a small earthquake.

"Gemma, Saoirse…" Aiyana whispered, "the earth moving beneath your feet is normal. It is a sign that the portal is ready to receive you. Grandmother told me what to expect."

In silence, they approached the tree. Once they were within reach, Aiyana joined the two women's hands with hers and guided them to the circle carving. All three hands touched the top center of the circle at the same time.

Slowly they began circling in a clockwise direction, which Aaron had explained would take them forward in time. They passed through 90 degrees of arc, which would have taken them to 1742. Saoirse noticed that she felt compelled to maintain contact with the carving no matter what.

After 180 degrees, or 1832, the humming sound and ground vibrations intensified and a purple aura appeared to envelop the trio. Gemma's eyes were wide with fright as the vision of Chepi on the edge of the clearing began to blur.

Saoirse suddenly remembered when Aaron and Michelle disappeared. It was when their hands hit the 270-degree mark, which would have deposited them in 1922. Was that going to be their destination as well?

Aiyana continued guiding their joined hands towards top center once more. Reaching the top, there was a blinding flash, and their surroundings seemed to completely disappear. Gemma sensed that they were floating through time, seeing vivid images of the atrocities in King Philip's War against white settlers, the burning of New London and Groton during the Revolutionary War, and the body of Connectican Gordon Cartwright Jennings draped over a cannon at the Alamo.

The also saw William Howard Taft graduating from Yale, the end of World War I, the mushroom clouds over Hiroshima and Nagasaki, and the music of Yale graduate Cole Porter being featured in "Kiss Me, Kate."

The passage of time seemed to slow as they approached 2012. Before being deposited in that year, they saw President Obama expanding the rights and protections of LGBTQ individuals through legislation and Executive Orders. For each historical event, Gemma and Saoirse would later remember that they were fully aware of the event but were not participants.

They came to an abrupt stop in almost complete darkness. The air around them was damp and cool, and a musty odor assaulted their sense of smell. It reminded Saoirse of some of the tombs she had opened during her digs.

As the fog of time travel cleared from her senses, Saoirse recognized that she was once again naked, as was Gemma. They both noticed a dim light glowing from a nearby wall. Gemma immediately saw that it was another Hecate's Wheel.

Looking around, Gemma once again went into detective mode. She observed that there was a steep stairway, not much more than a ladder, leading up to a trapdoor about fifteen feet above their heads.

Piquing Gemma's curiosity even more than the room itself was a steamer trunk a few feet from the base of the ladder. She also noted one other oddity: Aiyana was still fully clothed in her Quinnipiac attire.

"Saoirse, I think that trunk contains something that is meant for us. We should investigate," said Gemma.

Saoirse reached the steamer trunk first and lifted the unlatched lid. Inside, she found two brand-name track suits, female undergarments, and shoes. Mysteriously, everything was perfectly sized. There was also a flashlight in the trunk, which Saoirse suggested should be used to climb the ladder up to the trap door and in case there was darkness on the other side.

"Why are there only two of everything, when there are three of us?" Saoirse asked rhetorically, but at the same time suggesting she wanted an explanation from Aiyana.

"Miss Saoirse, Miss Gemma…" Aiyana said meekly, "I am not meant to remain here with you. That's why I am not naked. I am going back to my time as soon as I am sure you are safe."

"That sounds as if you coming with us was planned," Gemma suggested.

"Yes, it was. Grandmother Chepi sent me on this quest as the final part of my training. Someday, I will be allowed to travel and not return," Aiyana said with a smile, "and it will have to be for the right reasons, with the right person."

Now devoting their full attention to the contents of the steamer trunk, Saoirse and Gemma dressed quickly. As they bent over to put on their shoes, they were startled by a blinding flash. Turning towards the Wheel, they saw that Aiyana was gone.

"She was serious that she wasn't staying here," said Gemma. "I hope she gets her wish."

The two women quickly finished dressing. Once their eyes recovered from the bright flash that took Aiyana away from them, they were able to take in more of their surroundings.

On a table under the ladder, there were stacks of papers. They all appeared to be handwritten using quill pens. One of the stacks had a paper that was dated October 9, 1701, with a heading "An Act for Liberty to Erect a Collegiate School." It was signed by ten Congregational ministers, all of whom featured prominently in Connecticut history.

"I wish Michelle were here to help us determine the importance of these papers," Saoirse said. Her tone conveyed the sadness that both she and Gemma felt at being separated from their friends, Aaron and Michelle.

"We can't be in 1701," Saoirse said after a short pause. "The clothes from the trunk – and the flashlight – are not from that time."

"Perhaps this dark room is a repository for long-lost historical records?" Gemma asked.

"It certainly is possible, but the dampness should have caused these old papers to deteriorate a lot more than they already have," Saoirse explained.

"I'm dying to find out what lies in store for us at the top of the ladder," Gemma said expectantly.

"Let's go find out!" Saoirse said with obvious excitement in her voice.

*   *   *   *   *

Michelle and I opened the little shack and found male and female garments inside. It was clearly the nondescript attire of the working class and matched what Michelle had seen in black-and-white family photos of the 1920s. It more or less confirmed her assumption of where they were in time.

As we dressed, Michelle was the first to notice that, despite the moonless night, we were able to see what we were doing. Turning around, back towards the center of the clearing, she noticed the glow once again coming from the tree carving.

"That's odd," Michelle said to get my attention. Her brow was deeply furrowed.

"What is odd, my dear?" I replied.

"A few moments ago, we were in pitch black darkness, but now we can see – thanks to the light from that… whatever it is… that seems to have brought us here," said Michelle.

"I'm just as confused as you are right now, but I think it is a safe assumption that Gemma and Saoirse have gone their own separate way," I explained. "It is the only logical conclusion to be drawn from the fact that there are only two sets of clothing here. I'm also pretty sure that the glow means the time portal is closed."

Underneath the clothing, there was a stack of seemingly fresh newspapers from around Connecticut. On top was the Meriden *Morning Record*, dated March 29, 1922. It seemed odd that the paper started with page 13, but the story at the top center of the page was written by Royal S. Copeland, MD, the New York City Commissioner of Health. The headline read: "What Cholera Really Is and How to Guard Yourself." The story went on to describe the symptoms of and morbidity rates from the disease. Other papers described the spread of the disease from Russia and the Philippines.

As I read the stories aloud to Michelle, she recognized immediately that we had landed in the middle of a burgeoning global pandemic.

"Aaron, were you vaccinated against cholera before you went to England?" she asked.

"Yes, I was," I answered emphatically.

"So was I, and the immunity should carry through to our child, at least for the short term," Michelle said more to comfort herself than to explain the situation to me.

As we sat in silence, I could see that Michelle was searching her memory for information about such an epidemic. I hoped her gift of total recall would provide us with more information.

Our attention to our circumstances was broken by a sudden squeal from Michelle.

"My darling, I think I just felt our baby move," she cooed with delight. "It was like a little mouse running around inside me."

"Do you think I might be able to feel it, too?" I asked, hoping that I could share in the moment.

"I doubt it," Michelle replied. "A baby's first movements are usually something uniquely private for the mother. It won't be for another month or so that you'll be able to feel him... her... move on the outside of my belly."

"Well, let's get back to our predicament, shall we?" I suggested. We needed to come up with a plan or risk running afoul of the local authorities.

"Aaron, when the pandemic hits New York City this summer, people will be leaving the city in droves, most abandoning their possessions and leaving their documents behind. We could use that as a cover for our existence and convince the authorities that we are newlywed refugees. It should be easy for us to create new identities here."

I considered what my wife was telling me: she was prepared to remain here in 1922 rather than risk another jump through time. Because we were not transported back (or was it forward?) to 2012 from the Quinnipiac village, we had to do something that would give us a believable story.

"Aaron, if we do this, I am sure the authorities will ask your occupation. What do you intend to tell them? You certainly don't look the part of a college professor. A ditch digger, maybe, but certainly not anything of a professional nature," Michelle said as she stifled a laugh. Once again, she was able to find humor in a situation.

I shared a chuckle before offering my opinion. "Michelle, my darling, let's cross that bridge when we come to it. Knowing that there is no national database of information in 1922, there is almost no chance that our story won't be accepted as true. All we have to do is convince *whoever* that anybody who could confirm our stories was in New York City and likely quarantined – or worse."

40: Unbelievable

August, 2012

The Sunday SUN

Sunday, August 19, 2012

Missing for nearly a year, Detective Sergeant Gemma Royce-Smallworth of the West Mercia Police and her partner, Leeds University Professor Saoirse Donoghue, PhD., miraculously turned up in the town of New Haven, Connecticut in the United States.

The pair disappeared from an archaeological dig at the Roman ruins in Wroxeter in September last year, along with two American archaeologists, Aaron Shepherd, PhD., and his assistant, Michelle Whitcomb, both from the state of Michigan. An exhaustive search lasting several months turned up no reliable leads and the West Mercia Police eventually suspended their investigation. At the time, the disappearances were considered to have been the results of foul play.

The couple would not comment on how they managed to end up in Connecticut.

Insiders are speculating that Royce-Smallworth and Donoghue faked their own disappearance in order to take advantage of the more liberal same-sex marriage laws in the United States. Connecticut was second only to Massachusetts in recognizing same-sex marriages.

When challenged by our correspondent in the United States, neither Detective Sergeant Royce-Smallworth nor Professor Donoghue offered any confirmatory comments as to the state of their relationship.

41: Closure

August, 1922

"Next!" the police officer bellowed. There was a long line of people outside New Haven's City Hall awaiting their turn to provide the authorities with details of their departure from New York City and the growing cholera epidemic there.

Having already been in line for several hours, Michelle and I were elated to have finally reached the point where our statements would be taken by one of the city's magistrates. We hoped that Michelle's gravid condition would be enough to draw the sympathy of the magistrate

Seated at a desk opposite the line of refugees was a magistrate, obviously uncomfortable in his black robe, and a clerk whose responsibility it was to record the statements of both the magistrate and the applicants.

The magistrate's flowing silver hair and well-groomed beard gave him a benevolent, grandfatherly appearance. The clerk, on the other hand, could easily have filled the role of Bob Cratchit in any theatrical production of Dickens' "A Christmas Carol." Michelle noticed the dichotomy of appearances and smiled.

"Names?" the magistrate asked, his voice devoid of any empathy.

"Aaron and Michelle Shepherd, husband and wife," I responded. The clerk wrote down the information, barely looking up at the couple.

Though they had been given the right to vote with the ratification of the 19th Amendment two years earlier, married women were still not allowed to speak on their own behalf in legal matters. Michelle knew this and remained conspicuously silent.

"Places of birth?" the magistrate asked.

"Michigan for both of us," I answered. Once again, they heard the scratching of the clerk's pen on the thick paper of the logbook.

"Dates of birth?"

"Myself, I was born in December 1890. My wife was born in June, 1895," Aaron answered as confidently as he could.

"Do you have any documents to prove your births or marriage?"

"Sir, we left New York City to escape the spreading cholera there. We had no time to gather more than the clothes on our back and our available money before leaving. As we were walking out the door of our building, the New York City Department of Health was condemning it. We were not allowed to go back inside," Aaron explained.

"What is the date of your marriage?" the magistrate asked.

"September 9, 1921," I answered.

Michelle began to sob at my explanation, daubing her cheeks with a somewhat soiled handkerchief.

"Aaron, I feel as though I may faint," Michelle whispered just loud enough for the magistrate and clerk to hear. I turned to face my wife and took her hands in mine. I knew it was a theatrical performance and winked at Michelle.

"Mr. Hutchinson," the magistrate said firmly, "please fetch Mrs. Shepherd a glass of water."

"Yes, sir," Hutchinson responded. A few moments later, he reappeared with a tumbler and pitcher full of iced water.

"Here you go, Mrs. Shepherd," Hutchinson cajoled as he poured Michelle a glass.

"Thank you, Mr. Hutchinson," Michelle said softly.

"Mr. Shepherd, what was your occupation in New York City?" the magistrate asked.

We had already discussed what this answer might be. The higher up we went in society, the more likely our story would be subject to verification, so we had decided that Aaron would assume the role of common laborer.

"I was a laborer, sir, and Mrs. Shepherd was a seamstress," I answered. Hutchinson scribbled the notes in his ledger.

"How did you come to live in New York City?" the magistrate asked.

"We were following our dream of living in a big city. Detroit offered only employment at the automobile factories and that was not something I wanted to do," I explained, "and Mrs. Shepherd's skill as a seamstress are wanted anywhere." Again, Hutchinson's pen scratched on the logbook.

The magistrate looked the us up and down, cocked his head, and closed one eye as if he was deep in thought. Tenting his fingers beneath his chin, the magistrate finally smiled and said, "Welcome to Connecticut, Mr. and Mrs. Shepherd."

"Mr. Hutchinson, please see that the Shepherds are given all the documentation they need to get employment and lodging here in our fair city," the magistrate ordered.

"Yes, sir," Hutchinson said as his pen scratched and scratched and scratched across some very rough paper. When he was done, he handed Aaron three sheets of paper. One was a substitute marriage certificate. The second was a voter registration document for both of them. The third was a letter of introduction for Aaron to present to the local housing authority.

"Thank you, sir," we said in unison as we turned and walked away. We were now safe in Connecticut as legal residents – in 1922.

Author Note and Acknowledgments

This book has been nearly a year and a half in the making, largely because of the deep research into the flight of Charles II from England to France after the Battle of Worcester in September, 1651.

As I wrote each chapter, I recursively researched the path Charles II and his entourage took to flee England. The timeline was as close as I could make it to the accounts provided by Charles (and others) to Samuel Pepys (pronounced "peeps") in 1680, 20 years after the Stuart monarchy was restored and almost 30 years after the Battle of Worcester. Some historians believe that some of the grandiose statements made by Charles were exaggerations that were further embellished by Pepys.

In the 17th Century, there were no internal combustion engines, no railroads, and not really much at all in the way of mechanization. Travel during that time was either on foot, horseback, or horse-drawn wagon.

Regardless, the route taken from Worcester to Shoreham and the channel crossing aboard the *Surprise* follow the legendary Monarch's Way, a meandering 625-mile route that includes numerous stopovers; one of those was as long as a fortnight. The Battle of Worcester ended on September 9, 1651, and Charles departed England on October 15 of that same year. That encompassed a period of 43 days – meaning that the royal entourage covered an impressive average of 14.5 miles per day, not adjusted for extended delays.

I'll leave it to my readers to sort out and I apologize (or is it "apologise"?) to any of my British readers if I have affronted their documented history – but also remind them that this is, after all, a work of fiction.

As with all of the Lineage Series novels released so far, "Take the Long Way Home" is loosely connected to my family tree. This connection is through the person of Colonel Charles Giffard and the Chillington Estate which encompasses both Boscobel House and Whiteladies Priory. It was one of Giffard's men, Richard Penderel who is believed to have spirited Charles II into hiding among the boughs of the Royal Oak in a woods adjacent to Boscobel House.

There are also a couple of more recent connections to my family tree: my father attended Michigan Technological University, Western Michigan University, and the College of William and Mary, earning a degree at each of those institutions. Michelle Whitcomb is also the maiden name of one of my maternal first cousins (but she spells it with one "L"); she knows I am using her name in the book, and I thank her for allowing me the privilege of doing so.

*   *   *   *   *

As with all of my other books, my first acknowledgement goes to my wonderful wife, Sandy. She has tolerated my late nights and supported the time taken to research each chapter – as well as listening to my often-incomprehensible babble about the facts I have uncovered.

Next on the list is my friend, Melissa Speed, who provided quite a few details on the Chillington Estate, having at one time been a volunteer docent/interpreter at Boscobel House. Melissa is an author in her own right and is a staff writer for the "*Living Medieval*" magazine in England.

Also of note are the other three authors in the Lineage Independent Publishing stable: Lisa Talbott, G. B. Carmichael, and Rebecca Conaty Bruce. Each of them has provided motivation when I was suffering from "writer's block."